# YORKSHIRE ROSE

*The first story in Margaret Pemberton's powerful new Yorkshire trilogy.*

Disappointed by his daughter's marriage to a mere working-man, mill-owner Caleb Rimmington has disowned her and refused contact with her three children. Rose, Noel and Nina long to meet their grandfather and their Rimmington cousins whom they read about in the gossip columns of the local paper. When Caleb dies this dream becomes reality. Intense, passionate relationships follow. There are broken marriages and broken lives. Throughout it all, Rose is the warp and weft that keeps the family intact.

*Rose Sugden is a Yorkshire girl through and through.*

# YORKSHIRE ROSE

# YORKSHIRE ROSE

*by*

Margaret Pemberton



**Magna Large Print Books**
Long Preston, North Yorkshire,
England.

British Library Cataloguing in Publication Data.

Pemberton, Margaret
Yorkshire rose.

A catalogue record for this book is available from the British Library

ISBN 0-7505-0772-1

First published in Great Britain by Severn House Publishers Ltd., 1996



Published in Large Print 1997 by arrangement with Severn House Publishers Ltd.



Magna Large Print is an imprint of Library Magna Books Ltd.
Printed and bound in Great Britain by T.J. International Ltd., Cornwall, PL28 8RW.

For my sister Janet—a Yorkshire girl.

## Chapter One

'Look at that, Rose!' Laurence Sugden said with Yorkshire pride, one arm around his daughter's slender shoulders, the other making a great sweeping gesture from the far right of the view in front of them, to the far left. 'From up here you can see nearly the whole of Bradford. There's Lister's Mill.' He pointed to the smoking, awesomely high mill chimney dominating a sea of smaller chimneys. 'It's the highest mill chimney in the country and the top is so broad they say a man could drive a horse and cart around it!'

Rose giggled. She was twelve years old and for as long as she could remember her father had been telling her the story of the horse and cart.

'The man would have to get the horse and cart up there first,' she said, as she always said.

It was the 5th of May, 1908, and they were standing on Odsal Top on the far side of the city. It was the first time she had ever seen Lister's Mill, which was the nearest of the city's score of mills to her terraced home, from such a distance.

'And there's Drummond's Mill chimney,' her father continued, 'and Black Dyke Mills chimney, and Whiteheads. And there's the Cathedral, lying in the very bottom of the bowl.'

Laughter bubbled up in Rose's throat. Her father sometimes had a very funny way of describing things, but he was right about the bowl. All the hills around Bradford, with the moors stretching out beyond them, cupped the city in what looked, from this distance, to be a giant, smoke-hazed bowl.

'And there's Lutterworth's,' her father said, his hand tightening slightly on her shoulder.

Rose covered his hand with hers. Her father was Head Tapestry Designer at Lutterworth's. It was a position he was rightly proud of. Tapestry designers weren't common-or-garden mill workers, like weavers or spinners. A man had to have artistic talent to be a tapestry designer. And to be Head Tapestry Designer at a mill as big as Lutterworth's, he had to have a lot of artistic talent.

The bulky Kodak camera that hung from his shoulder, and that was the reason for their excursion to a part of the city's outskirts Rose had never visited before, slipped forward slightly and he heaved it back, saying, 'Have you ever seen such a grand sight, Rose? All those chimneys belching smoke, all that power and energy? Bradford may be a mucky city, but it's also a mighty city. Can you see how individual many of the chimneys are? Lister's chimney is square with decorative fluting on all four sides and the upper third is pedimented and decorated with dummy window-arches, just like an Italian bell-tower.'

Laughter fizzed again in Rose's throat. It was typical of her father that he would see the beauty in the might and power of Bradford's mills, where another man would have seen only the grime. She, too, was fascinated by the sheer size and majesty of some of the city's mills. Lister's, of course. And, out of loyalty to her father, Lutterworth's. But most of all to a mill her father hadn't mentioned by name. A mill he never mentioned by name.

Rimmington's.

It lay very close to Lister's, its chimney looking small in comparison. It wasn't small, though. Built in 1865, it was two hundred feet high. She knew the exact height, because ever since she had been a small girl she had gone out of her way to find out everything she could about Rimmington's. Rimmington's wasn't just any mill. Rimmington's was owned by Caleb Rimmington and that made

Rimmington's very special indeed to Rose, for though she had never met him, Caleb Rimmington was her grandfather.

'I think we can be on our way home now, little love,' her father said, removing his arm from her shoulder and picking up his collapsible tripod. 'I've got some fine pictures of the city. They may even find their way into the *Yorkshire Observer.*'

Rose hoped so. She knew how much such photographic successes meant to him. Her father regarded photography as an art, taking as much pride in the pictures he took as he did in the paintings he occasionally sold.

As they began to walk away from their magnificent viewpoint and towards the distant tram terminus she said, her thoughts still on Rimmington's, 'If Grandfather Rimmington hadn't fallen out with Mother, when you and Mother married, would you have been Head Tapestry Designer at Rimmington's, not Lutterworth's?'

Laurence Sugden's handsome face, as classically sculpted as a Greek statue's, tightened. 'Now as to that, Rose lass, who's to say?' he said, keeping his voice light and indifferent as he always did whenever he was obliged to make any comment concerning either Caleb Rimmington or his mill.

Rose knew that he didn't want her to pursue the subject, but if she didn't, how would she ever *know* things?

'Do you think Grandfather Rimmington is ever curious about us?' she asked, as the houses that marked the tram terminus came into view. 'Do you think he ever wishes he *hadn't* fallen out with Mother when you and Mother married?'

Laurence sighed. He could understand Rose's mystification as to why her grandfather never made any contact with her, or with Noel and Nina, but how could he possibly explain it? He could hardly say that her grandfather was a pig-headed autocrat who, having once taken the attitude that his daughter had demeaned both him and herself by marrying one of his employees when he had had a much finer marriage marked out for her, would never change his mind about cutting her out of his life, not even if he lived to be a hundred.

'It's impossible to tell what other people think, Rose, or why they often do things which seem totally inexplicable.'

He looked down into her troubled eyes and his heart contracted. He had three dearly-loved children but this child, his youngest child, was the child of his heart. Unlike her elder sister Nina who, at fourteen, was already showing signs of becoming a head-turning beauty, Rose hadn't inherited his classical features. Her flaming red Rimmington hair had far too much ginger in it to be described as titian, her toffee-brown eyes were a little too large, her freckled nose a little too short, her generous shaped mouth far too wide. And from the first moment she had been placed in his arms, her unfocusing, Pekingese eyes meeting his, his heart had gone out to her in complete and utter love.

In the intervening years he had often wondered if the special feelings she had aroused in him had been occasioned by the knowledge that, without the armour of beauty, she would perhaps be vulnerable in a way her more favoured brother and sister never would be.

Despite his unhappiness at the subject under discussion, an amused smile touched the corners of his mouth. If, when she had been new-born, he had been thinking along those lines, then he couldn't have been more wrong. Rose's merry little personality was far from being that of an introverted plain Jane. She was totally unselfconscious and exuberantly outgoing, completely unenvious of the compliments her elder sister's delicately oval face, double-lashed sea-green eyes and gold-red hair, so ceaselessly garnered.

His smile deepened. Rose possessed a quality far rarer than physical beauty.

Like her mother, she possessed an infinite capacity for happiness and for making others happy, which was why, seeing her usually radiant eyes so troubled, his heart felt as if it were being painfully squeezed within his chest.

His fingers tightened around the strap of his camera case. Damn his father-in-law! His money and his mill meant nothing to Lizzie, but his affection did. And so, it seemed, it did to at least one of her daughters.

'Your Grandfather Rimmington strongly disapproved of your mother's wish to marry me,' he said at last, judging that she was now old enough to be told the truth of the matter.

'Because you were poor?'

He flicked a circling bee out of the way. 'Being poor is a relative thing, Rose. In your Grandfather Rimmington's eyes I undoubtedly *was* poor, but compared to lots and lots of other young men I was wealthy. I lived in a house that had an outdoor privy to itself. I never went barefoot. And I won a scholarship to Grammar School. No one who's ever received a good education can ever consider themselves to be poor.'

Rose digested this information in silence for a minute or two. She'd always known how much her father valued education and she'd always tried hard to make him proud of her where schoolwork was concerned. Not that she wanted to be a blue-stocking. She wanted to be a tapestry designer, like him. She was *going* to be a tapestry designer.

'If Grandfather Rimmington didn't want Mother to marry you,' she said, making the most of her father's sudden willingness to talk about a subject that had previously always been strongly discouraged, 'who *did* he want her to marry?'

Laurence's jaw tightened. The conversation was getting into deep waters, but now that it had been embarked upon there was nothing for it but to see it through to the end.

'Someone who could consolidate his social position,' he said, striving not to let his bitter feelings towards his wife's father show in his voice. 'Your great-grandfather Rimmington was a self-made man, Rose, and your grandfather wanted a son-in-law with a title, even if the title was only that of a Sir Somebody-or-other.'

Rose wrinkled her nose, unable to imagine her mother married to anyone else but her father. 'So that Mother would be a lady?' she asked, wondering just what a social position was, and if it was as uncomfortable as it sounded.

They were nearly at the tram terminus

now and though there was a tram waiting to make the return journey down into the city centre, her father didn't increase speed so that they could catch it. Instead he stopped walking and looked down at her gravely.

'Never be fooled into thinking that a title can turn anyone into a gentleman or a lady,' he said, with a note in his voice that Rose knew meant he was being very, very serious, 'because they don't. It takes far more than that, little love. It takes good manners and compassion and a love for everything that is beautiful and good. Your mother never had need of marrying a baronet in order to be a lady. She simply *is* a lady. And she would be a lady even if she'd been born in the poorest of Lister's or Lutterworth's mill cottages.'

Rose nodded. That her mother was a lady she understood very well. Everyone said so. Johnny, the milkman. Mr Jabez, who delivered their coal. Mr Todd, the headmaster of Toller Lane Junior School, who lived next door to them. Mrs Mellor, who lived next door on the other side of them and who rarely had a good word to say about anyone.

As, hand in hand, they resumed their walk towards the tram terminus, she said musingly, 'And do you think that Mother's brother's children know that Mother is a lady?'

It was a tortuous way of referring to her uncle and of bringing her cousins into the conversation but, as she had never met either her uncle or her cousins, she didn't know how else to do so.

'Your cousins?' Her father stared down at her bewilderedly. 'Well of course they know that Mother is a lady! She's their aunt and the only other family they have, apart from you and Nina and Noel. Grandfather Rimmington's refusal to allow any contact between Walter and your mother, or between Walter's children and you and Nina and Noel, doesn't alter that one jot.' His bewilderment gave way to bemusement. 'You really do ask the most peculiar questions sometimes, little love. You'll be asking me next how to spell Constantinople.'

Despite the weight of her thoughts, she grinned. Constantinople was the name of a pen and paper word game they often played and she'd been able to spell it ever since she'd been three years old.

There was no one else at the tram terminus and the tram that had been waiting there had left for its steeply downhill journey several minutes ago.

As they seated themselves companionably inside the welcome shade of the tram shelter she again referred to her cousins. 'Have *you* met them?' she asked curiously. 'Do they know all about us? Do they know our names?'

Laurence smoothed his neatly clipped moustache with his thumb and forefinger. It was only to be expected that Rose was curious about her cousins. Nina certainly was, though it was the difference in their lifestyles that most aroused Nina's curiosity. 'Is their house very, *very* big? Do they have maids? Does cousin Lottie go to school or does she have a governess?'

Knowing that Rose's questions would be far different and realizing that the subject was one she was going to pursue at least until the next tram arrived, he said patiently, 'I haven't seen them for a long, long time, little love.' Not since the day of your grandmother's funeral, he could have added, but didn't. 'And I'm sure they know your names. Just as you know theirs.'

Rose retrieved a Glacier Mint from the pocket of her blue and white gingham dress, removed some fluff that had accumulated on it and popped it into her mouth. 'And who is the eldest, William or Harry?' she asked, deeply interested.

Laurence set his cumbersome camera case and tripod down on the floor between his feet. Giving her information about her

Rimmington cousins was less traumatic than talking about her grandfather.

'William is the eldest,' he said, taking a pipe out of one of his jacket pockets and searching in the other for his tin of tobacco. 'He must be seventeen by now. Harry is a year younger. He was born the same year as Noel. And Lottie is just a little bit younger than Nina and a little bit older than you.'

'Then she must be thirteen,' Rose said, wondering if Lottie had the Rimmington red hair and, if she did, if it was a gingery marmalade colour, like her own, or a sizzling titian, like Nina's.

'Do William and Harry paint and play music, like Noel?' she asked, wishing she could meet them, wishing they lived as a proper family, spending Christmas and birthdays together and going for picnics together on Shipley Glen and Baildon Moor.

Laurence tamped tobacco into the bowl of his pipe. 'The Rimmingtons aren't artistic,' he said wryly. 'The artistic talent you and Noel have inherited comes from the Sugden side of the family. The Rimmingtons are all physical action. One of your great-uncles died fighting the Zulus. Another emigrated to the wilds of Canada and became a fur trapper.'

'And Grandfather became a wool baron?'

There was pride in her query and Laurence frowned slightly. 'That's how he likes to think of himself, yes,' he said, lighting his pipe, not wanting her to admire in any way the ruthless autocrat who had come damn near to ruining all their lives.

A tram trundled into view and they rose to their feet. 'I'm going to visit my Grandfather Rimmington when I'm older,' Rose said with fierce determination. 'Whether he wants to meet me or not, I'm going to meet him!'

Laurence clamped his teeth hard on his pipe stem. If this was the result of speaking frankly to her then the next time she asked for information about the Rimmington side of her family, he would exercise more caution. The very thought of her, or Nina and Noel, turning up on the doorstep of Caleb Rimmington's ostentatious mansion made the hair on the back of his neck stand on end. He and Lizzie had suffered enough explosive confrontations with her father to last them a lifetime and they most certainly didn't want any more.

'I don't think that would be a very good idea, little love,' he said as they stepped inside the tram. 'In fact, I think it might be a very, very bad idea.'

'Did Pa say *why* it would be a bad idea?'

Noel asked, frowning in concentration as he applied glue to a difficult join on the model monoplane he was making.

It was after tea and they were in the parlour. Unlike every other parlour they had ever been in, it wasn't a stuffy, uncomfortable room used only for when company called. Whenever it was even the slightest bit chilly a coal fire glowed in the black-leaded grate. Books vied for space with precious knick-knacks behind the glass-fronted doors of a walnut display cabinet. Against one wall was an upright Broadwood piano, its top crammed with silver-framed photographs. In the wide window-bay there was a mahogany table covered with a floor-length rust-coloured plush cloth, fringed at the hem. It was at this table that Noel was now working, intricate pieces of chamfered balsa-wood laying in neat piles on the sheet of newspaper that was protecting the plush from drips of glue.

'Well of course he didn't,' Nina said impatiently, anticipating Rose's answer and replying for her. 'It's a miracle he even *mentioned* Grandfather Rimmington by name. Mother certainly wouldn't have done. I can't count the times I've tried to wheedle information out of her but it's like getting blood from a stone. Absolutely impossible.'

She eased herself into a more comfortable position in the armchair that flanked the table and the open window, making sure that her bilberry-blue, ankle-length pinafore dress didn't get crushed in the process.

Outside in the neatly-kept garden Alba roses gave off a heady, sweet scent. A Jeanne d'Arc rose-bush was clustered with cascades of milk-pale flowers. At the window's edge a Félicité Parmentier positively ached with dense, hanging clusters, the colour of pale-pink coconut-ice.

'And it's so *frustrating,*' she added, picking up the ivory-backed nail-buffer that was laying in her lap. 'For all we know, Grandfather Rimmington might be as curious about us as we are about him.' She began polishing her nails with vigour, her glorious hair held away from her face with two heavy tortoiseshell combs. 'And think of the difference it would make to our lives if we were on good terms with him! There would be trips out in motorcars! Maybe even trips abroad! In another year or so, when he's eighteen, Noel would be able to study art in Paris or Florence and I—'

Before she could embark on a litany of the many material advantages bound to come her way if only they were on proper familial terms with Grandfather Rimmington, Rose said disapprovingly,

'Those aren't the right kind of reasons for wanting to be on friendly terms with Mother's family. The *right* reason is simply because they are our blood relations, our *only* blood relations.'

'Well, yes, of *course,*' Nina conceded, as if it were a fact too obvious for her to have bothered mentioning. 'But think how wonderful it would be if we were regularly invited to Crag-Side. A house that size must be marvellous for parties and dances. I bet it has a ballroom and a conservatory and—'

'It's a wool baron's house in Ilkley, not a Blackpool pleasure dome,' Noel said dryly, holding up to the light his near-finished model of the monoplane Louis Blériot had crossed the Channel in, so that he could inspect it more clearly. 'And as Uncle Walter is widowed I don't suppose they have many dances there. It's not as if our cousins are of age, is it? William's only a year older than me and Harry and Charlotte are only fourteen and fifteen, or is it fifteen and sixteen?'

'Pa said Harry was sixteen, like you, and that Charlotte was a little younger than Nina and a little older than me,' Rose said, glad that Noel was curbing Nina's exotic flights of fancy. 'Only he didn't call her Charlotte. He called her Lottie.'

Noel set the monoplane back on the table and pushed a tumbled lock of mahogany-red hair away from his eyes. 'Then there must be *some* contact between Ma and Pa and the Rimmingtons, or how else would Pa know that Charlotte was known as Lottie?'

It was a perceptive remark, voiced with little real interest. Noel had gleaned enough information about his Rimmington relatives over the years to have long ago come to the conclusion they were all Philistines. Blessed with wealth, neither his maternal grandfather nor his uncle patronized the Arts. It was an omission Noel found incomprehensible.

He said now, truly curious, 'Did Pa say if William was interested in art and design? He might be a student at Bradford Tech or at Leeds Art School.'

Rose was seated on a leather pouffe and she drew her feet up on to it, circling her gingham-skirted knees with her arms. 'Pa said *none* of the Rimmingtons are artistic. He said that they were all physical action and that one of our great-uncles died fighting the Zulus and that another emigrated to Canada and became a fur trapper.' She plucked a dust fluff out of one of the pouffe's buttoned dimples. 'I suppose that means that William will become a soldier or an explorer or something else wonderfully exciting.'

Noel gave a snort of derision and Nina said dreamily, 'I think officers look very handsome. I wonder if cousin William is handsome? He'll certainly be very rich when Grandfather Rimmington dies.'

'Aren't you forgetting Uncle Walter?' Noel asked dryly, swinging himself round on his chair, away from the table. A Félicité Parmentier petal fluttered in at the open window, settling on his hair. 'Cousin William won't be master of Rimmington's mill until his father dies, and I don't expect that will be for years and years and years.'

'But he'll be the *heir* during all those years,' Nina pointed out practically, 'and heirs are always able to borrow lots and lots of money.'

Rose felt an upsurge of irritation. Why was it that Nina was so mercenary-minded? Neither their mother or father were and Noel certainly wasn't. 'You think about money too much,' she said chastisingly, aware of how much their father would hate to hear Nina speaking in such a way. 'And it's cocoa time now and as Ma has gone to the Ladies Meeting at church one of us is going to have to make it, and I don't think it should be me because I made it last time Ma was out.'

'Pa isn't in either,' Noel said, as Nina

rose reluctantly to her feet, 'it's his teaching night at the Mechanics Institute so it's only cocoa for three and *please* make them with milk and not water, Neen. If there's one thing I can't abide it's thin and watery cocoa.'

Nina gave an exaggerated sigh as she crossed the room towards the door. 'I bet cousin Lottie doesn't have to skivvy around Harry and William,' she said, no real bad feeling in her voice. 'I bet cousin Lottie only has to ring a bell for a maid to come scurrying in to wait on them hand and foot.'

'Maybe she does, but I bet she doesn't have French roses in her garden,' Rose said, as Noel flicked the pale pink petal from his hair. '*No one* has as many roses in their garden as Ma has planted in ours.'

Noel grinned. 'And there's something else they don't have, little Rose. Artistic talent. Thanks to Pa, that's something we all have, even Nina.'

Nina paused at the doorway, determined to have the last word. 'I'd like my talent to be peppered with a little family money,' she said stubbornly. 'Just enough for me to go to Paris to study dress design, or perhaps Rome...'

Noel gave a roar of exasperation and threw a cushion at her. Nina burst into laughter, slamming the door adroitly against it.

'You forgot to ask her to bring some chocolate biscuits in with the cocoa,' Rose said, well used to such shenanigans. 'And I really wish Nina wouldn't harp on and on about the way the Rimmingtons have lots of money and we have only a proper amount of it. Pa doesn't like it. He says it shows a false set of values and it makes him unhappy.'

'Does it?'

Noel rose to his feet, crossing the room and sitting down beside her on the battered pouffe. He slid an arm lovingly around her narrow shoulders. 'Then I'll have a serious word with her about it. We don't want Pa being upset over a nonsense subject like the Rimmingtons, do we? Where did you and he go today to take photographs of the city? Odsal Top? Queensbury?

'Odsal Top.' Now that Noel had promised to seriously talk to Nina she perked up. 'And did you know that the upper third of Lister's mill chimney is pedimented and decorated with dummy window-arches, just like an Italian bell-tower? Rome is in Italy, isn't it? Do you think the bell-towers in Rome look like Lister's mill chimney?'

Noel gave a shout of laughter. 'What a marvellous thought! I'd love to believe they do, little Rose, but somehow I doubt it.' He hugged her close, continuing to chuckle. 'As Bridlington or Filey is the nearest we're likely to get to Rome we'll never know though, will we? Do you want a game of Halma before you go to bed? There's just time, or there is if you don't play every move as if your life depends on it!'

'Rome? In *summer?*' Thirteen-year-old Lottie Rimmington, clad in white from the broad silk ribbon holding her long fair hair away from her face to her neatly booted feet, stared at her father in disbelief. 'No one goes to Rome in summer, Papa. Even I know that.'

Walter had no doubt that she did. Despite the angelic way she was dressed she was a proper little madam and had been ever since she'd been able to walk and talk.

He adjusted his stance in front of Crag-Side's Italian marble fireplace, trying to look suitably parentally authoritative. Where his only daughter got all her unnerving self-assertion from he couldn't think. Certainly not from him. Even to think of the way his father had browbeaten him as a child brought him out in a cold sweat. And the browbeating hadn't ended when he had become an adult.

Behind his tweed-jacketed back his clasped hands tightened. As a young man he had wanted to enlist in the Army. It had been an ambition his bull-necked father had vetoed immediately. 'The Army? The *Army?'* Bradford's premier wool baron had thundered. 'The Army's for the second sons of minor gentry and the Rimmingtons aren't piffling minor gentry! We're money, lad! Wool money! And you're not a second son! You're my *only* son, and as heir to the biggest, most lucrative mill in the whole damn country, you'll damn well learn how to run it!'

It had been the same when he had fallen in love and wanted to marry.

'A Ramsden? A *Ramsden?'* Caleb had been so enraged his Yorkshire diction had become broad enough to cut with a knife. 'Who't bloody 'ell are t' Ramsdens when they're at 'ome? You'll marry a lass wi' a bit o' class and clout my lad, and Polly Ramsden 'as neither!'

Even at a distance of all these years anger spurted through Walter at the remembrance. His father had been wrong where Polly was concerned. She may not have come from a family that had the kind of social clout Caleb so hungrily yearned for, but when it came to sheer good manners and niceness she had had class in abundance. And what had he, Walter, done when faced with losing her? Why, he'd done what he'd always done. He'd crumpled spinelessly before the sheer force of his father's will, and he'd let her go.

Shame and regret coursed through him. She'd married someone else, of course, a weaver at Lister's, but not until he, also, had married.

He sighed heavily, oblivious of his daughter's slightly impatient scrutiny, looking down through the long tunnel of the years, remembering.

Lizzie hadn't been spineless. Lizzie hadn't made the mistakes he had made. As he thought of his sister the tension lines around his mouth eased. When Lizzie had fallen in love with Laurence Sugden she hadn't let Caleb's rantings and ravings deter her in the slightest. Faced with a choice of giving up the man she loved and continuing to enjoy their father's favour and all the material comforts such favour brought, she had opted for what their father had vengefully predicted would be a life of back-breaking penury with Laurence.

A glimmer of a smile touched his mouth. His father's passionate hopes had come to nothing there. Laurence Sugden was talented and hard-working enough to have been able, even in the early years of his marriage, to provide a modestly comfortable home for his wife and family. One of their next-door neighbours in Jesmond Avenue was headmaster of a local school; another was a doctor. And when it came to his father's pet subject 'class', Laurence had the easy, impeccable manners of a natural-born gentleman.

Walter's smile deepened. Laurence's speech didn't betray his mill cottage upbringing either, a fact he knew infuriated Caleb, whose broad northern vowels proclaimed his roots the instant he opened his mouth.

'What are you thinking of, Papa?' Lottie asked, giving in to her impatience. 'Are you still thinking about Rome? Because if you are—'

'I was thinking about your Aunt Elizabeth,' Walter said with unexpected frankness. 'I was thinking about how much I miss her companionship.'

And not just now, at this very moment, he thought heavy-heartedly. I've been missing it for nearly twenty years. I've been missing it ever since I allowed myself to be forbidden contact with her.

'Aunt Elizabeth?' Lottie forgot all about Rome. 'Aunt Elizabeth whom Grandfather won't let us mention and who lives in a slummy Bradford mill cottage?'

'She doesn't live in a mill cottage!' Walter shouted, taking Lottie so much by surprise that her jaw dropped and she gaped at him in disbelief. Her father never shouted. He never shouted at *anyone*. 'She lives in a large, newly-built family terrace house in an exceedingly pleasant part of the city!'

'Then why don't we ever visit her?' Lottie asked, recovering her composure with typical speed. 'We haven't got any other relations to visit and—'

'And if your Aunt Elizabeth *did* live in a mill cottage, it wouldn't be a slum,' Walter continued vehemently. 'It would be as pin-neat as many, many mill cottages are.'

Lottie was beginning to passionately wish William and Harry were in the room. She'd never, ever, seen her father so roused before.

'And just remember, young lady,' he continued with even greater vehemence, 'your own roots aren't worlds removed from slum housing. Rimmingtons haven't always lived in state at Crag-Side. Your great-grandfather was born in a cottage at Thornton that had earth floors and relied on a nearby beck for water.'

Lottie's eyes, the colour of bluebells before they opened, nearly popped out of her head.

'And when your great-grandfather dragged himself up by his boot straps and laid the foundation stone of his first mill, he didn't give a thought to the miserable living conditions of his workers,' Walter continued, stunning even himself at the thoughts he was, for the first time ever, putting into words. 'And neither did your grandfather when he approved the design for the present mill. Other mill owners did, though. Out at Saltaire, Titus Salt built a village for his workers. Housing, schools, places of worship, an institute, the lot. It's something Rimmington's could have done, and didn't. And because we didn't, it's something we should be eternally ashamed of.'

Lottie stared at him, transfixed. He was a radical, like William! Whoever would have thought it? Certainly not William, who had learned long ago that at Crag-Side it was prudent to keep his growing socialist conscience to himself. Should she tell her father that his seventeen-year-old son was a secret Labour Party sympathizer and that he even approved of the cause of the Suffragettes? She remembered her grandfather's often spoken intention that William was to be his heir where the mill was concerned, not their father, and thought better of it. A careless word from Papa in their grandfather's hearing about William's political sympathies and there might be no end of trouble.

Having relieved himself of thoughts that had festered for years Walter blinked. The vast drawing-room was very quiet, the only sound the ticking of the French ormolu clock on the marble mantelpiece.

Reading his mind all too clearly Lottie said with touching gravitas, 'Don't worry Papa, I won't let Grandfather know you think we should all be eternally ashamed.' She paused for a moment, her head tilted thoughtfully, 'Titus Salt became *Sir* Titus Salt, didn't he? Was that because of the workers' village he built? Might Grandfather have become a Sir as well if he had done something similar?'

Walter didn't answer her. He was in need of a brandy and he couldn't drink one at ten in the morning before his young daughter. Well aware that for the last few minutes he had been behaving completely out of character and wondering if he was coming down with influenza, he walked unsteadily past her and out of the room.

'And he said that he missed Aunt Elizabeth's companionship and that she *didn't* live in a slummy mill cottage,' Lottie said to her fascinated audience as they lay sprawled on the lawn after an energetic game of croquet, '*and* he said that not all mill cottages are slummy, though how can he know?'

Harry pushed a sleek lock of dark hair away from his forehead. 'Perhaps Pa's a secret visitor of the poor?' he suggested, vastly amused.

'*And* he said that Great-grandfather Rimmington was born in a cottage that had to rely on a beck for water and that when Great-grandfather dragged himself up by his boot straps and built his first mill—'

William rolled onto his stomach. 'If Great-grandfather was born into such poverty, where did the boots come from in the first place?' he interrupted. 'I've always wanted to know and never been able to find out. If—'

'If you interrupt again I shall forget something,' Lottie said crossly. 'Now, where was I?'

'When Great-grandfather had built his first mill,' Harry prompted obligingly.

'When Great-grandfather built his first mill he didn't make any provision for housing for his mill-workers,' Lottie continued, 'and he said Papa didn't do so either when the present mill was built and that their not having done so was to our eternal shame.'

Harry's eyebrows shot nearly into his hair. William looked incredulous.

'And the annoying thing is,' Lottie continued, her voice heavy with disgust, 'if Great-grandfather or Grandfather *had* made provision for their workers, as Titus Salt did, they'd have probably been knighted by the King and I would be Lady Charlotte Rimmington, not just plain Miss Rimmington!'

At this guileless disclosure of where her true indignation lay, Harry whooped with laughter.

William pursed his lips.

Seeing his look of disapproval, Lottie said defensively, '*And* there would have been statues of Great-grandfather and Grandfather all over Bradford, just as they are statues of Titus Salt, and you can't tell me you wouldn't have liked *that*, William!'

'No, I can't,' William said truthfully, 'but I'm fairly sure my reasons for doing so would be different to yours.'

Before Lottie could indignantly retaliate, Harry said speedily, 'Did you know that Aunt Elizabeth and her husband have three children, two girls and a boy? It's strange to think we have cousins we've never met, isn't it. I wonder what they're like? I wonder if we would like them?'

Lottie didn't know and didn't care. She'd just remembered something else; something her father's subsequent conversation had put completely from her mind. She sat bolt upright, saying in happy self-importance, 'Papa said something else as well. Something you're never going to believe. He's taking us on a foreign trip next month. He's taking us to *Rome!*'

## Chapter Two

On a beautiful May morning in 1910, Lizzie Sugden stood on her front doorstep, a spotlessly clean apron tied around her waist, the sleeves of her boot-skimming, raspberry linen dress pushed high to her elbows. 'Rose! *Rose!*' she shouted, looking up and down the cobbled street for a glimpse of her daughter's distinctive head of hair.

'You're wasting your time, Mother,' Nina, now a very grown-up sixteen, said from the room the front door opened immediately onto, 'she went out with Jenny Wilkinson an hour or so ago.' She held her sketch pad out in front of her, the better to judge the summer walking dress she had just outlined. Should she have made it arrow-straight all the way down to the ankle-length hem, or should she have given the skirt a little more width so that it fell in narrow fluted folds?

Deciding that it looked far more elegant arrow-straight, and that the edging of silk piping she had given the collars and wrist-length cuffs would look even more effective if it also ran in parallel lines from points midway on the shoulders, curving in a little to delineate the waist before continuing on down to the hem, she said a little peevishly, 'I don't know why Rose spends so much time with someone who comes from the mill cottages. It's a wonder she doesn't catch nits.' She gave an exaggerated shudder, mindful of her own crowning glory. 'And if she did, she would give them to *all* of us!'

Lizzie gave up the task of trying to call Rose in and turning her back on the street, said with unusual tartness, 'That's quite enough High and Mightiness Miss, Jenny's mother was Polly Ramsden before she married and Rose won't catch nits, or anything else, from any of Polly's children.'

Nina forgot all about her dilemma of whether to colour the walking-dress navy blue, with emerald silk piping, or whether to opt for lilac with deep mauve piping. 'How do you know anything about a family who come from the mill back-to-backs, Mother?' she asked, addressing her mother, as she always did, in the way she was sure her pampered and privileged cousin Lottie addressed hers.

'Never you mind,' Lizzie said, deciding that if she wanted to speak to Rose about the letter that had arrived that morning, confirming she would be attending Bradford School of Art when the new term started in September, she would have to go out and look for her and, remembering the time, long ago now, when her brother had been in love with Polly Ramsden, the prettiest weaver to ever enter Rimmington's vast loom room.

She untied her apron. Rimmington's. Why was she thinking of it now, when she had schooled herself so strictly never to do so? Was it because she was well aware of Rose's ambition to one day be Head Tapestry Designer there?

'Keep your eye on the kitchen-range, Nina,' she said, as she set a wide-brimmed black straw hat on top of her hair. 'There's a custard tart on the bottom shelf of the oven and I don't want the nutmeg burning to a crisp.'

She turned on her heel, walking speedily and yet with head-turning grace, out of the house and down the short front path to the street. That it would be absolutely impossible for Rose to achieve her ambition both she and Laurence knew only too well. No matter how extraordinary her talent, their daughter wouldn't be allowed over the threshold of Rimmington's in any capacity, let alone one customarily only entrusted to men. Lutterworth's would be a possibility, though. Even though women designers were virtually unheard of, the management at Lutterworth's might just allow Laurence to employ her.

With her sleeves now rolled down and buttoned at the cuffs she walked down the neat, respectable street to the busy road that lay at its foot. What she was doing was utterly pointless, and she knew it. The news of Rose's acceptance into art school would keep until hunger eventually brought Rose home again. And yet...in all the years she'd lived with Laurence in Jesmond Avenue she had never ventured across the busy road that separated it from the long streets of smoke-blackened, back-to-back cottages that sprawled downhill on its far side, reaching almost as far as the beck that ran into, and through, the centre of the city.

For the past couple of years she had known that Rose, on a trip to nearby Lister Park, had made friends with a girl who came from the cottages, a girl whose widowed mother worked as a weaver at Rimmington's and whose name was Polly.

As Lizzie began to make her way carefully across the road, side-stepping a temporarily stationary horse-drawn rag-and-bone cart and narrowly avoiding a horse-drawn omnibus, she wondered if Polly Wilkinson, née Ramsden, the girl Walter had fallen in love with and wanted to marry, would recognize her?

There was no reason why she should do, of course. They had only met once when Walter, eager to have at least one member of his family's approval of the girl he hoped would be his wife, had introduced her to Polly in a little café just off Forster Square, in the city's centre.

By now she was half-way down a steeply cobbled road of terraced back-to-back mill cottages, and poverty was becoming more apparent with every step she took. Many of the children playing noisily in the street were barefoot. Other, luckier ones, wore clogs. Doorsteps were clean, though, scrubbed and painstakingly white-stoned, and line after line of washing was strung across the street, blowing gently in the summer breeze.

'Do you know which house the Wilkinsons live at?' she asked a woman standing at one of the many open doorways.

The woman settled her weight against the door jamb, her beefy arms folded across her ample chest. 'And what if I do?' she asked, her eyes raking Lizzie from head to foot and taking in the quality of Lizzie's plain and practical week-day dress and her neat, cared-for boots.

'I'm looking for my daughter. She's a friend of Jenny Wilkinson's.'

The woman shifted her stance a little, her eyes brightening with interest. 'Are ye the ma of that funny-faced imp wi' the carroty hair?'

Lizzie, recognizing the description as being a reasonably accurate one of her much-loved daughter, nodded.

The interest in the woman's eyes deepened. 'The Wilkinsons live rahnd t'back of number twenty-six,' she said, nodding her head in the direction of a house a couple of doors down. 'Lah-di-dah talk won't cut any ice wi' Polly Wilkinson, mind. She used to have a reet fancy boyfriend in her young days if everything ye hear is true.'

Lizzie hadn't taken two steps towards the dark, built-over passage leading through to the house backing on to number twenty-six when there came the sound of footsteps running through it and girlish shouts of laughter. A second later a fair-haired girl in a rough calico dress and boots, Rose at her heels, burst out of it into the narrow street.

She stopped abruptly at the unexpected sight of a stranger. Rose ran into the back of her, her eyes flying open so wide they were the size of a marmoset's. 'Mother! What on earth...? How did you know...? Why...?'

'You've been accepted at Bradford School of Art, love.'

Rose gave a choked gasp and then dashed

past her friend, throwing herself into her mother's arms. 'Oh, isn't that wonderful, Ma? Isn't that just too wonderful for words!?'

Lizzie hugged her. As far as she was concerned, what was truly wonderful was the artistic talent all three of her children possessed. Noel, at eighteen, wasn't remotely interested in putting his talent to use in the commercial world, but was determined to find fame and fortune as a practising artist. Nina burned to be a dress designer and dreamed of working for one of the great fashion houses in London or Paris or Rome. And Rose...Rose wanted to be like Laurence. She wanted to make designs for cloth—worsteds and tapestry—designs that would put the mill she worked for into the small league of mills known world-wide.

On the face of it, Rose's was the most modest of their three ambitions, but even her ambition would take every little bit of her energy and tenacity and obstinate will-power.

With a radiant face and shining eyes Rose said, 'And you don't mind me visiting Jenny? I don't usually. I usually meet her in Lister Park when she's finished work and I've finished school. Jenny's been working in the mill for a month, ever since she was fourteen, and—'

'Shut up, you silly ha'porth,' Jenny said, giggling with nervousness and flushing scarlet. 'Your mam don't want to know that!'

Lizzie looked into Jenny's bright, intelligent eyes, wondering if she was a mill girl at Rimmington's; wondering if she knew that Rose's grandfather was Caleb Rimmington.

*'Jenny!'* Polly Wilkinson's voice carried clearly as she walked with quick, light steps, through the echoing passageway. 'I've made bread and dripping for both of you and if you don't come in for it, it's going to go dry.'

She emerged into the sunlight of the street and smiled at Lizzie. 'Nice to meet you. Are you Rose's ma? I was just...' her voice died away.

Lizzie read the recognition in Polly's eyes—and the disbelief. Elizabeth Rimmington in a serviceable linen dress and plain black straw hat? And in a street of mill cottages? Polly's incredulity was blatant.

'Yes, it's me, Polly,' she said, stepping towards her, unknowingly just as distinctively stylish in her modest, week-day clothes as she had been in the days when she had been Miss Elizabeth Rimmington of Crag-Side, the only daughter of one of the richest men in Yorkshire. 'I'm

Mrs Sugden now. My husband works at Lutterworth's and we live not far from here, just the other side of Toller Lane.'

Polly's work-roughened hand flew to her throat. 'I knew Rose was a cut above us, but I never thought...I never imagined...'

'Have you a kettle on the boil?' Lizzie asked, knowing the only way to put Polly at her ease was to do so over a friendly cup of tea, 'Because if you have, I'd love a cup of tea. My throat's parched.'

Polly giggled suddenly—a giggle not very different from that of her daughter's. 'All right, then, Mrs Sugden. Come in and have a cup for old time's sake.'

As the two women turned and began to walk together through the covered passage, Rose and Jenny stared at each other. They were both old enough to know that their own friendship was unusual enough, but that their *mothers* should be on friendly terms?

'I wonder if my Pa knows?' Rose said. 'I know my elder sister doesn't. My elder sister wouldn't believe it in a million years!'

'Of course I don't disapprove, love,' Laurence Sugden said that evening as he and Lizzie sat in the pleasant coolness of their back garden. 'I don't want Rose to ever start choosing her friends on the basis of where they live, or don't live, but you have to remember that I've worked all my life to get away from the poverty of the mill cottages and that I never expected to see any of my children frequenting one.'

Lizzie took hold of his hand, to show that she understood. In retrospect, her impulsive urge to visit Polly Wilkinson had not been very sensible, and nor had her easy acceptance of Rose's presence there. She didn't totally regret her actions, though. She had liked Polly from the first moment of being introduced to her and, if Walter had had the backbone to have followed his own inclinations and married her, would have been more than happy to have had her as a sister-in-law.

'I don't suppose it's a friendship that will last once Rose starts art school,' she said comfortingly. 'I'm going to take her shopping tomorrow to buy a portfolio case and a new set of brushes. Nina's coming with us.'

Beneath his moustache Laurence's mouth tugged into a smile. 'No doubt Nina's doing so in the hope that if shopping's being done, something might just come her way.' He gave her hand a loving squeeze. 'You don't mind if I sit out here a bit longer and enjoy a smoke, do you love?'

Lizzie shook her head. 'I'll be getting

on with some ironing,' she said, rising to her feet.

The scent of nightstocks and roses were heavy in the evening air as she crossed the grass to the kitchen door. At the step she turned, looking back towards her husband. He was the picture of contentment, his pipe in his hand, blue smoke wisping upwards, a man at peace with himself and with the world.

'Now that we've done our shopping can we have tea and toasted teacakes somewhere?' Nina asked Lizzie as, with Rose clasping her new, brown-paper-wrapped portfolio case and brushes, the three of them walked along Market Street in the city centre.

It lay in the very bottom of the bowl that was Bradford, one of the very few streets that was not uncomfortably steep. Horse-drawn wagons and carts and omnibuses clattered along it, vying for space with bicycles and the occasional motorcar. On their right-hand side were the ornate window displays of Brown & Muff's, the city's smartest department store. In one window Nina glimpsed a walking dress of blue serge decorated at the neck with a lace fichu. It wasn't a quarter as stylish as the walking dresses she had sketched the previous day.

'I'm too tired to walk up Ivegate to

Kirkgate Market,' Lizzie said, referring to the covered market where they usually stopped for tea and toast. 'As a way of celebrating Rose following you and Noel to art school, let's have tea in Brown & Muff's instead.'

Nina almost purred with delight. Tea at Brown & Muff's! It was a practically unheard-of treat. There would be cream cakes instead of common-or-garden tea-cakes; cream cakes that would be served on doily-covered plates; cream cakes that had to be eaten with little silver cake-forks.

'And can we look in the fashion department?' she asked as Lizzie led the way to Brown & Muff's imposing entrance.

Lizzie nodded, not at all averse to looking in Brown & Muff's fashion department herself, though she wouldn't, of course, be able to buy anything. However adequate Laurence's wage as Head Tapestry Designer at Lutterworth's, it wasn't *that* adequate, not when they had three artistic, ambitious children to support.

She was just about to say 'yes' to Nina's request when a motorcar the size of a ship chugged to a stop at the kerb-edge. The paintwork was a gleaming blue-green, the upholstery cream calfskin. Chaos was caused as the drivers of more mundane vehicles slewed round at their wheels to have a closer look; a horse harnessed to a lightweight cart shied in panic; pedestrians on both sides of the street stopped to gawk.

Lizzie stopped too. She hadn't see her niece or nephews for eight years, not since her mother's funeral, but she recognized them with ease. William, dark-haired and tall and rangy, like his father. Harry, even darker-haired and with broad shoulders and an easy athleticism about him that spoke of perfect physical fitness. Only Lottie, a white straw hat perched on top of mouse-fair hair that hung straight as a dye down her back to her waist, would she have had difficulty in recognizing.

'Who are they?' Nina hissed as the trio began to cross the pavement to Brown & Muff's main entrance.

Lizzie, grateful that Nina, despite all the many local newspaper cuttings she had collected about her cousins over the years, hadn't yet recognized them, didn't reply.

Instead, as Rose and Nina took a noseying step nearer to Brown & Muff's entrance, she took a step backwards, adjusting the wide brim of her purple, weekend-best hat, so that it shielded her face a little more. Not, she thought wryly, that her niece and two nephews were likely to recognize her, or acknowledge her even if they did so.

A wave of regret surged through her. She would have liked to be on loving terms with them. At nineteen, William, the elder boy, was the very spit of Walter at the same age, even down to his air of self-conscious awkwardness. No such awkwardness blighted his younger brother. Despite her discomfiture she felt a glimmer of amusement. Where on earth had Harry's air of utter assurance come from? It was so blatant it was almost indecent. As for the demurely dressed Lottie... Lizzie could recognize a handful when saw one and the stubborn tilt of Lottie's chin told her she was seeing one now. Her amusement deepened. How on earth was her easily brow-beaten brother going to keep his two younger offspring in line?

Only feet away from Brown & Muff's entrance, Rose shifted the awkward parcel in her arms into a more comfortable position. What on earth were Nina and her mother waiting for? They'd been approaching the entrance first, hadn't they? Why should they be waiting for people to go before them, simply because the people in question had arrived in a grand motorcar? And what if they, too, were on their way to Brown & Muff's café and there was only one table free?

She stepped forwards, intent on reaching the entrance before the girl with the long mousy hair could do so. The girl, startled, didn't stop in her tracks soon enough. As the inevitable collision took place Rose's precious new portfolio case skidded from her arms.

Dimly she was aware of Nina's cry of embarrassed mortification; of the girl's cross expletive; of the elder of the young men saying in concern, 'Are you all right, Sis?'

Uncaring of them all she bent down to retrieve her portfolio case. The younger of the young men beat her to it.

'Here you are,' he said with an easy grin as they faced each other, both of them still hunkered down. 'The wrapping's got a little bit scuffed but I'm sure whatever is inside is unmarked.'

A lock of near black hair had tumbled low over his brow and he looked suddenly very approachable and not at all like a sniffy young man who had just alighted from an outrageously expensive motorcar.

'Thank you very much,' she said gratefully, taking it from him. 'It's an art portfolio case and—'

From somewhere above them the girl said impatiently, 'Do come *on,* Harry!'

For no reason she could think of Rose found herself grinning back at Harry. His sister had spoken to him just as Nina often spoke to her.

'At least you're not hurt,' he said, as their amused eyes held and complicity flashed between them. 'Do you want to open up your parcel and check to see if your portfolio case is damaged?'

He stood upright and, suddenly aware that for the last couple of minutes the many pedestrians who had stopped to gawk at the motorcar were now gawking at them, Rose also straightened up, saying hastily, 'There's no need. I'm sure it's all right.'

The older young man and the girl had already disappeared into Brown & Muff's elegant interior and as Nina darted eagerly to Rose's side, Harry flashed Rose a last, disarming, down-slanting smile, and turned to follow them.

'Well!' Nina said expressively, indignant at Rose's crassly clumsy behaviour, envious at the encounter the clumsiness had resulted in and crushingly disappointed that she, too, hadn't managed to exchange a few words with what had to be the most handsome, eligible young man she had ever seen, or was ever likely to see. 'You really surpassed yourself there, Rose! Fancy dashing rudely in front of people like that! What *must* they have thought?'

She looked around for their mother,

saying as Lizzie walked up to them, 'Do you think we should hurry after them and apologize to them for Rose's behaviour, Mother? After all, it was very kind of the young man to pick up Rose's parcel for her and he was...was...' She flushed in confusion. She could hardly say to her mother that he was the most gorgeous looking young man she had ever seen in her life, '...and he was *thoughtful,*' she finished lamely.

Lizzie, well aware of her sixteen-year-old daughter's true feelings, said crisply, 'I don't think that is necessary, Nina. And I don't think we'll take tea in Brown & Muff's after all. It's bound to be crowded with wool-mens' wives. If we walk up Ivegate to Kirkgate Market I can buy some sewing thread from the haberdashery stall.'

Nina's disappointment was so intense she was robbed of speech. Rose, not similarly inconvenienced, said chattily as they walked towards the bottom end of steeply climbing Ivegate, 'That young man was nice, wasn't he? He's called Harry, just like one of our cousins, and...'

Nina stopped dead, the blood draining from her face. She remembered the photographs that had appeared in the *Yorkshire Observer* when the Rimmington family had come back from their Italian trip a couple of years ago. Her Rimmington cousins had altered quite considerably since then, Harry in particular had grown much handsomer, which was why she hadn't put two-and-two together immediately she had set eyes on them. She knew now, though. Their approximate ages alone were a sure giveaway. William nineteen or twenty. Harry eighteen, the same age as Noel. Lottie fifteen, a year older than Rose.

'It was them!' she croaked, looking almost as if she was going to faint. 'It was our cousins!' She turned anguished eyes on her mother who had stopped and turned towards her. 'And you knew, Ma, didn't you?' she said, for once forgetting to call Lizzie 'mother'. 'That's why you hung back when everyone else was staring at them, and at their motorcar! It's why we're now walking to Kirkgate Market instead of going into Brown & Muff's café!'

Well aware that Nina was on the verge of making a minor spectacle of herself in the street, as Rose had just inadvertently done, Lizzie said unhappily, 'Yes, I'm fairly sure it *was* your cousins, but we could hardly have introduced ourselves to them on the street, could we? And besides, what would have been the point? They've been brought up to have nothing to do with us whatsoever, and so our introducing ourselves to them could only have led to deep embarrassment, for them as well as for us.'

'Was that young man truly cousin Harry?' Rose asked, goggle-eyed. 'He was very nice!' She remembered her cousin Lottie's cross exclamation when her collision with her had taken place. 'And I'm sure cousin William and cousin Lottie are as equally nice,' she said generously.

'Oh, do be quiet, Rose!' Nina's voice was strangled with frustrated tears. 'You're such a baby you simply don't understand!'

'Whether Rose does, or doesn't understand, *I* understand that I have no intention of standing in the middle of Ivegate while you make a spectacle of us all,' Lizzie said, her frayed nerves beginning to show. 'Unless you begin to walk in a proper manner towards the market I shall simply take you both home.'

As Lizzie turned on her heel and began walking up the steep street with purposeful speed Nina felt tears sting the backs of her eyes. How could her mother be so dismissive of such a wonderful opportunity lost? Didn't she realize that if they had made themselves known to their cousins they might now be sitting in Brown & Muff's café, taking tea with them? And that afterwards they might even have been given a ride in Grandfather Rimmington's sumptuous, *wonderful* motorcar?

'Come on, Neen,' Rose said, entranced at the realization that the young man she had felt such instant rapport with, was her cousin Harry. Her father had certainly been right about the Rimmingtons being men of action. It would be *very* easy to imagine cousin Harry in uniform and on horseback, or cutting his way through unexplored jungles, or climbing previously unconquered mountain peaks. She remembered the very different impression cousin William had given. Perhaps her father hadn't been *utterly* right after all. Perhaps cousin William was more dreamy and artistic; more like Noel.

'Come on,' she said again as they began to lag behind Lizzie. 'We don't want to be taken home without having toasted teacakes, do we?'

Nina clenched her fists so tightly in frustration that she split the stitching on her wrist-length summer gloves. 'To *hamlet* with the teacakes!' she said explosively, using the worst expletive she knew. 'Don't you understand that though we now know who *they* are, *they* don't know who we are?'

Rose's eyebrows lifted in surprise. 'But they will one day, Neen,' she said with absolute certainty, 'and when they do, cousin Harry will remember picking my parcel up for me. Just you wait and see.'

'I wonder what would have happened if Walter had been with them?' Laurence said musingly to Lizzie as they lay that night in the sublime comfort of their brass-headed, feather-mattressed bed. 'I know he's never risked your father's wrath by making any communication with you, but surely in those circumstances, taken by surprise as he would have been, he would have acknowledged you?'

'I'm not sure,' Lizzie said, as she lay in the loving embrace of his arms, her white, broderie anglaise trimmed nightdress as demure and virginal as a young girl's. 'If his children hadn't been with him, he would certainly have done so. But he could hardly have asked his children not to say a word of such a meeting to their grandfather, could he?'

Laurence gave a grunt of exasperation. As far as he was concerned, his brother-in-law could certainly have done such a thing. Why Walter hadn't stood up to his father years and years ago, Laurence couldn't even begin to imagine. If he'd done so, he wouldn't have lost the girl he'd so dearly wanted to marry and he wouldn't have lost Lizzie's loving companionship either.

'As far as your Walter's concerned, all that can be said is that there's nowt so queer as folk,' he said, grateful that none of their children showed any of their uncle's spinelessness. He pulled her closer, brushing the top of her hair with his lips. 'Let's be getting a little shut-eye love. I've felt a bit under the weather today.'

'It's the heat,' Lizzie said, wondering if she should mention Nina's quite obvious instant infatuation with Harry. She shrugged the thought away. The disturbing question of Nina's fast blossoming womanhood could be left for another day. She closed her eyes, wondering how Harry would have reacted if he had known that Rose was his cousin; how William and Lottie would have reacted.

'Good-night, God Bless,' she said to Laurence, sad that her children, and her brother's children, were being denied the pleasure of growing up together as loving friends.

'He was very nice and he looked sort of...buccaneering,' Rose said next morning at breakfast in answer to Noel's query about Harry. 'I didn't notice William or Lottie very much because I didn't speak to them. I only spoke to Harry.'

Nina cut a slice of buttered bread into 'soldiers' and laid them on the side of her plate, next to her egg and eggcup. She'd given her three cousins a great deal of thought during the night and she wasn't so sure now that Harry had been *quite* as handsome as she had first supposed. William, who would one day eventually inherit both Rimmington's mill *and* Crag-Side, had really looked very...distinguished. Thoughtfully she sliced off the top of her egg. Yes, distinguished was the word—and sensitive. There was, after all, something just a little common in the way Harry had so swiftly squatted.down to scoop Rose's portfolio case from the flagstones—and he way he had remained in that undignified position when talking to her.

'Do you want a cup of tea, Pa?' Rose was asking their father.

'Yes, pet.' Laurence walked across to the kitchen table, lines of strain edging his mouth. He paused before sitting down, rocking slightly on his feet.

'Steady on, Pa,' Noel said, glancing up at him in concern.

Laurence raised a hand to his high starched collar, as if to loosen it, saying with surprise in his voice, 'I don't feel very well, son.'

As they all turned to look towards him he said again, 'I don't feel very well at all,' and then, in a moment of horror they were to remember for the rest of their lives, his face contorted and he pitched forwards over the table, sending milk jug and teapot, eggs and eggcups, cutlery and crockery, flying.

## Chapter Three

*'Run for the doctor, Rose!'* Noel shouted as he leapt to his feet.

Rose was aware of Nina screaming, of her mother crying out 'Laurence! *Laurence!'* as she rushed ashen-faced towards him.

*'The doctor, Rose!'* Noel shouted at her again as he tried to break their father's terrible slither to the floor amid steaming scalding tea and rivulets of milk and dribbles of egg yolk.

For a second that seemed to last a lifetime Rose was unable to force her legs to move and then, with a choked gasp, she spun on her heel, running as she had never run before in her life.

Dr Todd removed his stethoscopes from around his neck and laid them back in their case. His patient was lying on his side on a horse-hair sofa in the parlour, covered with a light blanket. Not even with the help of Noel and a neighbour would he have been able to manoeuvre Laurence up to a bedroom and nor had he desired to do so. It was his belief that a room central to the day-to-day doings in a house was far more suitable for a bedridden patient than the isolation of an upstairs room. And he had absolutely no doubt that Laurence Sugden was going to be bedridden for a long, long time.

He said now to Lizzie, 'Your husband has suffered a severe stroke, Mrs Sugden. He may eventually recover some power of speech, but he's never going to communicate with ease again. As for the use of his right side...' He shook his head unhappily. 'I doubt he's ever going to be able to use his hand and arm, or leg, again.' He placed his stethoscope case in his capacious black bag. 'Your husband's been very effectively crippled, Mrs Sugden. My advice to you would be to turn this room into his bedroom. A bed positioned so that he can see out of the window and take pleasure and interest in what is going on in the street...'

Lizzie swayed, grasping hold of a winged-back chair for support, wishing that Dr Todd hadn't asked to speak to her in privacy; wishing that her children were with her. 'But Laurence is only forty-three, Doctor! What about his job? What about his *talent?*'

Her knuckles whitened on the maroon leather of the chair. Until now, all she had felt was dizzying, all-engulfing relief that Laurence was still alive; that he wasn't going to die; that she wasn't going to have to live the rest of her life without him. Now, for the first time, a glimmer of understanding of what lay ahead, dawned.

Her eyes were black pits in the chalk-white pallor of her face. 'My husband is an *artist,* Doctor! He's Head Tapestry Designer at Lutterworth's! He *has* to be able to have the use of his right hand!'

Alan Todd sighed and picked up his battered black bag. How was it that shock so annihilated commonsense? Hadn't he just told her that her husband had suffered a stroke so severe it was doubtful he would walk again? That being the case, how could she still have been under the impression he would one day return to work? Things would be hard for her financially, of course, though if the rumours he had heard were true, not as hard as it was for others in her position. Caleb Rimmington would no doubt ease her now harshly straitened circumstances—and she had two children of working age and one of near working age. With the elder two in the mill the Sugdens would manage all right. It was those who had no such advantages he felt sorry for; those for whom the loss of ability to work meant utter destitution.

'You must reconcile yourself to the fact that your husband's working days are over,' he said bluntly. 'I shall call in and see him regularly, of course, but his general nursing care will be up to you and your daughters. Give him easily digestible food that doesn't need chewing, pobs will be sufficient over the next two or three days—and change his position frequently so that his paralysed limbs don't take up unnaturally cramped positions.'

He picked up his Homburg. 'There are no hard and fast rules about strokes, Mrs Sugden. If the will-power is there a measure of speech and movement may be regained, but there'll be no more painting, of that I can assure you.' He nodded a courteous goodbye, put his Homburg on his head, and walked out of the room and out of the house.

Lizzie stared after him, numbed by the horror coursing through her. On the sofa Laurence lay immobile, no longer a man in the prime of life, fit and virile, but a man suddenly old before his time. His eyes were closed, but whether he was asleep or not she wasn't sure. Had he, perhaps, heard all that Dr Todd had said? And if he hadn't, how would she be able to bring herself to break the news to him? Distraught sobs rose high in her throat. Why, oh why, hadn't it been his left side that had been affected? If it had been his left side he would still be able to draw and paint and life would be bearable for him. As it was...

The pain she felt on his behalf was so intense she didn't know how she was going to bear it. 'Oh my love,' she whispered brokenly, sinking down beside him and taking one of his inert hands in hers. 'Oh, my dear, dear love!'

There was a nervous tap on the parlour door and Noel put his head around it, his face almost as ashen as his father's. 'We heard the doctor leave. What did he say? Is Pa going to recover? Is he going to have to go into hospital?'

Lizzie rose heavily to her feet. 'It's best if we talk in the kitchen,' she said, not wanting to discuss things in Laurence's inert presence.

The short walk into the kitchen seemed to take forever for she knew that at the end of it, when she had told Noel and Nina and Rose of the dependent, disabled future their father faced, nothing would ever be the same for them again. Noel's dream of becoming a working artist and Nina's ambition of becoming a dress designer would be ground into dust. They would have to leave art school and find jobs in order to bring money into the house.

She stumbled, feeling as if her heart was being squeezed dry in her chest. Noel and Nina in one of the local mills? It didn't bear thinking about, not after all the soaring dreams she and Laurence had encouraged them to have. Yet if they didn't go into a mill, what was the alternative? She couldn't go in a mill in their stead. She was too old old to begin to learn spinning or weaving or even burling and mending, and besides, she was going to have to nurse Laurence.

As she entered the kitchen Nina and Rose turned pinched, frightened faces towards her.

'What did the doctor say?' Nina demanded quaveringly. 'Is Father going to have to go into hospital? Is...'

Rose ran towards her, throwing her arms around her, both giving and receiving comfort and Lizzie hugged her close, shaking her head in response to Nina's question.

'No,' she said in a cracked voice. 'Your father isn't going to have to go into hospital.' As she felt Rose's tremor of relief and saw the same vast relief flash through Nina's eyes, she added swiftly, 'But that's only because there's nothing that can be done for him in hospital, or at least nothing that we can't do for him ourselves, at home.'

Rose looked up at her, her toffee-brown eyes almost black with concern. 'Shall I go and sit with him now, Ma?'

'It's apoplexy, isn't it?' Noel said tautly.

'Pa's suffered an apoplectic stroke, hasn't he?'

Lizzie nodded. Noel would probably know what that signified, but would Nina and Rose?

She sat down at the kitchen table, waiting until they were seated around her before saying, 'Your father is going to need a very great deal of care...'

'I'll help care for him!' Nina was almost buoyant at the thought. Caring for a sick father seemed so romantic somehow. Perhaps her cousin William would hear of it and...

Lizzie clasped her hands together very tightly. There was no easy way of saying what had to be said, and the sooner it was said the better. 'Your father's stroke has paralysed his right side...'

'But it will get better, won't it?' Rose's voice was thick with urgent hope. 'When I sprained my wrist I couldn't move it for ages and ages it was so painful, but the swelling went away eventually and—'

'A stroke isn't a sprain, darling,' Lizzie kept her voice steady only with the greatest difficulty. 'There may eventually be improvement, but Dr Todd doesn't think your father will ever speak clearly again or...or...' her hands were clenched so tightly together the veins in them stood out like those of an old woman's, rigid and blue, '...or walk again, at least not unaided.'

There was a choked, incredulous cry from Noel. Nina's jaw sagged. Rose didn't move a muscle. It was almost as if she had stopped breathing. Somewhere in the background a clock ticked. Through the open window there came the sound of a distant lawnmower being trundled up and down.

'And nor is he likely to ever recover the use of his right arm and hand again,' Lizzie finished.

The clock chimed the half-hour. The lawnmower grated on the edge of a flagged pathway. Three blank, uncomprehending faces stared at Lizzie.

'But Pa *has* to have the use of his right arm and hand,' Noel said at last, as if somehow she, and Dr Todd, had not understood the obvious. 'He's an artist. You did tell Dr Todd that, didn't you? I mean, Dr Todd does *know*, doesn't he?'

Lizzie couldn't speak. To speak would have been to break down completely.

Slowly, with terrible finality, understanding dawned in the three pairs of eyes holding hers.

*'No!'* Noel roared, catapulting to his feet so violently that his chair fell over backwards. *'Jesus God!* NO!'

No one had ever heard such a profanity

uttered in their house before. No one cared.

Nina choked, pressing her hands to her mouth. Rose's monkey face was all sharp angles, as if the skin had been pulled tightly up and over her cheek bones.

Lizzie passed a hand across her eyes, waves of panic beating up into her throat. Should she tell them what the consequences of Laurence's stroke were going to be? It was obvious that they hadn't, as yet, thought out what his inability to work was going to mean for them all. And when she did tell them, what then? How would they come to terms with the grim reality that was now their future?

Noel solved her dilemma for her. Spinning on his heel he rushed blindly for the back door, yanking it open with such force it rocked on its hinges. Seconds later the gate slammed after him. As his running footsteps faded into the distance up the cobbled guinnel dividing the rear gardens of Jesmond Avenue from the rear gardens of the next street, Nina began to cry in earnest.

Rose stood up unsteadily, saying in a voice as brittle as glass, 'I'm going to sit with Father. And I'm going to pray. I'm going to pray *very hard!*'

Lizzie nodded, grateful for the stay of execution Noel's abrupt departure had given her. She, too, was going to pray. And she was going to do something she had never done in all her married life; she was going to go through the bureau where their household papers were kept. If God was very, *very* good, a scrutiny of their finances might show that with frugal management they could survive without Nina or Noel having to leave art school or, at the very worst, of only one of them having to do so.

Rose sat with her father until her mother came into the parlour with a bowl of warm milk in which small pieces of white bread were soaking.

'I'm going to see if your father will eat some pobs,' she said, sitting down in Rose's place at the side of the sofa as Rose rose to her feet. 'Would you go in search of Noel for me?'

Rose nodded, saying helpfully, 'Pa's not asleep. He keeps opening his eyes and trying to talk, but his face is all lopsided and I can't understand what he's trying to say.' Barely suppressed tears made her voice wobbly, 'And every time the words don't come out right his eyes look *frightened.*'

She, too, looked frightened.

Lizzie's heart went out to her. 'It's going to be all right, Rose,' she said gently, praying to God she was speaking the truth. 'Somehow or other we're going to manage, and somehow or other your father will be able to communicate with us again.'

Comforted, Rose managed an unsteady smile. Of course it would be all right. How could it be otherwise when her father was still alive and they were still a close, united little family?

She found Noel down by the Bradford Beck. He was seated on its shallow grassy bank, his clasped hands hanging loosely between his bent knees as he stared sightlessly at the tumbling, gurgling water.

Rose sat down beside him. Ever since they had been small children they had loved playing in, and near, the Beck. Just a short distance from where they now were it went underground, emerging after a short distance to run behind warehouses and mills before going underground again, this time not emerging until it had run beneath the city centre and was well on its way to the River Aire, at nearby Shipley.

Everyone Rose knew referred to it affectionately as 't' mucky beck', and she had never been able to understand why, because at Bull Royd, where they were now, and above Bull Royd towards

Thornton and Allerton, the Beck ran like a country stream between narrow fields, its banks speckled with kingcups and marsh marigolds and ragged robin.

'It's mucky when it reaches the mills,' her father had often said to her, 'the mills pump their waste into it and have done ever since the first mills were built on its banks.'

Rimmington's mill wasn't built on the Beck's banks and for that Rose had always been very glad. She would have hated Rimmington's to have been one of the mills which disposed of its waste in such a heedless manner.

As Noel picked up a small pebble and threw it desultorily into the water, she said, 'Everything's going to be all right. Mother says so. She says Father will soon be able to communicate with us in some way or other and that—'

'How?' Noel demanded with a ferocity that made her flinch. 'By sign language? By making noises like a toddler learning to talk? And what does it matter even if he *is* able to speak properly again, if he can't draw and paint? What does *anything* matter if he can't draw and paint anymore?'

Rose looked at his still averted head with troubled eyes. Art was so all-important to him that he couldn't conceive it might not be equally all-important to their father, and with sudden insight Rose knew that it *wasn't* so all-important to their father. Their father loved art passionately and was proud and respectful of his talent, but it had never dominated his life as it dominated Noel's. Too many other things made their father happy. Their mother. Themselves. Sitting in the garden in the summer dusk with his pipe. Listening to the local brass band whenever it played in Lister Park. A game of draughts or Halma with her or Nina. A game of chess with Noel.

She said with utter certainty, 'Lots of other things will still matter to Pa; lots of other things are precious to him. Mother. You and me. Nina.'

Noel groaned and ran a hand through his fiery hair. There were times, and this was one of them, when Rose's ability to always think positively almost drove him to distraction.

'Why are things so simple for you, Rose?' he demanded, wishing with all his might they were so simple for himself. 'You may have oodles of artistic talent but you don't have an ounce of artistic temperament.'

Rose shrugged. She wasn't sure she wanted an artistic temperament. All she wanted to do was to handle fabrics and design patterns for them.

She picked a daisy and twirled it round between her fingers. 'Pa's not going to be able to work anymore, is he?' she said perceptively. 'And if he's not even going to be able to get out of the house we're going to have spend lots and lots of time with him so that he doesn't get bored.'

Noel frowned, a sudden thought occurring to him. It was so ridiculous he shrugged it away. There would be insurances and his mother very probably had a small private income of her own.

'I'm going back home,' he said, springing to his feet. 'I'm in the middle of painting a self-portrait and I'm curious how my reaction to Pa's stroke is going to affect it. I can't possibly look the same, can I? And even if I do, it's not mere physical resemblance I'm after. It's my psyche.'

Rose remained where she was. Noel didn't need her. When his head was full of creative fervour he didn't need anyone. As he strode off over the grass towards the crowded streets that ran down to the Beck's fields she hugged her knees with her arms, aware that life had changed dramatically and might never be the same, ever again.

Lizzie pushed her chair away from the mahogany bureau and tucked a straying wisp of hair back into the loose knot on top of her head. It was the fifth time she had gone through their rent-book and bank-book and bills, and the conclusion was inescapable. Without Laurence's wages from Lutterworth's they couldn't possibly afford to live as they had been doing. Their rent, which had once seemed reasonable, now seemed monstrous. The figures in Laurence's bank book, instead of offering comfort, merely seemed to mock her. All their married life Laurence had earned enough to keep them in modest comfort but his income hadn't been such that he had been able to amass any notable savings. He had no pension to look forward to. No sick benefit.

She rubbed her temples with her fingers, trying to ease the build-up of pressure behind her eyes. Could she take a lodger in? It would mean either her, or Nina and Rose, moving into the attic and that in turn would mean Noel no longer having a studio of any kind. And how much would a lodger bring in? Would it be enough to keep Noel and Nina from going into one of the mills? And if they did go into a mill, which mill would they go into? They couldn't go into Rimmington's. She would *die* before she allowed them to work as mill-hands in their grandfather's mill. And Lutterworth's would be nearly as bad. How could they enter the weaving or spinning sheds at a mill where their father had one held such a respectable position?

She leaned her head back, stretching out her throat muscles, gazing sightless up at the prettily moulded ceiling. There was one solution to the problem that would keep Noel and Nina from mill work, but it was so extreme, would have been previously so utterly unthinkable, that she didn't know how she would be able to confront Noel and Nina with it. Rose, she knew, would immediately see the sense of it and adapt willingly and with sunny cheerfulness. Noel, too, as long as he was able to continue with his Fine Art studies, might very well be understanding about it. But Nina would certainly not be understanding. Nina would be devastated. Her heart hurt as she thought of the distress that was going to be caused whatever the action she took. In the end, all she could do was set the choice before them. She only hoped that when it came to making it, they would be unanimous in their decision.

'Do you like this idea for a ladies evening shirt?' Nina asked Rose that evening when they had cleared the table and washed and dried the dishes together. Their mother was in the parlour with their father. Noel was in his makeshift studio. She passed her sketch pad across to Rose. 'It's to be worn over a skirt and it would be cut like a djibbah and edged at the hem and neck with braid.'

'What's a djibbah?' Rose asked, interested.

'It's a loose-sleeved garment they wear in the Middle East.'

Rose was impressed. When it came to clothes, there was hardly anything Nina didn't know.

'And would you make it out of silk?'

Nina shook her head, her titian hair tumbling so thick and loose around her shoulders that she looked as if she had just stepped from a Burne-Jones painting.

'No,' she said, removing the sketch pad from Rose's hand and beginning to pencil in the braid, 'chiffon. I thought it would look best in a really glorious searing pink. Or maybe a patterned chiffon. Pink and orange or pink and purple.'

Rose nodded in approval. There wasn't a wool-man's wife in a fifty-mile radius of Bradford who would be seen in anything so Orientally exotic, but the *clientèle* Nina dreamed of dressing wouldn't be wool-men's wives. They would be society women; maybe even French or Italian society women, or even New York society women.

The door clicked open and their mother walked into the kitchen. 'Would you ask

Noel to come down?' she asked Nina, her high-cheek-boned face pale and strained. 'There's something I want to say to you all.'

'It might be best to leave it till tomorrow,' Nina said, still sketching and not looking up. 'You know how Noel hates being disturbed when a piece of work is going well, and this latest self-portrait is going well, it's—'

'I want Noel down here, *now,*' Lizzie said, such an odd expression in her voice that Nina's head jerked upward, her eyes meeting her mother's eyes in blank astonishment.

'I'll go.' Rose pushed her chair hastily away from the table. She'd never heard her mother speak in that tone of voice before. Not *ever.*

Before Nina could protest she scampered from the room. Perhaps Dr Todd had been back to see their father when they hadn't been around. Perhaps he had made a fresh diagnosis. Perhaps their father *was* going to go into hospital after all.

'Go away, I'm busy,' Noel said, standing before his easel in his old painting clothes, a much-used palette in one hand, a brush in the other.

'Mother wants you,' Rose said, panting slightly after her hurried climb up the steep attic stairs. 'I think it's about Pa and I think it's very important. She looked very...*taut.*'

Noel sucked his breath in between his teeth in frustration. He loved his mother dearly but, being a Rimmington, she didn't truly understand what being an artist *meant.* She seemed to think a creative urge was something that could be turned on, or off, like a tap. He wondered if Van Gogh had ever been similarly plagued by his family. If he had, it was no wonder he'd gone mad.

'I'm coming,' he said, curbing his irritation with difficulty and putting his palette and brush down on the nearest available, cluttered surface. 'I can't imagine what can be so important, though. We've all come to terms with Pa's condition, haven't we? We all know it's going to be a long slow haul before there's any improvement. I thought if I could finish a really grand piece of work it would buck him up no end.'

'It will,' Rose said as she clattered down the drugget-covered stairs in his wake. 'He's taking much more of an interest in things now and he's stopped looking so frightened when he tries to speak and only makes funny sounds. Ma told him he *had* to make funny sounds because we would all soon begin to understand what he meant by them. While you're downstairs you should look at Neen's latest dress design. It looks like something out of the *Arabian Nights.*'

They burst into the kitchen, Noel with paint splodges on his face and hands, his hair standing up in tousled spikes where he had run his fingers through it.

'Rose said you wanted a word with me,' he said to Lizzie, straddling a wooden kitchen chair and resting his folded elbows on its back.

'I wanted a word with all of you.' Lizzie looked round at her dearly-loved, oh so talented children. 'This isn't going to be easy, my loves. It's going to be very, very difficult.'

Nina put her sketch pad down on the table, more bewildered than ever. Noel wondered if the radically different, more loosely applied brushwork he was now practising expressed inner emotion in the way he intended it to. What he was after was an effect of tension between the image depicted and the paint on the picture's surface. If he perhaps used a far more crude and violent colour tone...

'There simply isn't going to be the money to continue living as we have been doing,' Lizzie said gravely, breaking in on his thoughts. 'The rent on the house is considerable and over and above that, we have to have money for day-to-day living expenses. If your Father is unable to work again...'

They all three stared at her with rapt attention, waiting to hear what the solution would be. An insurance policy, Noel thought, his thoughts again straying to the possibility of applying non-natural colour in his self-portrait. If he did so, his self-portrait would look even more distorted and, in doing so, would hopefully express his inner emotions in a much more direct manner.

'Whatever money Grandmother Rimmington left Mother when she died,' Nina thought, wondering if she could take her Oriental theme even further by designing daring 'harem' trousers. They would be worn beneath a skirt, of course, and be just visible.

'If Pa can't work, perhaps we'll have to,' Rose thought, her tummy muscles knotting tightly and giving her a queasy feeling. It would mean no art school for her—and if she didn't go to art school, how could she ever achieve her dreams.

'If your father is unable to work again,' Lizzie repeated, her clasped hands tightening until the knuckles showed white, 'then we are going to have to drastically reorganize the way we live.'

There was silence.

At last Nina said perplexedly, 'I'm sorry,

Mother, I don't quite understand. In what way will we have to reorganize how we live? I know Father's going to need a lot of care, but—'

'We're going to have to go out to work, aren't we?' The speaker was Rose. There was no horrified disbelief in her voice, only troubled acceptance. After all, if their father couldn't work any more, *someone* would have to, and it was obvious that their mother couldn't, for their mother would need to be home in order to nurse their father.

With a violent exclamation Noel sprang to his feet, running his hands through his already chaotic hair. 'For the Lord's sake, stop talking rubbish, Rose! If Ma could just explain what she means by our having to reorganize our lives...'

'I mean that there is not enough money for you to continue at art school and that—'

'*No!*' Nina pushed her chair sharply back from the table, her eyes so panic-stricken she looked almost deranged. 'I won't leave art school! I can't!' Her voice was shrill with rising hysteria. 'I'm going to be a dress designer! You and Father have always agreed I should become a dress designer! How can I ever become one if I have to work in a shop...'

Her voice tailed off in stupefied horror.

In a gesture straight from Greek tragedy she clasped her throat with both hands. 'You don't intend for me to work in a shop, do you?' The pupils in her green cat-eyes had widened so much the irises could barely be seen. 'Shop girls don't earn enough money, do they? You mean for me to work in a mill—and for Noel to work in a mill as well!'

Noel made a strangled, choking sound. Rose's eyes remained fixed on her mother's. She could tell that her mother had more she wanted to say to them. Perhaps she was going to explain an alternative. Perhaps...

'There must be some Rimmington money somewhere!' Noel's voice was barely recognizable, hoarse with naked fear. 'I mean, when Grandma Rimmington died you went to the funeral, didn't you, Ma? You and *Grandma* Rimmington never fell out, did you? And Grandma Rimmington must have had *some* money of her own and left you a bequest in her will!'

Rose could almost feel Nina holding her breath—and she knew that Nina was wasting her time. For anyone with eyes to see, the anguish on their mother's face was answer enough to Noel's question.

Wearily Lizzie shook her head. 'No, Noel,' she said, knowing the terrible blow she was dealing him. 'My mother never disobeyed my father once in her entire life, and she didn't do so where her will was concerned. No money, or possessions, were left to me by her.'

No one spoke. No one could think of one earthly thing to say. Nina began to cry. Rose moved nearer to Lizzie, sliding her hand in hers. At last Noel said in strangled tones, 'There must be an alternative! There *must* be!'

Lizzie's hand tightened on Rose's. 'Oh yes, there is an alternative,' she said, knowing that the moment of decision-making had come. 'If I began to take in sewing and we lived very, very frugally, we could perhaps make ends meet—but only if we no longer had to pay such a high rent on our home.'

Noel wiped beads of sweat from his forehead with the back of his hand, so grateful at the thought of a reprieve, *any* reprieve, he didn't give a thought to what the alternative of not paying a high rent might be. Nina stared at her blankly. How could the rent they paid on their home be reduced? Even she knew that rents never went down, that they only ever went up.

Rose blinked, a glimmer of understanding beginning to dawn in her eyes. Of course! Why hadn't *she* thought of it? What Noel would think of what she was sure their mother's solution to their problem was going to be, she didn't know, but she knew that Nina would hate it. She frowned. Nina couldn't possibly hate it as much as she would hate not being able to continue with her studies at art school. No one could. It simply wasn't possible. And there would be compensations. They would be nearer Bull Royd and the Beck and...

'It would mean our moving into another, smaller house,' Lizzie said, breaking in on Rose's racing thoughts, 'and one in not such a nice area.'

'Blow the area,' Noel said, again running his hands through his hair but this time in a gesture of infinite relief. 'I could do some work evenings and weekends to help out, maybe even give some private art lessons.'

'Where?' Nina asked tautly, her eyes locked fearfully on her mother's. 'Where would we move to that we could afford? *This* area is hardly staggeringly smart, is it? I know it's nice enough and our neighbours are professional people, but we're still in sight of Lister's mill chimney and the mill back-to-backs are only a stone's throw away. Where on earth could we move to that would be cheaper?'

Lizzie felt her heart twist in her breast. She had never once regretted her action in turning her back on a life of luxurious ease in order to marry Laurence, but she did bitterly regret her father's oxlike obstinacy in refusing to acknowledge her children. It meant that none of them enjoyed even a taste of the lifestyle Walter's children enjoyed and though Noel seemed uncaring of the fact, and Rose oblivious, she knew that Nina longed for the kind of clothes and travel and society that were so well within her cousin Lottie's reach—and as far from her own reach as the moon. And she knew that for Nina, the move she was about to suggest would be a fate worse than death.

She hesitated for one last, agonizing second and then, knowing there was no acceptable alternative, she answered Nina's fear-filled question, 'The mill cottages,' she said. 'There's one empty next to the Wilkinsons and the landlord says we can move in immediately.'

## Chapter Four

Ever after, Rose was to look back on the next few moments of time as being nearly almost as bad as the moment when her father had lunged senselessly across the kitchen table, plunging their lives into previously unimagined upheaval.

Noel's reaction had been one of stunned incredulity, but even as his eyebrows had shot high and his jaw had sagged, reluctant acceptance had flared through his eyes. He would be able to continue his studies. What did it matter where he lived as long as he didn't have to risk injury to his hands by working at a loom or a twisting machine?

It was Nina's reaction that touched the moment with unforgettable hideousness. She hadn't protested, hadn't even spoken. She had simply screamed.

Lizzie had sprung to her feet with a speed of movement totally alien to her usual effortless grace. Seizing hold of both Nina's hands she had tugged her to her feet, shouting at her for the first time ever. *'Stop that, Nina! Stop that this minute! What on earth will your father think is happening?*

*Do you want him to have another stroke? Do you want to make things even worse than they are?'*

'I'll go in to Pa and reassure him,' Noel had said, his thoughts already turning to how he would find room, in a back-to-back, for a makeshift studio.

'It won't be so bad, Neen.' Rose had felt physically sick at the depth of Nina's distress and her voice had been fraught with urgency as she had tried to offer some comfort. 'Polly Wilkinson's mother is ever so nice and she and Ma are already friends.'

Nina hadn't been remotely comforted. Stunned with shock at being shouted at in such a way by her mother she had ceased screaming and, sobbing hysterically, had gasped, 'Why should we have to live in a mill worker's back-to-back? We're *Rimmingtons* as well as being Sugdens! What will our cousins think if they find out? They'll never have anything to do with us, will they? Not ever, ever, ever!'

'Somewhere along the line your values have got exceedingly misplaced, Miss!' Lizzie had let smartly go of Nina's hands and had breathed in deeply, her fine-etched nostrils pinched and white. 'And unless your cousins' values are equally cock-eyed, and I sincerely hope they aren't, where we live will make not the slightest difference to them.'

Nina had shaken her head, her hair tumbling wildly around her shoulders. Her mother was wrong. She *knew* her mother was wrong. And she knew that she would never be able to become accustomed to living in a house with no plumbed-in bath and no indoor lavatory and amongst neighbours who wouldn't even know what a dress designer was; neighbours who would wear clogs instead of shoes, and shawls instead of hats and coats.

'It isn't fair!' she had whispered, her face blotched and streaked by tears. 'It isn't *fair!*'

Lizzie had known it wasn't fair, and that other things weren't fair either. It wasn't fair Laurence having been struck down and left unable to move unaided and unable to communicate articulately. It wasn't fair that when her father had such vast personal wealth she wasn't able to go to him in their time of trouble and have that trouble eased.

Her spurt of anger, occasioned only by her own distress, had vanished and with an aching heart she had drawn Nina into the comfort of her arms, saying with loving compassion, 'Life isn't fair, my love. It never has been and never will be, and it is something each and everyone one of us has to come to terms with.' Smoothing

Nina's fiery, turbulent hair as if she were a child she had added gently, 'And we have to contain our distress, my pet, for if we don't your father is going to be aware of it and then *he* is going to be distressed even further and that won't help his recovery. It won't help his recovery one little bit.'

As Nina had drawn in a shuddering, steadying breath the stairs had creaked and Rose, knowing what the sound signified, had walked out of the kitchen. Noel was returning to his paints and brushes and their father was on his own again. As she crossed the foot of the stairs, heading towards the parlour, she wondered how her father would feel at moving from their modestly substantial home into a mill cottage—a mill cottage near identical with the cottage he had been born in and had worked so hard to escape from.

'I suppose the mercy is, Mr Sugden won't be aware of where you're having to move to,' Rose overheard Mrs Mellor saying to her mother a week later as her mother stood at their front garden gate supervising the loading of their belongings on to a removal cart.

Lizzie checked there was enough crushed newspaper packing a crockery-filled tea-chest and said evenly, 'My husband has lost some power of movement and speech,

Mrs Mellor, not his wits. He's quite well aware of where we're moving to—and he's grateful that our new next-door neighbours are a family Rose and myself have long been friendly with.'

'Is that so?' There was arch disbelief in Mrs Mellor's voice. She didn't for one moment believe stylish Lizzie Sugden had, as yet, had anything to do with any of her new neighbours-to-be. How could she have? The social gulf dividing the residents of wide, tree-lined Jesmond Avenue from the mill workers and similar who inhabited the long narrow streets of the back-to-backs, was as deep as a chasm.

Rose's arms tightened around the bedding she was carrying. 'The house we're moving into is next door to my *very best friend's house,'* she said fiercely, well aware of Mrs Mellor's scepticism.

Mrs Mellor sniffed. Where Rose was concerned, nothing would surprise her. She resisted the temptation to ask Rose if it would have been more correct to have described her friend's house as being back-to-back with the house they were moving in to, not next door, but Lizzie Sugden was still within earshot and she thought better of it, saying instead. 'And how is your poor father going to be moved into your new home? He's not going to be able to walk there, is he?'

Lizzie saved her from replying. She had been having a brief word with the removal man's boy and she now stepped away from him, saying as she began to walk back up her garden path, 'Dr Todd has kindly offered to chauffeur my husband to our new address,' and then, turning her attention immediately to Rose, 'Don't stand dawdling and chatting, love. I want the eiderdowns and pillows on the cart before the beds and mattresses are loaded.'

As Rose obediently hurried off in the direction of the removal cart with her bulky cargo, Mrs Mellor watched Lizzie re-enter her now half-empty house, an expression of grudging respect in her eyes. 'Chauffeur' indeed! Lizzie Sugden might be suffering a severe reversal of fortune but she'd certainly lost none of her annoyingly effortless style. She folded her arms across her chest and sniffed. Stylishness, as Lizzie Sugden was so painfully finding out, was all very well but it didn't pay the rent, nor would it go down too well in a street of back-to-backs. Lizzie Sugden was going to have to trim her sails in more ways than one when she moved in amongst her new neighbours. Mrs Mellor sniffed again. She wouldn't want to be in Lizzie Sugden's shoes—not for all the tea in China.

'We're ready, Missus,' Albert Porritt, the

removal man, said an hour or so later as he patted his horse's muzzle, his shirt sleeves rolled high, a battered trilby pushed to the back of his head. 'You're flitting into number twenty-six Beck-Side Street, aren't you? I don't want to be off-loading all your worldly goods at t'wrong house.'

'Neither do I.' Lizzie kept control of her composure with difficulty. The moment had come; was finally here. Noel and Dr Todd had already, and with the greatest difficulty, manoeuvred Laurence into Dr Todd's motor car. The house behind her, her home for all her married life, was stripped bare. Nothing was left but the roses in the garden. She stood at the gate for the last time, breathing in their scent.

On the far side of the street a muslin curtain twitched and another was pulled discreetly aside to enable the watcher behind it to see more clearly. A flare of anger, white-hot, spurted through her. What were her neighbours, who for years had been civilly friendly towards her, afraid of? Did they think the bad fortune necessitating her family's move might be contagious? Whether they did or not, it was obvious none of them intended coming out into their front gardens in order to say goodbye to them.

Rose slid her hand into hers. 'We'll make *real* friends in Beck-Side Street,' she said, reading her mother's thoughts all too clearly. 'Did you know Mr Porritt lives there? Do you think he'd let me ride there on the cart? I'm sure there'd be enough room up on the front of it.'

Lizzie squeezed her hand. It wouldn't be a very dignified way for Rose to arrive at their new home, but what did that matter? She was the only one taking the move in her stride and if she wanted to arrive on the removal cart, and if Mr Porritt didn't have any objections, then neither did she.

Nina, seated in the rear seat of Dr Todd's motorcar, her arms around her father in order to keep him at least half upright, hadn't been nearly as understanding.

'She's doing *what?*' she had said, the last vestige of blood draining from her face. 'But how can you *allow* it, Mother! People will think we're tinkers!'

'People will think what they want to think,' Lizzie said crisply, determined not to enter into a conversation that would cause Laurence even more distress than he was already suffering.

With Dr Todd's gentlemanly assistance she settled herself in the front passenger seat, aware of an unnerving sense of *déjà vu.* This wasn't the first time she had turned her back on a way of life. Before, it had been in order to pursue her own happiness; now, it was in order that her children could keep their precious dreams and one day, God willing, attain them.

'I think we're ready to leave, Dr Todd,' she said steadily, adjusting her black straw hat with a net-gloved hand. 'Noel has gone on ahead with the key to open up the house and Mr Porritt has promised that the instant he arrives, he and his boy will unload the sofa so that Laurence can rest while the remaining furniture is moved in.'

Dr Todd made a noncommittal noise in his throat. He wasn't accustomed to letting his patients' lives touch him so closely and wasn't overly enjoying the experience. Beck-Side Street was no sort of address for a family like the Sugdens and just why they were moving there, instead of the older children finding employment and compensating for Laurence Sugden's loss of income, he couldn't for the life of him understand.

Albert Porritt, ignorant of the fact that the insipid-looking young fellow who had gone ahead to open up the house, and the dramatically pale young woman tending her sick father in the rear of the motorcar had, between them, never done a day's paid work in their lives, was equally flummoxed. He'd moved all sorts of families in his time, and under all sorts of conditions, but he'd never moved a family quite as hard to fathom as this one.

They didn't talk right, for one thing. Here they were, about to move in to a mill back-to-back, and even the friendly little lass now wedged between him and his lad, spoke as if she were a nob from Harrogate or Ilkley. He wondered if the sick head of the household had been a Grammar School teacher. Lots of Grammar School teachers were very particular about how they spoke and how their children spoke. He cracked his whip over the head of his horse in order to hurry it up a little. One thing was for sure; the entire blooming family would have to learn to speak a little differently if they were to feel at home amongst their new neighbours.

'That newfangled motorcar'll 'ave arrived at t'house by now,' his son, Micky, suddenly said, awe at the very thought of Dr Todd's motorcar, thick in his voice. 'I bet there's nivver bin a motorcar in Beck-Side Street afore. I bet its mekkin' a right commotion.'

'T'Lord Mayor has one,' Albert said knowledgeably. 'And if I had a cart wi' a motor instead of this 'ere old 'oss, I'd be able to do that many jobs, that blooming quick, I'd be as rich as t'bloody Lord Mayor mesself.'

Rose listened to the conversation with

interest. She liked Mr Porritt. He'd let her hold his horse's reins all the way down Jesmond Avenue, only taking them from her when the horse had clip-clopped out into the busier roads.

'My grandfather has a motorcar,' she said artlessly. 'It's much bigger than Dr Todd's and it isn't black, like Dr Todd's, it's a lovely blue-green colour.'

'Oh, aye?' Albert looked down at her, disbelieving amusement in his eyes. She might speak all lah-di-dah but she wasn't lah-di-dah enough to have a grandad with a motorcar even posher than the one now ferrying her father to Beck-Side Street, because if she had been, she and her family wouldn't be moving into Beck-Side Street in the first place. 'And I suppose it has a flag in front, like t'King's?' he said affably.

Rose, well aware that he was teasing her, grinned. It didn't matter that he didn't believe her. All that mattered was that he was yet another resident of Beck-Side Street she was on friendly terms with. She wondered whereabouts in Beck-Side Street he and his son lived, and where he kept his horse. She wondered, if she asked nicely, if he would let her help him look after it.

'There's a right crowd gathered to see t'motorcar,' the previously silent Micky now said, as the horse turned into the top end of Beck-Side Street and they could see clear down to the bottom end of it, and the fields and the Beck beyond. 'I knew it'd cause a commotion. I bet that cheeky Jenny Wilkinson is pestering to have a ride in it.'

'Jenny Wilkinson isn't cheeky,' Rose said, immediately defensive. 'She's my best friend.'

Micky shifted his feet against the board they were resting on, his heavy wooden clogs making a grating noise. 'I know,' he said, not looking at her as he had carefully avoided looking at her all morning. 'I've seen you and her laiking together in t'street.'

His father's eyebrows rose slightly. If the freckled-faced baggage so enamoured of his horse had, indeed, already a friend in Beck-Side Street, then she wouldn't have much of a problem in quickly feeling at home there. He couldn't imagine her elder sister having a friend there, though. He couldn't imagine her elder sister having a friend there *ever.*

As Dr Todd's motorcar putt-putted over the cobbles of Beck-Side Street and people crowded out on to their front steps to gawp at it, Nina's arms tightened around her father, not so much to steady him as to gain some comfort from him. The street was even worse than she had imagined it would be. Long and straight, it seemed to stretch downhill into infinity, only the arches of the built-over passageways leading through to the 'backs' breaking up the uniform tedium of smoke-blackened stone.

'I'm so so...orry li...ittle l...ove,' her father said with immense effort, patting her arm lovingly with his still mobile left hand.

She blinked away the tears that had been threatening to fall. 'There's no need for you to be sorry, Father,' she said fiercely, feeling instant remorse at having allowed him to read her feelings so clearly. 'You couldn't help having a stroke. And we won't live in Beck-Side Street forever.' Her eyes were brilliant as emeralds with the force of her determination. 'We won't live in Beck-Side Street a day longer than is absolutely necessary!'

'We're going to be living in Beck-Side Street till kingdom come,' Noel said bitterly six months later as he and Nina walked morosely by the side of the Beck heading aimlessly in the general direction of Allerton. 'The trouble is, Rose and Ma *enjoy* living cheek-by-jowl with the Wilkinsons and all the other friends they've made. I don't. I find it utterly impossible. There's no room to work. I'm trying to stretch a four-foot by five-foot canvas and it's impossible in a room eight-foot by three, especially when there's a bed in it into the bargain!'

Nina was sympathetic. She was also envious. Despite the unsatisfactory smallness of Noel's room at least he didn't have to share it. She had to share with her mother and Rose and when the three of them were all in the room together there wasn't room to swing a cat. Nor was there an inch of space anywhere else in the house. Downstairs there was only one all-purpose room. Stone-flagged and, unlike most of the other houses in Beck-Side Street, carpeted, it had a door leading to the short, steeply curving flight of bedroom stairs, a door leading to the cellar-head and another door which led straight out on to the street. One wall was dominated by a vast black-leaded kitchen range containing both oven and fireplace. Their father's bed took up a large amount of room beneath the only window, a hand sewing-machine was almost permanently in evidence on top of the table.

'Even if you had room to work, there wouldn't be any peace and quiet to work in,' she said dryly, letting her fingers trail over the tips of high-growing grass. 'If Jenny Wilkinson isn't helping Rose do the laundry in the cellar-head sink, and laughing and chattering and slopping water all over the place as she does so, then her mother is on our doorstep gossiping with Mother or Albert Porritt is sitting chin-wagging with Father.'

Noel grunted. He didn't object on any deep-down level to either Jenny Wilkinson and her mother, or Albert Porritt and young Micky, or any of the host of other neighbours who were always in and out of their house. It was just that he had never been accustomed to having his home treated as if it were an extension of the street. In Jesmond Avenue, friendliness had been restricted to chats on the pavement or in the local shops and when people *had* called at the house, they had knocked at the door first. No one knocked at doors in Beck-Side Street. In Beck-Side Street, doors were always off the latch and in good weather, nearly always ajar or wide open.

He said musingly, 'It's strange, isn't it, how Ma, brought up in a house as vast as Crag-Side, has so easily adapted to taking in sewing and living in a mill cottage no bigger than a rabbit hutch.'

They'd reached a point on the Beck's banks where a cluster of trees grew close to the water and Nina halted. This was as far as she intended walking. If Noel wanted to mooch on as far as Allerton he could do so on his own.

'Mother's happy if Father's happy,' she said perceptively, 'and she knows that Father's happier living in Beck-Side Street, and having you and me and Rose still at art school, than he would be living in Jesmond Avenue waiting for us to come home from the mill every day.'

Noel made no response. It was unlike Nina to be so prosaic but for once she had stated a truth there was no escaping from and she had also lobbed in a reminder of just why their present living conditions had to be endured. He plunged his hands even deeper into his flannels pockets and as he did so, a thought occurred to him, a thought that immediately seized all of his attention. Why, instead of merely enduring the living conditions of Beck-Side Street, didn't he capitalize on them? Why didn't he capture images of the street and its inhabitants in paint? And why didn't he do so using Expressionist techniques?

'Oh for goodness sake! Are you listening to me or am I speaking to myself?' Nina said exasperatedly, having asked for the second time if he knew that their father's replacement at Lutterworth's had invited Rose up to the design offices for a look around.

Noel took his hands out of his pockets, excitement racing through him. He had a canvas already primed and he knew now what he was going to sketch out on it. 'You're speaking to yourself,' he said with brotherly bluntness. 'I'm sorry about this, Neen, but I have to go.' He began backing away from her over the daisy-starred grass. 'There's something I have to do. There's something I have to do *immediately!*' and without any further explanation he rounded on his heel, breaking into a run, sprinting back down the side of the Beck in the direction of Bull Royd.

Nina said a word she had heard Micky Porritt use when he hadn't known he was being overheard, and plonked herself down on the grass with uncharacteristic gracelessness. It really was too bad. Although Noel didn't *enjoy* living in Beck-Side Street, it didn't truly trouble him. As long as he was able to paint, *nothing* truly troubled him.

As for Rose... She plucked moodily at a daisy. Rose was far happier in Beck-Side Street than she'd ever been in Jesmond Avenue. She and Jenny Wilkinson were well near inseparable and both of them were fast friends with Micky Porritt, though why they were was beyond her, *she* had never been able to get a word out of him. Rose's ambition, too, was an ambition perfectly attainable even with a Beck-Side Street address. The designer who had stepped into their father's shoes at Lutterworth's was a man who had worked for their father for years and who had enormous respect for him. Via him, contact with Lutterworth's had been maintained and the present invitation for Rose to visit the design offices was a strong indication she might be offered a position there when she left art school.

Lucky Rose. Not so lucky Nina. Tears of self-pity burned the backs of her eyes. Unlike Rose, she had no friends. She had abandoned all her previous friendships because she couldn't, *wouldn't,* endure the humiliation of those friends visiting her in Beck-Side Street. She had made no new friends for the same reason. And she had made no friends *in* Beck-Side Street because she had nothing in common with anyone who lived there and, even if she had, to have made friends with them would have seemed an admission that she now *belonged* there, and that was an admission she would never make. Not ever!

She circled her knees with her arms, hugging them to her chest. If Noel hadn't dashed off so unceremoniously she had been going to tell him of how their cousins were, at this very moment, visiting London and enjoying a far, far different lifestyle. The Olympic Games were being held at the new White City stadium and according to the *Bradford Observer,* 'Mr

*Caleb Rimmington and his grandchildren are in attendance at them.'*

'Not all of his grandchildren,' she had thought when she had read this latest snippet of information about her estranged family's activities. Glumly she had wondered where they would be staying. A smart hotel almost certainly. Very possibly even the Ritz.

'Bugger,' she said now, aching at the unfairness of it all and reduced to uttering an expletive that would have shocked even Micky. 'Bugger, bugger, bugger!'

Gertie Graham, the massively built neighbour who lived directly opposite number twenty-six and who, on Lizzie's first visit to Beck-Side Street, had informed her as to which house the Wilkinsons lived in, lowered her bulk into a chair that had once graced the tastefully furnished parlour in Jesmond Avenue.

'There's nowt like a nice cup of tea,' she said to Laurence as Lizzie pushed the sewing she had been working on to one side and went into the cellar-head to fill the kettle. 'And nowt like having a nice chin-wag while you're supping it.' She looked round the pin-neat room. 'And where's my little ray of sunshine?' she asked, 'Out laiking with Jenny Wilkinson and Micky Porritt?'

'Ro...ose is vi...sss... it...ing Lu...u ...ter ...worth's,' Laurence said with difficulty.

Gertie never had the slightest trouble understanding Laurence's impeded speech, though she did think he was daft still troubling to talk so hoity-toity. Visiting Lutterworth's indeed! Why couldn't he just say she was up at t'mill like anyone else would have done? And what the heck was she doing up there, anyhow?

As Lizzie walked back into the room to put the kettle on the hob, her vibrant blue dress as clean and pin-neat as the room, her hair glossily brushed and parted in the middle, waving symmetrically around her ears as low as the lobes and then gathered in a shining knot in the nape of her neck, Gertie shook her head in affectionate despair. Whatever it was young Rose was up to, it would be something arsey-fairy. Never, in all her life, had she come across a family with so many rum ideas.

'I'm going to be a dress designer,' Nina had once said to her loftily when she'd asked her why she wasn't in one of the mills, earning some brass. 'I'm going to be famous like Mr Worth and Madame Paquin and Monsieur Poiret and Lucile, of *Maison Lucile* in Hanover Square.'

Gertie had lived in Bradford all her life and had never heard of Hanover Square and she'd certainly never heard of the other fancy names Nina had spouted at her. 'Go wash your mouth out with soap and water,' she had said to her tartly, adding for good measure, 'Cheeky little baggage!'

They got all their fancy ideas from their mother, of course. Tea was never drunk from pint pots in the Sugden house, it was drunk from fiddly cups set on even fiddlier saucers. There were no clogs on their doorstep, either, and no shawls hanging on the peg behind the front door.

At the thought of Lizzie Sugden with a shawl over her head and shoulders, Gertie cackled. From the day the Sugdens had arrived in Beck-Side Street, Laurence Sugden riding like a crippled king in the back of the first motorcar to ever trundle over Beck-Side Street's cobbles, Lizzie Sugden had worn a hat and gloves whenever venturing more than a few yards from her front door. 'Lady Muck,' she'd been called by everyone but Polly Wilkinson. Then she'd let it be known that she took sewing in for very reasonable rates and gradually, as people got to know her and her family, the nickname had lost its sarcastic edge and become almost a pet name.

'So what's Rose doing up at Lutterworth's?' she asked now, determined not to remain in ignorance and knowing it was bound to be something fancy.

'Sh...ee's lo...oo...king round the de...sign room,' Laurence said, an odd, almost wistful note permeating his voice. Gertie wasn't aware of it, but Lizzie was. She looked across at him, her heart hurting with love. It should have been Laurence now accompanying Rose around the design room. It should have been Laurence, fit and strong and virile, proudly introducing their daughter to his working world.

Gertie grunted, not truly understanding what a design room was, but not wanting to show ignorance. As far as she was concerned mills had weaving and spinning sheds, and carding and combing sheds, and dyehouses. Unlike Lister's, which was a silk and worsted mill, Lutterworth's, like nearby Rimmington's, was a worsted only mill. That somewhere in the process of producing a bolt of Lutterworth's cloth a pattern had been designed for it, was a thought that had never previously occurred to her, and it had certainly never occurred to her, and still didn't, that anyone she knew could possibly be responsible for such a task.

'It's t'weaving shed she needs to be in,' she said practically as the kettle began to steam. 'It's weaving that brings in the brass and Rose'd make a grand little weaver. All she needs is someone to give her a proper bit of encouragement.'

## Chapter Five

'You've certainly got an eye for colour,' Ted Rawlins, once her father's most talented protégé, said encouragingly to Rose as she fingered the swatch of cloth he had given her to examine. 'The brown does need lifting. A more tan shade would make the check much more effective. Now what do you think of this?' This time the swatch he turned to was a heather mixture, the overall effect a soft, misty green.

Rose screwed up her eyes and focused intently on the cloth. It had never occurred to her before that straightforward worsted fabrics could be as interesting in shading and pattern as ornamental tapestries.

'It's lovely, isn't it?' The feel of the fine wool cloth sent ripples of pleasure down her spine. And it didn't only look good and feel good. It smelt good too. 'I like the hint of yellow in the weft,' she said, thinking of the avant-garde designs Nina could make for such lovely material.

Ted Rawlins grinned. How had she known there was yellow in the weft? How, never having been in a mill before, had she known which *was* the weft?

'Let's have a mosey round the rest of the mill,' he said, heaving the heavy swatch book back onto a shelf. 'Have you ever been in a twisting shed? Or a weaving shed?'

She shook her head, excitement tightening her tummy into knots. 'No. If we're going in the weaving will I have to pin my hair up?'

'You will if you don't want to risk being scalped,' Ted Rawlins said cheerily, leading the way out of the cluttered design room and into a long, narrow, stone-floored corridor. 'The overlooker will have a spare headscarf handy. Has your Dad warned you about the noise in there? It can be quite frightening if you're unprepared for it.'

'I won't be frightened.' Her eyes shone in happy anticipation. 'I've always wanted to look around a mill.' She didn't add that the mill she had always wanted to look around was Rimmington's and that Lutterworth's was merely a stepping stone to that ambition. 'My friend, Jenny, works in the weaving. I hope we see her. It will give her the surprise of her life!'

'I nearly dropped dead with shock,' Jenny said, giggling. 'Specially at the sight of you with your hair all turbanned up in a mucky headscarf!'

The mill hooter had shrilly sounded the end of the working day and they were walking across the mill yard, jostled on all sides by a crush of women, some young and some not-so-young, all eager for a breath of fresh air after being cooped up in the noisy weaving sheds all day.

Rose's monkey-face split into a wide grin. The headscarf had made her feel like a proper mill girl. It had also made her head itch. 'I hope whoever wore that headscarf before me didn't have nits, she said as, hemmed in on all sides, they streamed out through the mill gates and into the narrow street beyond.

'I think they had sum'at worse than nits,' Jenny said mischieviously. 'If I remember rightly, the lass that wore that headscarf afore you had great round bald patches in her hair and her mam had painted them with iodine!'

Rose screamed and clutched at her ginger-red mane of hair and Jenny shrieked with laughter. 'You'll not get a fancy job in t'Design Room if you have purple-painted bald patches!' she gasped, holding her side she was laughing so much. 'You'll have to work with me in the weaving and wear a headscarf all day, every day!'

They were still laughing when they turned into the top end of Beck-Side Street.

'Blooming heck!' Jenny's laughter died abruptly, her eyes widening in incredulity. 'There's a motorcar outside your house! And it isn't the one that brought your dad to Beck-Side Street the day you moved in. It's far posher than that. It's *blue-green,* like something out of a fairy-tale! Have you ever seen anything like it afore in all your life?'

Rose stood stock-still, staring down the street. 'Yes,' she said, sucking in her breath, her eyes feverishly bright. 'Oh, yes! And the last time I saw it, it was outside Brown & Muffs! It's my grandfather's motorcar, Jenny! Grandfather Rimmington has come to visit Mother!'

It was a moment she had waited for as long as she could remember. A moment she had always hoped for and often prayed for.

'Isn't it wonderful?' Her face was ablaze with elation, the strength shock had robbed from her legs, fast returning. 'Isn't it *marvellous?*'

Without waiting for Jenny to answer she began to run, her feet flying over the paving stones and ringing out on the shallow cobbled indents that led to the covered passageways. Her grandfather wanted to be reconciled with her mother! For the first time in her life she would meet him face to face! And soon, perhaps, she would meet her Uncle Walter and her cousins! She ran as if there were wings on her heels. A bare-bottomed toddler scrambled hastily out of her way. Bonzo, the Porritts' Staffordshire Terrier, began racing along beside her, barking for all he was worth. A group of children playing hopscotch scattered in order not to slow down her breakneck speed.

*'Where's the perishin' fire?'* a wit called out to her as he lounged in an open doorway, his shirt collarless, his trousers bunching cumbersomely over the top of a broad leather belt, his clogged feet crossed at the ankles.

*'You're winning, lass!'* a woman pegging washing on a line strung across the street, called out jokingly. *'There's nobbut fresh air behind ye!'*

Rose waved a hand in good-natured acknowledgement and kept on running, her heart feeling as if it was going to burst with happiness. How long had her grandfather been in Beck-Side Street? Did Noel and Nina know of his arrival? Were they in the house now, already introduced to him? Chatting to him? Perhaps being invited to visit William and Harry and Lottie at Crag-Side?

'Father's dead,' Walter Rimmington said baldly to Lizzie, his tailored Savile Row, tweed suit making him look incongruously out of place in a room dominated by a black-lead kitchen range, a sick-bed, and a working-table crowded with a sewing-machine and pieces of cloth. 'It happened last night. He was in London with the children. They weren't with him when...when... He was asleep, Lizzie. He died in his sleep.'

Lizzie stood on the gaily-coloured, home-made rag-rug that fronted her hearth, staring at her brother almost catatonically. How could her father be dead? He and she were still estranged. He couldn't have died without their estrangement finally being healed. He couldn't. It wasn't possible.

'A...re you all ri...ight, lo...over?' Laurence asked with difficulty. He had struggled to his feet when their unexpected visitor had arrived and with the aid of a walking-cane was standing shakily upright.

She didn't answer him. She simply stared at, and through Walter, looking down through the long tunnel of the years, seeing in her mind's eye the big, bullish, domineering father who had once so petted and cossetted her. Her very first memory was of him throwing her high into the air in Crag-Side's vast, Chinese-papered drawing-room, catching her in his strong, safe arms as she screamed with terrified delight. And now he was dead and he would never see her children; never tell her he had lived to regret his harshness towards her; never tell her that he had, all through the years of their estrangement, continued to love her as she had continued to love him.

'Ma?' Noel's clothes were paint-streaked, his hair spikily dishevelled. 'Ma?' he said again awkwardly, not knowing what to say or do in such a disorientating situation. 'Do you want a cup of tea?' he asked inadequately. 'Have I to put the kettle on?'

Lizzie didn't answer him. Her eyes held Walter's. 'How can he be dead?' she whispered. 'How can he be dead and not have asked to see me?'

Walter lifted prematurely stooping shoulders in a gesture of helplessness. 'I don't know, Lizzie love. I don't know why he was as he was.' He passed a hand unsteadily across his eyes. 'And now I'll never know, and nor will anyone else.'

The sight of her brother's distress pierced Lizzie's frozen immobility. With a strangled cry, tears streaming down her face, she stepped towards him. 'Oh, Walter!' she sobbed as his arms closed around her. 'I always thought the day would come when Father and I would be friends again! And now it never will! Not ever!'

As she sobbed and sobbed, a little girl again, a little girl longing for paternal love and understanding, Laurence and Noel stood by, anguished and appalled.

All through the long years of his marriage it had never occurred to Laurence that Lizzie was suffering such inner hurt over her father's refusal to communicate with her, and the realization that he had been ignorant as to some of her deepest feelings shocked him profoundly.

Noel, too, was seeing a side to his mother he had never suspected existed. Always, before, no matter how grave the situation and how great her inner distress, as when his father had suffered his stroke or the decision had been taken to move from Jesmond Avenue to Beck-Side Street, his mother had remained outwardly composed. Now, however, she was utterly distraught, sobbing like a child for a father he had always assumed she no longer had feelings for and doing so against the inadequate chest of a man who, though her brother, was a man who had never before set foot across their threshold.

Deeply disconcerted he looked across at his father and saw, with a fresh stab of shock, that his father looked almost as distressed as Walter Rimmington. His eyes widened. His father couldn't be grieving over his grandfather's death, for to the best of his knowledge his father and Caleb Rimmington had never been on friendly terms. As his mother was rocked, still weeping, against the fine tweed of Walter Rimmington's jacket, understanding dawned. It was his mother's grief that was so distressing his father. His love for her was so deep, her pain was his.

The realization made him more embarrassed than ever and he cleared his throat, saying again, tentatively, 'Have I to put the kettle on?'

This time his father, at least, responded to him. 'Ye... es, lad,' he said, swaying as he struggled to stay upright.

Noel took two swift strides, taking hold of his father's useless right arm, pressing him back down into his armchair.

'There's no need to remain standing, Pa,' he said gruffly, wishing that his mother would stop crying and attracting the attention of the entire street. He didn't have to look through the window to know that every Nosy Parker from the bottom of Beck-Side Street to the top, were standing on their front doorsteps or at the ends of the passageways, goggling at the unbelievable ostentation of Walter Rimmington's motorcar and pruriently speculating as to the cause of the grief-stricken sobs issuing from their home.

Wishing fervently that Nina or Rose would put in an appearance, he picked up the fire-blackened kettle and, side-stepping his mother and his uncle, went into the cellar-head to fill the kettle at the tap.

Tapped water, in Beck-Side Street, was a very recent luxury and he remembered how indignant Jenny Wilkinson had been when she had told him that all the houses in Beck-Side Street now had indoor cold taps, and he had failed to be suitably impressed.

He turned the tap on. Jenny would be on her way home from the mill, but where would her mother be? Mrs Wilkinson wasn't quite as much of a Nosy Parker as their other mutual neighbours, but even if she wasn't standing with folded arms at the end of the passageway she would certainly be able to hear his mother's sobs through their shared wall and would be anxious as to their cause.

He wondered if, when he had put the kettle on the hob, he should nip round the back and have a word with her. She was too good a friend to his mother to be left worrying that his father had had another stroke, or that something had happened to Nina or Rose. And where *were* Nina and Rose? He turned off the tap. He'd left Nina by the Beck an hour or so ago. She couldn't *still* be there, surely? And what the devil was she going to make of the news that their grandfather was dead?

He stepped back into the room, dripping water droplets from the heavy kettle as he did so, relieved to see that though his mother was still crying, she wasn't doing so with such disturbing abandon and that someone, presumably her brother, had given her a large, serviceable handkerchief.

As he set the kettle on the hob Walter Rimmington spoke to Laurence. 'My father's body will be home by tonight,' he said awkwardly, painfully aware that, because he had allowed his father to forbid him contact with Lizzie, Laurence Sugden's opinion of him was not very great. 'William is accompanying it. Harry and Lottie returned to Ilkley this morning, by train. It's been a terrible experience for them. So far from home...no mature person with them to handle things...'

As his father struggled to make a suitably sympathetic reply, there came the sound of running feet. The feet were female and lightly-booted, not clogged, and as they drew nearer and nearer Noel swung round to face the door. It was Rose. It had to be Rose. Only Rose would race down the steep street so heedlessly fast. She would have seen the Rimmington motorcar and would have assumed...

As he realized what her assumption

would be, he took a swift step towards the door. With luck he'd be able to halt her pell-mell run and break the truth to her before she burst into the house. He was seconds too late.

The door rocked back on its hinges before he was even within reach of it. 'Where's Grandfather?' she demanded breathlessly, whirling into the room, her hair flying around her shoulders, her cheeks rosy with excitement, her eyes shining. 'I've run and run in order that he wouldn't leave before I got here! Are you my Uncle Walter? I'm Rose and...' the expression on his face checked her instantly.

Her mother was now standing by her father's chair and she spun to face her. At the sight of her mother's tear-ravaged face her eyes flew to her father's face, and then to Noel's.

Her father's obvious distress and Noel's equally obvious deep discomfiture, banished every shred of her fizzing elation.

'What is it?' Her voice was hoarse, thick with rising panic. 'What's the matter? Why is Ma crying?' and then, not waiting for a reply, she rounded on her uncle, 'Where's my grandfather?' she demanded with fierce urgency. 'Why have you come here without him? *Where's my grandfather?*'

It was Noel who finally spoke. Walter Rimmington, acutely aware of being in another man's home, felt good manners decreed her father or mother broke the news of her grandfather's death to her. Laurence, aware of his agonizingly undignified speech defect, was reluctant to do so. Lizzie, knowing how Rose had longed and longed to one day meet her grandfather, was incapable of it.

'Grandfather Rimmington is dead,' Noel said, wishing fervently that Walter Rimmington wasn't still present. 'He was in London with our cousins, to see the Olympic Games, and he died there, in his sleep.'

The blood drained from Rose's face. Dead? How could her grandfather be dead? She rocked back on her heels unsteadily. He couldn't be dead. She hadn't met him yet. He couldn't die before they had met; before they had had a chance to become friends. It wasn't possible. It couldn't be. It just couldn't be.

Her father said gently, 'I...I'm so...orry, li...ttle lo...ove.'

She looked into his loving face, saw the compassion in his eyes, and knew that her world had changed and would never be the same, ever again.

'Excuse me,' she said in a taut, stilted voice—a voice that didn't seem to be hers at all. 'I think...I want... Excuse me.'

She was at the door. Had opened it. Was

on the pavement. Dimly she was aware of her mother calling after her and of Noel saying that it would be best if she were let be.

She paused for a second as the door clicked shut behind her. The throng clustering around the motorcar fell silent.

'What's up, Rose love?' someone finally ventured. 'Have your Ma and Pa got trouble?'

'Has someone died, lass?' another neighbour asked sympathetically. 'Has your Ma suffered a sad loss?'

Rose didn't answer. She couldn't. Jenny came up to her, wide-eyed and anxious, scraps of weaving thread still clinging to her hair. 'Wasn't it your grandad come to visit? I heard your mam crying. Nowt's happened to Nina, has it? Or to your pa?'

Rose shook her head, unable to put the awfulness of what had happened into words. 'No,' she said, desperate to put as much distance between herself and the prying eyes of her neighbours as possible. 'I'm going down to the Beck to be on my own for a while, Jenny. I'll tell you everything when I get back.'

Her voice was dangerously unsteady and Jenny, aware that Rose was close to breaking down and knowing she wouldn't want to do so in front of an audience, merely nodded. She'd seek Micky out while Rose was down by the Beck. Micky was the only other person, besides herself and her mother, who knew that Rose was related to the Rimmingtons and he would be as curious as she was about the Sugden's visitor.

She watched Rose run out of sight around the bottom right-hand corner of the street, knowing it would be useless to question her mother.

'Rose's mother's family is Rose's mother's business, not ours,' she had said crisply when Jenny had once asked her if Rose's grandfather really was Caleb Rimmington of Rimmington's mill, and not just a gentleman who happened to have the same name. 'No good ever comes of being a Nosy Parker, Jenny, so no more questions about the Sugdens relationship to the Rimmingtons, if you please!'

'House door's opening!' said one of the Nosy Parkers at present clustered around the Rimmington motorcar.

There was an immediate shuffling of feet as, almost in unison, the small crowd shifted themselves to a more respectful distance.

'Well, he isn't t'Lord Mayor!' Gertie Graham, who had a ringside view of the proceedings from her doorway, pronounced as Walter Rimmington stepped out of number twenty-six and on to the hop-scotch-chalked pavement. 'If he was t'Lord Mayor he'd have a bloomin' great chain around his neck!'

'P'raps he's the toff that knocked Mr Sugden down and crippled him,' the man who had earlier teased Rose as she ran down the street, said speculatively. 'Mebbe he's come to give t'Sugdens a bit o' brass as compensation, like.'

It was the first anyone in Beck-Side Street had heard of Mr Sugden having been run down by a motorcar and though there were a few murmurs of dissent and the words 'stroke' and 'seizure' were heard, they were not heard very loudly.

Walter crossed the pavement, doing his best to seem unconcerned at the unwelcome attention he and his motorcar were receiving. Though he felt acutely uncomfortable in the narrow, dingy street, he had every intention of quickly returning to it. Now he was again on close, loving terms with Lizzie, he was going to remain on close, loving terms with her.

'Hey! Are you the Mister that knocked poor Mr Sugden over?' Nellie Miller's young daughter-in-law called out bravely. 'Because if you are, you should be ashamed of yourself!'

Walter flushed with indignation. 'Certainly not!' he said, beginning to crank the Renault's starting-handle with as much dignity as the operation allowed. As the motor began to rumble into life he felt echoes of the shock that had reverberated through him when he had first realized the extent of Laurence Sugden's disablement. So that was what had happened, was it? His handsome, talented brother-in-law had been mown down by a motorcar.

Sombrely he seated himself behind the Renault's steering wheel. It certainly explained why the family were no longer living in a pleasant family villa in Jesmond Avenue, but were instead enduring the cramped conditions of a mill cottage.

He released the brake, filled with a sensation of fierce resolution. They wouldn't be enduring such conditions for much longer, he would make sure of that. And he would make sure that his family, and Lizzie's family, were united at the earliest opportunity. What William and Harry would make of their artisan-looking eldest cousin he wasn't quite sure. The boy had been as paint-spattered as a labourer. As for the gamine-faced whirlwind that was his youngest niece... He felt his sombreness begin to lighten. She was obviously just as full of spirit as Lottie was and he was sure the two of them would get along splendidly.

Narrowly missing a horse-drawn coal

cart he manoeuvred the Renault limousine out of the top end of Beck-Side Street and began heading in the direction of Ilkley. Lizzie had another daughter, too. He wondered if she would be as engagingly hoydenish as Rose, and if she would be as touchingly upset at the news of her grandfather's death as Rose had been.

Nina paused as she neared Bull Royd, shielding her eyes against the last flare of sun, the weight of her hair looking as if it were nearly more than her slender neck could bear. Was that Rose running down the narrow strip of sloping meadow-land toward the Beck's banks? And if it were, why was she running so erratically? It was almost as if she couldn't see, almost as if she were crying.

She drew in a sharp breath. Rose *was* crying! Icy fingers seized hold of her heart. Had their father had another stroke? Was that why Rose had so obviously come looking for her? Lifting her skirts well clear of her ankles she broke into a run, shouting as she did so, 'Rose! I'm here! What's happened, Rose? *What's happened?*'

Rose hiccupped on a sob and came to a floundering halt. She'd come down to the Beck so that she could cry for her lost dreams in privacy and now here was Nina and she was going to have to tell her about their grandfather's death and Nina wouldn't understand why she was so distressed about it. Nina would think only of the possible benefits; the possibility that their Uncle Walter might now start treating them as family again; that they would meet and make friends with their cousins; that their lifestyle would change and become far more Rimmington-like.

She dashed the tears from her eyes and took a deep, steadying breath. 'Grandfather's dead,' she said bleakly as Nina raced breathlessly up to her over the rough grass. 'It happened last night, in London. Uncle Walter came to tell Ma and...'

Nina's eyes widened to the size of gob-stoppers. 'Uncle Walter Rimmington is in *Beck-Side Street?*' she demanded incredulously. 'Does that mean Grandfather's death is going to lead to a family reconciliation?'

Rose could almost see Nina's mind racing.

'Are we invited to the funeral?' Nina demanded urgently. 'Did Grandfather Rimmington have a deathbed change of heart? Has he left Mother a legacy?'

Rose shook her head, wondering how it was they could be sisters and yet, in so many ways, be such complete strangers to each other.

'No,' she said stiltedly, 'I don't think so. I don't know.'

Nina's excitement blazed, crackling from her like electricity. 'This could change *everything,* Rose! We'll be able to visit London and Paris! Perhaps even Rome!'

'We'll never know him,' Rose said, cutting across Nina's excitement with almost brutal terseness. 'He'll never know us. He'll never know how talented we are; never be proud of us.'

Nina blinked. There were times when it was awfully difficult to follow Rose's thought processes. Sometimes, as now, she positively *rambled.* Their grandfather had never shown the slightest intention of one day acknowledging them, or of being proud of them. Their Uncle Walter would acknowledge them, though. Their Uncle Walter would invite them to Crag-Side and would treat them as they should always have been treated; he would treat them not only as Sugdens but as *Rimmingtons.*

'Let's go!' she said, lifting her skirts clear of her boots again, not wanting to waste another second of time. 'I can't believe I'm going to meet Uncle Walter at last! Does he look like Mother? Is it obvious they're brother and sister?'

'You go,' Rose said dully, shocked that, at such a time, Nina could be so eagerly curious about something so utterly trivial.

'I want to be on my own for a while.'

Nina didn't trouble to ask her why. With her heart soaring she broke again into a run. They would all have to wear black for the funeral. Black would suit her. It would intensify the creaminess of her skin and the fox-red fieriness of her hair.

Rose stared after her. How was it possible that Nina's reaction to the news of their grandfather's death was so different to her own? All through their childhood she and Nina had talked and talked of Grandfather Rimmington, wondering how old they would be before they finally met him; wondering what circumstances they would meet him in. And now that meeting would never come and Nina had not expressed an iota of regret. All she cared about was the heightened chances of at last visiting Crag-Side; of meeting their cousins; of being openly accepted by them as family.

She turned towards the Beck, buttercups brushing against her ankle-length skirt. For as long as she could remember she had believed that one day her grandfather would rejoice in knowing her and that, a wool-man to his fingertips, he would exult in her passion for textiles and pattern, that she would, perhaps, prove to be the granddaughter of his heart.

The Beck eddied over the rough stones,

gurgling and tumbling, and she stared down into the shallow water, tears scalding her cheeks, grieving for what had never been, and now never would be.

# Chapter Six

'There's never been owt like it in t'street before, and I don't suppose there ever will be again,' Gertie Graham's daughter-in-law said to another of the Sugdens' neighbours as they stood in a doorway opposite number twenty-six on the morning of Caleb Rimmington's funeral. 'First we have a blue-green motorcar parked in t'street and now we have a black funeral motorcar! It's been outside t' house for nearly an hour now so it shouldn't be much longer afore they're out.'

'And Lizzie Sugden's a Rimmington, did you say?' There was awe in her friend's voice. 'A real, proper Rimmington? A Rimmington of Rimmington's Mill?'

Gertie's daughter-in-law nodded, enjoying her moment of self-importance.

'Then why is she living in Beck-Side Street?' her friend asked, mystified. 'Why is she living with ordinary folk when she could be living in a posh house in Ilkley?'

It was a question that was completely unanswerable and that had the entire street flummoxed. And not just the street.

'*Why*, Mother?' Nina asked, her voice cracking in disbelief. 'Why do you want to stay on in Beck-Side Street when we could be living in Ilkley, at Crag-Side? It doesn't make sense! It...'

All of them, apart from Laurence, were about to leave the house.

'For me to go to your fa...ather's fu...uneral would be li...ike thu...umbing my nose at him when he co...ould no longer reta...aliate,' he had said. 'It wo...ouldn't be a ma...ark of re...espect. It wo...ould be a ma...ark of disre...espect.'

Lizzie looked unseeingly at her reflection in the small mirror that hung near the door. She was wearing a black cloth coat that no one had ever seen before and that could only have come from the most exclusive section of Brown & Muffs' fashion department. The buttons were of jet, the revers and cuffs edged in black watered-silk binding. Her black hat was wide-brimmed and heavily veiled, the crown swathed in ebony ostrich feathers. She looked exactly what she was. A stylish, graceful, middle-aged woman whose father had been one of the city's most prosperous mill owners.

'It's nei...ther the pla...ace nor the ti...ime for su...uch co...mments, Ni...ina,' Laurence said as sharply as he was able, acutely aware of his wife's ash-white face and the depth of her suffering. 'Pu...ut a scarf o...o...ver your ha...at, it will be wi...indy in the mo...otorcar.'

With unsteady hands Nina secured a black chiffon driving-scarf over the black velvet hat she had made herself and which so perfectly complimented her fiery hair and the austere severity of her home-made, black, broadcloth suit. Where had the money for their funeral clothes come from? Did Uncle Walter perhaps know that her mother was a beneficiary of his father's will? And had he told her so? And had she accepted money from him as some kind of an advance on that legacy? It was impossible to think of her mother accepting money from him under any other circumstances. She was too fiercely proud.

As she followed Lizzie out of the house and across the pavement to the waiting motorcar, her frustration was so intense she had to clench her leather-gloved knuckles into fists in order to contain it. Her mother wasn't only fiercely proud. She was ridiculously proud. Why, why, *why* had she turned down Uncle Walter's suggestion that they make their future home with him, at Crag-Side?

She was dimly aware of Rose giving a little wave to Micky Porritt who was standing on Gertie Graham's doorstep, enjoying a ringside view of their departure. A flare of annoyance complemented her frustration. What on earth did Rose think she was doing? Surely on this occasion at least she could act with a little dignity and decorum?

As Noel, looking strangely alien in a sober black suit, his white shirt sporting a high, waxed collar, his hair gleamingly slicked down, settled himself in the front passenger seat, Nina shifted herself into a more comfortable position between her mother and Rose, and laced her fingers together in her lap.

*Why* would her mother refuse the offer to live at Crag-Side? It didn't make any sense. It wasn't as if her father's pride was at stake. How could it be when he was disabled and no longer even able to work? And it wasn't as if the offer of a home at Crag-Side could be interpreted as being an offer of charity. Crag-Side was her mother's family home, for goodness sake! She, and they for that matter, had every *right* to be living there!

As the motorcar began to slowly trundle away over the cobbles, she saw that the curtains were closed at every window. It was a traditional mark of respect when there had been a death but only, usually, if the death had occurred in a neighbouring house. Had their neighbours drawn their curtains out of sympathy with their loss, or would they have drawn them anyway on the day of Caleb Rimmington's funeral? The vast majority of Beck-Side Street residents had, after all, been employed by him. Which only made her mother's refusal of her Uncle Walter's offer more incomprehensible than ever, because her mother must surely realize that no one in Beck-Side Street would continue treating them with unselfconscious neighbourliness. How could they, now they knew they were related to the Rimmingtons? They would be cold-shouldered and ostracized just as surely as a mill worker's family encroaching on middle-class, or upper-class, territory would be.

Rose shot her a covert, perplexed look. Squeezed up close to Nina she could positively *feel* her tension, but she didn't understand it. Nina's remark to their mother, that they could be living at Crag-Side if they wanted to, was news to her. No one had told her that their Uncle Walter had made such an offer, but then over the last few days she'd very rarely been home for anyone to be able to tell her anything.

'If you want me to come with you, for company like, I won't talk if you don't want to,' Jenny had said on more than one occasion.

Rose had appreciated her sensitivity but had declined her offer. Not usually a person to brood, her grandfather's death had affected her profoundly and she had wanted to be on her own for long periods in order to come to terms with it.

Even now, five days after learning of his death, she felt *strange*. It was as if the world had shifted on its axis and had still not righted itself. She wondered if her cousin Lottie felt the same. As the motorcar eased on to the Ilkley road at a suitably funereal speed, she wondered if her cousin Lottie would understand that even though she, Rose, had never met their grandfather, she had always loved him—and would always miss him.

'Our cousins?' Lottie, dressed in black from the silk-ribboned boater on her head to her ebony buckled shoes, stared at her father, her tear-stained face pale and bewildered. 'Why are you asking me to be mindful of their feelings, Papa? They didn't even *know* Grandpa! *We* were the ones he loved, and who loved him! He wouldn't have *wanted* the Sugdens at his funeral! It's...it's like inviting strangers!'

Walter pressed a hand towards his temples. Why was everything in life so difficult? Why couldn't Lottie be just a little more understanding?

'I think your grandfather's spirit will be far more at peace knowing that all his family will be at his graveside, mourning him, than it would be if the situation had been otherwise,' he said, speaking with as much patience as his fraught nerves would allow. 'And as your cousins are going to find it very strange being at Crag-Side for the first time, a little thoughtfulness from you would be—'

William, who had been standing looking out of the window at the gravelled drive and the four black-plumed horses in the shafts of the ornate, as yet still empty hearse, turned around, his eyebrows high.

'They're coming to Crag-Side? I hadn't realized. I thought they'd simply be at the Cathedral and the cemetery.'

Walter cleared his throat. He had yet to tell any of his children that he had offered Lizzie and her family a home at Crag-Side. He wondered whether he should break the news to William and Lottie now, unhappily aware that it wasn't the most ideal of moments, not when his father's body was lying in almost royal state in the Chinese drawing-room and Lizzie and her children were expected at any moment. Perhaps if he impressed on them that as Crag-Side had been Lizzie's childhood home...

'William...Lottie...' he began, his headache intensifying.

The door opened and without stepping into the room Harry said tersely, 'A funeral car has just turned into the end of the driveway. I assume it means Aunt Elizabeth and our cousins are arriving.'

'Harry makes it sound as if they're *proper* cousins,' Lottie said to William with deep, hurting resentment as their father, vastly relieved at the interruption, joined Harry at the door and strode off with him towards the Italianate entrance hall.

'However strange it may seem, Lottie love, they are,' William said, not able to understand why she was making such an issue of it. He put an arm around her shoulders, giving her a loving hug, adding comfortingly, 'Weddings and funerals are always the same. People turn up at them that no one's seen or thought of for years and then, when the niceties have been observed, they disappear back into the woodwork again. The Sugdens coming to Grandpa's funeral is typical funeral manners, that's all.'

Lottie longed to be convinced but was full of terrible doubt. It seemed so *wrong* to have strangers intruding at such a time, especially when those strangers were claiming they had been as closely related to her grandfather as she, and William and Harry, had been.

Did it mean that all the time she had

thought she was her grandfather's pride and joy and little love, she had really not been so special after all? When she had been enjoying outings with him had he sometimes been thinking of the Nina person, or the Rose person? Jealousy roared through her, intensifying her grief. She didn't want her grandfather to be dead. She didn't want the Sugdens to be coming. She didn't want to feel as if nothing in life could ever again be regarded as being fixed and certain. Her throat choked with tears. She wanted it to be *before* they had gone to London. She didn't want it to be *now*. She wanted it to be *then*.

Walter Rimmington strode across the marbled floor of Crag-Side's circular entrance hall to greet his sister and his nephew and nieces. 'Lizzie, dear,' he said, his voice cracking with emotion as he took hold of her hands and kissed her on her cheek. 'Oh Lizzie dear! I'm so glad you're here! The coffin is open and is in the Chinese drawing-room. I haven't been in to pay my last respects yet. I couldn't. Not by myself. Perhaps when we have done so together, Noel and Nina and Rose could do so and—'

'Only Noel,' Lizzie said thickly, and though her arm was resting in his, it was obvious to everyone present that emotionally and mentally *he* was leaning on *her*. 'It wouldn't be fair to subject Nina and Rose to such an ordeal, not when they never met Father whilst he was alive.'

Nina opened her mouth to protest and then thought better of it. She'd never seen anyone dead and she didn't want to do so now.

Rose was looking at her cousin Harry. She would have recognized him anywhere. Even though he was dressed very formally, in black trousers and morning coat with his hair, like Noel's, brushed into total submission, there was still an overwhelming sense of vigour and good temper about him.

'The rotunda is no place for family introductions,' Walter said, aware that his nephew and eldest niece were standing in stiff discomfiture and that William and Lottie had not even had had the good manners to put in an appearance, 'but as Harry is here...'

Harry dutifully stepped forward.

'Lizzie, my second son, Harry. Harry, your Aunt Elizabeth.'

'I'm very pleased to meet you, Aunt Elizabeth,' Harry said. And meant it. Why on earth had he imagined she would be an embarrassment? No matter how unsuitable her marriage there was nothing clogs-and-shawl about her. She carried herself with grace and style and great dignity. And despite the fact that, until his grandfather's death, she and his father had had little or no contact for years and years and years, there was obviously a bond of great affection between them. As for his cousins...

'I'd like to introduce you to your cousin Nina,' his father was saying, and he was looking into green-gold eyes, wide-spaced, black-lashed, and a creamy-skinned face of flawless perfection framed by the most glorious coloured hair he had ever seen in his life.

As she proferred him the tips of her gloved fingers a charge like that of a jolt of electricity jarred through him, all-engulfing horror following hard on its heels. He was in a state of urgent physical arousal for God's sake! And with his much-loved grandfather laying in state only rooms away!

'And Rose,' his father was saying.

Aghast at the indecency of his reaction to her sister he murmured something polite—shook her hand—but her face barely registered and neither, when he was introduced to him, did her brother's. All he could think of was the incredible experience he had just undergone. What did the French call it? *Coup de foudre?* Instant, unreasoning, overpowering sexual attraction. And for his *cousin* for goodness sake! For a *Sugden!*

'William and Lottie are in the small drawing-room,' he heard his father saying to his aunt as, her arm still in his, he began to lead the way out of the rotunda. 'Other mourners who are leaving for the cathedral from the house are gathered in the west wing drawing-room. We'll be going to the cathedral and on to the cemetery in carriages, of course. Much more dignified than funeral cars. But first...his father's voice shook slightly, 'First, Lizzie, you and I must pay our last respects to Father.'

Harry, eager for the opportunity of escorting Nina. and putting his violent physical attraction to the test, said swiftly, 'I'll take Noel and Nina and Rose into the small drawing-room and introduce them to William and Lottie.'

His heart was racing as if he had been running. What was going to happen when he fell into normal, natural conversation with her? Was the magic going to vanish into thin air? And if it didn't? If it persisted? What then?

'William and I have already paid our respects to Grandfather,' he said to Noel as his father shepherded his aunt into the sombrely curtained confines of the Chinese drawing-room. 'It will be rather strange for you, I expect, with you never having known him.'

Noel looked across at his cousin sharply, wondering if he was being condescended to, but one look at Harry's handsome, bold face assured him he wasn't. Whatever Harry's faults might prove to be, Noel was certain snide sarcasm would not be among them.

Every single fibre of Nina's being was struggling to remain outwardly composed. So this was Crag-Side! This was where her mother had been born and had spent her childhood! This was where she, too, if her grandfather hadn't so disapproved of her father, would have spent childhood holidays and weekends and Christmases! That she had never done so, hurt like a physical pain. How could her mother have never resented being denied all this opulence and grandeur? How, after being brought up in a house that seemed as vast as a palace, could her mother have ever happily settled for life in Jesmond Avenue, let alone life in Beck-Side Street! To Nina it was unimaginable. Inconceivable.

'William, cousin Nina,' her unnervingly personable cousin Harry was saying, and she was shaking hands with the young man who would one day inherit the great Gothic magnificence that was the Rimmington family home.

Ever since her first glimpse of him, as he had escorted Lottie into the glittering bright interior of Brown & Muffs, she had known that he was far more *intellectual* looking than his brother. Now she saw that he was also extremely attractive in a reserved, understated way. His hair was darkish and straight, with a suspicion of a cow's lick which, today, had been brushed into near annihilation. He was tall and lean and there was a preoccupied expression in his eyes that she felt wasn't there just because of the sombreness of the occasion but was, instead, part and parcel of his intriguingly reserved personality.

'Lottie, our cousin Nina,' Harry was saying smoothly.

A girl a year or two younger than herself, and dressed to look *far* younger, stared stonily at her. For a heart-stopping second Nina's composure threatened to desert her. On his many visits over the last few days to Beck-Side Street her Uncle Walter had been so *unequivocally* accepting of all of them as family, that she had forgotten all her earlier fears of *not* being accepted by her Rimmington cousins.

In the sophisticatedly black broadcloth suit she had designed and made herself, she had felt as if *no one* could view her as not being their equal. She had stepped from the funeral car into the marble-floored splendour of her mother's family home and had immediately felt as if she *belonged* there. She hadn't felt out-of-place or overawed or intimidated. She had felt herself to be what she knew herself to be—a Rimmington, as well as a Sugden, a Rimmington who had inherited all her mother's head-turning grace and innate sense of style. And if her overpampered and cossetted younger cousin was going to try and make her feel socially inferior then she was in for a big disappointment!

As Harry introduced Lottie to her, Rose took one look at her cousin's pale, pinched face and felt immediate empathy with her. Lottie had *known* their grandfather. His home had been her home. She had spent time with him, been taken out on treats and visits by him. And if she hadn't been with him when he had died, she had been very, very near—in the next hotel room perhaps. It must have been a traumatic experience for her, for it was quite clear by the grief and suffering in her eyes that whatever their grandfather's faults, he had had none where she was concerned. Lottie had loved their grandfather, and was grieving for him deeply.

'I'm sorry,' she said to Lottie simply,

meaning the words with all her heart. 'It must be terrible to lose someone you've loved so much, and who has loved you so much. I didn't know Grandfather but I wanted to. The world seems strange now he isn't in it anymore, doesn't it? It's as if nothing is the same. As if it never *will* be the same.'

Lottie's eyes widened and she drew in a deep, shuddering breath. This extra-ordinary looking girl with the almost saucerlike eyes and fiercely ginger hair was describing *exactly* how she felt. And they were cousins. First cousins. And nearly the same age.

'Grandpa would have found your hair... odd,' she said, speaking with an artless truthfulness that had William flushing with embarrassment and Noel reflecting that his youngest cousin and youngest sister had an awful lot in common, 'but I think he would have liked you. He never talked about you, though. He never even talked about your mother.'

This was something Rose had long ago accepted. It didn't mean, though, that he hadn't often thought of them all. It didn't mean that he hadn't made himself just as unhappy as he had made them unhappy.

'Our hair is Sugden hair,' she said, intrigued to note that though both William and Harry were dark-haired, Lottie's mousy hair was so light as to be almost blonde.

A little to the left of her she could hear Noel saying to William in obvious answer to a question, 'We're all at Bradford School of Art. I'm studying for a Fine Art Degree. Nina is studying Fashion Design. Rose is studying Textile Design.'

'Noel's the art school's star.' That was Nina, somewhere to the right of them and talking to Harry. 'He's been chosen by the College for a fellowship. There's a possibility of shows in Leeds and Manchester, maybe even London.'

Unsaid, but implicit, was that though they hadn't the benefits of the Rimmington name or Rimmington wealth, they were leagues ahead where sheer creative talent was concerned.

William looked across at his youngest cousin, intrigued. Textile design. He wondered if his father knew. If his grandfather had known. One thing was certain, the Sugdens weren't remotely the clogs-and-shawl Bradfordians they'd been led to believe they were. Not that it would have mattered to him. He'd far rather mix with plain-speaking, honest working men and women than with the upper-class chinless wonders his grandfather had always been so anxious he should mix with.

At the contemplation of plain-speaking honest men and women his thoughts, so ruthlessly held in check all morning out of respect for the occasion, immediately flew to Sarah and her family. Would things be easier for himself and Sarah now his grandfather was dead or, now that he was the immediate heir to the mill, would they be even more difficult? At least Sarah no longer worked at Rimmingtons. She hadn't truly seen how important it was for her not to do so, but she'd humoured him and was now one of the vast army of weavers employed at Lister's. A pulse throbbed at the corner of his jawline. Whatever people might say when their relationship became public knowledge, they couldn't say he was taking sexual advantage of one of his father's workers.

The door opened and his father entered the room, his face strained. William wondered if it was because of the difficult experience he had just undergone, or if his father was already feeling the pressure of his new burdens. He wasn't a man who enjoyed exerting authority and it was almost impossible to imagine him as an all-powerful mill owner.

As he crossed the Turkish-carpeted room Harry and Nina, Rose and Lottie, mindful of where he had come from and the message he was most likely bearing, fell silent.

Lightly he laid his hand on Noel's

shoulder. 'Your mother is waiting for you in the Chinese drawing-room,' he said, raw-voiced.

William sensed, rather than saw, Noel's sudden tension. He felt a shaft of sympathy for him. Neither he nor Harry had much relished saying goodbye to the waxlike corpse that had once been their vigorous, dynamic grandfather, and the experience would be even harder for Noel, for Noel had never known him. The pulse at his jawline continued to throb. It was a hell of a way for anyone to see their grandfather for the first time.

As Noel dutifully and reluctantly accompanied Walter out of the room, the silence was profound. A moment ago, the social ice had been thawing with remarkable speed. Now, reminded of just why they were all gathered together, it froze even Lottie into mute awkwardness.

Fifteen minutes later Caleb Rimmington's coffin was being carried with majestic solemnity out of Crag-Side, his formerly disunited family following unitedly behind it. Lizzie's black-gloved hand was tucked into the crook of her brother's arm. William followed them, Lottie protectively close by his side. Harry escorted Nina. Noel and Rose brought up the rear. Behind them came the myriad other mourners who had been invited to leave for the funeral service from the house. Noel wasn't sure, but he thought one of the distinguished looking gentlemen was the Rimmingtons' solicitor. Another he recognized as being Jacob Behrens, patriarch of one of Bradford's most prestigious wool families.

With almost royal respect the servants had lined up in parallel lines in the palatial entrance hall, and the coffin and mourners passed between them. Many of the servants had tears in their eyes and one young woman, a tweenie, was weeping openly. Noel was impressed. Until the last week or so he had never given much thought to his Grandfather Rimmington, and because of the way his mother had been treated by his grandfather, what thoughts he had given him had not been overly favourable. A man genuinely mourned by those who had worked for him in the intimacy of his home could not, however, have been all bad.

Noel thought back to the mesmerizing moment when, his mother by his side, he had looked on his grandfather's strongly-carved features. Even in death, Caleb Rimmington's face had been overpoweringly forceful. His first reaction had been that it was a face he would have loved to have painted. His second, that he now understood why the rift between his mother and her father had gone so deep and been so unbridgeable. Caleb Rimmington had not been a man who would take being defied lightly. With something like awe he realized just how courageous his gentle-mannered mother had been when she had so determinedly followed her heart and married his father.

When they alighted from the closed carriages and entered Bradford Cathedral it was to find it packed to the gunnels with mourners. Nina felt as if every eye in the world was on her as she took her place in the second front pew, Noel on one side of her, Harry on the other. Thank goodness money had come from somewhere to provide them all with suitable mourning clothes! She wondered if the ladies present would be wondering where her stylish costume had come from. She knew no one would assume it had been home-made. Nothing that she designed and tailored for herself ever looked home-made.

The congregation rose and the solemn notes of the organ led them into a deep-throated rendering of *Rock of Ages*. Rose's troubled eyes rested on the lily-covered casket before the altar. Instead of this stiflingly formal church service she would have much preferred something beautiful and barbaric. A funeral fit for a warrior. A pyre, blazing Vikinglike, high on the moors over Crag-Side.

Beside her Lottie gave a stifled sob, tears trickling down her cheeks.

Instinctively Rose reached out, taking Lottie's leather-gloved hand in hers.

For a long, long moment Lottie's fingers were frigidly unresponsive and then, as the congregation launched into the hymn's last verse, they slid curlingly between Rose's fingers, squeezing hard.

## Chapter Seven

'And so I s'ppose we'll soon be shut of you?' Micky Porritt said glumly as he, Jenny and Rose sat in their favourite spot on top of the middens and Bonzo sat disconsolately on the stone-flagged ground, barking mournfully every now and again in order to remind them of his existence.

'No. Why should you be shut of me?' Rose plucked at a blade of grass that was growing out of one the cracks in the midden's roof. 'I'm not going anywhere.'

'That's not what I 'eard.' Micky sat with his knees hunched to his threadbare jacketed chest, his arms circling them. 'I 'eard you'd all be buggering off to Ilkley now to live wi' your swanky uncle.'

Rose frowned, not because of the swear word but because she, too, had heard the same rumour. Ever since the funeral Nina had spoken of little else. 'Mother's bound to change her mind and agree to our going!' she had said time and time again. 'How can she not? How can *anyone* prefer to live in Beck-Side Street when they could be living at Crag-Side?'

'My Uncle Walter isn't swanky,' she said,

heading the conversation on to ground she felt more sure of. 'He just talks nicely, that's all.'

' 'E talks like a swank and 'e dresses like a swank and 'e drives a swanky motorcar,' Micky said, not about to let her off the hook, 'and he should keep to 'is own sort. 'e shouldn't come nosying down Beck-Side Street.'

Rose tossed the blade of grass over the midden's edge in a gesture of impatience.

Jenny, who hated disagreements of any kind, looked from Micky to Rose with troubled eyes. Ever since the afternoon when she and Rose had turned into Beck-Side Street and seen the swanky motorcar parked outside number twenty-six, nothing had been the same. Gossip about the Sugdens had become rife. Even Albert Porritt, Micky's dad, had put his two-penn'orth in, declaring that he'd known since the day he'd helped them to flit that there was something rum about them.

She said now, tentatively, 'Perhaps Rose's uncle won't visit so often now that her grandfather's been...now that the funeral is over.'

Micky cocked his head to one side slightly, eyeing Rose, waiting.

Rose's wide, full-lipped mouth, tightened. Why was everyone so persistently awkward about her Uncle Walter's visits?

Ever since they had begun, Albert's attitude towards her had changed and Jenny's mum no longer called at their house half as often as she had used to do.

'It's not because she thinks your Mam's too posh now,' Jenny had reassured her fiercely, 'It's just that she doesn't want to be there if your uncle makes one of his unexpected visits.'

'But why?' Rose had demanded, mystified. 'Why does it matter?'

Jenny hadn't known. She'd only known that it *did* matter, and that when she'd first told her mam that Rose's posh Uncle Walter had visited number twenty-six, her mam had dropped the jar of jam she was carrying and had looked as if she was about to faint dead away.

She sat back on her heels now, waiting for Rose's reply to Micky, her sense of unease growing.

'My grandfather's funeral isn't going to make any difference to my Uncle Walter's visits,' Rose said, unwittingly feeding her friend's anxieties. 'He's *family*, and family visit each other all the time, don't they?'

'Oh aye, *normal* families do,' Micky agreed, scooping a loose clod of earth from between the midden's stone roofing flags and throwing it at the barking Bonzo in an attempt to silence him. 'But your family isn't 'xactly normal, is it? You didn't even *know* your family till your grandpa died and they're posh, aren't they? They're not normal folks like my family and Jenny's family and Gertie's family and every other family in Beck-Side Street. And if *they're* posh, then it stands to reason *you're* posh, and if you're posh...'

Rose knew exactly what Micky was going to say. He was going to say that if she were posh then she didn't fit in to Beck-Side Street. Fighting back tears of exasperation she sprang to her feet. 'Don't say it, Micky Porritt! Don't ever say it or I'll never speak to you again! Beck-Side Street's my home and I've as much right to live here as you and Jenny have!'

Jenny, ever the peacemaker, scrambled to her feet, saying urgently, 'Micky didn't mean to upset you, Rose! It's just that he's confused. We've never had anyone in the street with swank family before and...'

Rose wasn't listening. She, too, was confused. If even Micky and Jenny were going to start treating her differently now that they knew she was related to the Rimmingtons, how were her other friends and neighbours going to begin treating her? And how were they going to treat Noel and Nina and her mother and father?

She ran to the midden's edge and laying flat on her tummy on the cold roofing flags, slithered backwards over it until she was hanging on only by her hands. Then, amidst a frenzy of barking from Bonzo, she let go, dropping lithely to the ground. Negotiated in this manner the drop wasn't very deep, though it always slightly winded her.

'Rose...please...wait for me...' Jenny was running across to where a high wall, dividing one set of backyards from another, abutted the middens, providing an easier and more ladylike method of descent.

With a hurting heart Rose saw that Micky was making no similar attempt to follow her. Tears stung the backs of her eyes. Why was the fact that the Rimmington side of her family had money, making so much difference to everything? She was still the same person. She still wanted to have the same friends. In a convoluted way, it was her Beck-Side Street friends who were being snobbish. Why shouldn't her Uncle Walter visit number twenty-six if he wanted to? Why shouldn't William and Harry and Lottie visit it as well?

'Which...ever way you lo...ok at it, lo...ove, it isn't go...ing to wo...ork,' Laurence said with difficulty. 'How can Wa...lter's child...ren vi...sit here? And if we sta...ay here and they regu...larly visit Crag-Si...de, they're go...ing to feel out of pla...ce both he...re and the...re.'

Lizzie sat, deep in thought, a sewing-basket full of socks waiting to be darned by her side. How could she move her family to her childhood home when, while her father had been alive, none of them had been welcome there? Somehow, in a way she couldn't explain, it seemed an underhand thing to do.

There were other things to take into consideration, too. The fact that when she had married Laurence she had done so knowing she was deliberately turning her back on the kind of lifestyle Crag-Side offered. Ever since she had met and fallen in love with Laurence, she had only ever wanted from life what he could offer her. And what he could offer her now was Beck-Side Street with all its sanitary inconvenience and cheering friendliness.

She clasped her hands together in her lap, her resolve growing. If they moved to Crag-Side there would be no big, booming-voiced Gertie Graham calling in every day in order to chat to Laurence. There would be no Albert Porritt calling in to give him a game of draughts or dominoes. No Polly Wilkinson popping in with a cheery word. No Jenny and Micky running in and out, treating the house as if it was their own. On his bad days, Laurence wouldn't be able to lay in bed and see people passing up and down the street. He wouldn't be able to wave to them and to feel part-and-parcel of a little community, as he did now—and nor would she.

Her fingers laced together, tightening. If they moved to Crag-Side she would leave friends behind it would be impossible to replace. True friends, like Polly and Gertie. Friends who would willingly help her out no matter what trouble she might face. And she didn't want to do that. Certainty flooded through her. Despite all the many physical comforts Crag-Side could offer, she didn't want to live there. She wanted to remain in the little back-to-back she had made their home. She wanted to remain in Beck-Side Street.

'I don't think Noel and Nina and Rose will feel out of place if they remain living here and yet regularly visit Crag-Side,' she said at last, looking across at him with a heart full of love. 'They're like me. Adaptable.'

Beneath his moustache, grown heavier in order to conceal the slight rictus at the side of his mouth, Laurence gave her a lop-sided smile.

'Ro...se certainly is. I'm no...t sure ab...out No...el and Ni...na though.'

Lizzie frowned slightly. She, too, wasn't sure how Noel and Nina would take the decision to stay on in Beck-Side Street. She said slowly, 'All that matters to Noel is his work, and now he's been chosen for a fellowship, and has a grant, he's indifferent to everything else.'

'And Ni...na?' Laurence prompted gently. 'All her li...fe she's drea...med of Cra...g-Si...de and of li...ving the ki...nd of li...festyle Wi...lliam and Ha...rry and Lo...ttie lead. If Wa...alter is ha...ppy for her to li...ve there, shouldn't we at lea...st ask her if she wo...ould like to?'

'Without us?' Lizzie stared at him. 'You mean for her to go and live at Crag-Side while the rest of us stay in Beck-Side Street?'

He fumbled awkwardly in a pocket for his pipe. 'She's a young wo...man, Li...zzie. She isn't a chi...ild any...more. It's a dec...ision she sho...uld be all...owed to make for her...self.'

Lizzie looked swiftly away from him, picking up the sock she had been darning, pricking herself clumsily on the thumb with her darning needle as she did so. He was right, of course. She knew he was right. And if it wasn't Nina moving away from home to live at Crag-Side, it would be Noel leaving home in order to live in Manchester or London. Even Rose was barely a child any more.

'The...re comes a ti...ime when we

ha...ve to let th...em all go, lo...ve' Laurence said, reading her thoughts, his pipe remaining unlit in his hand. 'And Cr...ag-Side is as go...od a pla...ce as any for Ni...na to ma...ake a sta...rt.'

Lizzie nodded, wryly aware that Laurence, like herself, thought it a foregone conclusion that when given the choice of moving to Crag-Side or remaining at home, Nina would opt for Crag-Side.

'But why only cousin Nina?' Lottie asked bewilderedly as her father settled himself at the breakfast table. 'Why aren't cousin Noel and cousin Rose coming to live at Crag-Side as well?'

'Because they're intelligent enough to know that living in an ostentatious mausoleum is not the be-all and end-all of existence,' William said, helping himself to kidneys and bacon from a silver dish on the sideboard. 'Noel uses the art school as his personal studio and doesn't want to be further than walking distance from it, and Rose simply prefers to remain living in Beck-Side Street with her parents.'

'But *why?*' Lottie persisted, struggling for understanding. 'The houses in Beck-Side Street are mill cottages, aren't they? How can anyone prefer living in a mill cottage to living at Crag-Side?'

'Some mill cottages are little palaces,'

William said, sitting down at the table, thinking of Sarah's parents' pin-neat cottage and not noticing the swift rise of Harry's eyebrows.

Lottie opened her mouth to say that their grandfather hadn't thought so, and then closed it again. Incredible though the conclusion had been, she knew now that her grandfather hadn't been right about everything. He hadn't been right about refusing to have anything to do with Aunt Lizzie, just because she had married someone he didn't approve of.

Though Lottie still hadn't met Rose's father she knew he must be a special person because it had been so instantly obvious that her Aunt Lizzie was a special person. Her cousin Rose, too, was very *very* special.

She toyed with the scrambled eggs on her plate, wishing it were Rose who was coming to live with them, wondering when Rose would next visit them, wondering if her father would allow her to go with him the next time he visited Beck-Side Street.

Harry, seated beside her on the opposite side of the table to William and their father, caught William's eye and frowned warningly. He'd always been able to read his elder brother like a book and he knew that William was sorely tempted to tell their father that his remark about some mill cottages being little palaces hadn't been based on hearsay, but on personal experience. Now, however, at the breakfast table and with Lottie present, was not the time for William to embark on a disclosure that would lead him into confessing he was in love with a mill girl.

'I'm glad you're not taking a snobbish attitude to your Aunt Lizzie's decision to stay on in Beck-Side Street,' his father was saying guilelessly to William. 'It may seem an odd decision to us, but she has her reasons and we must respect them.'

Harry speared a mushroom. Ever since their grandfather's death, their father had been showing a side of himself none of them had ever seen before. Where once he had rarely uttered their aunt's name, now it was on his lips continuously. For the first time it occurred to him to wonder if his father had been quite as appalled by their aunt's marriage to Laurence Sugden as they had always supposed him to be. He certainly wasn't behaving now as if the marriage had ever appalled him. And if, in the past, his ostracizing of the Sugdens had only been because he'd been too fearful of their grandfather's displeasure to behave otherwise, his reaction, when William were to tell him about Sarah, might not be the one William so fearfully anticipated.

It was an interesting thought, but not

nearly so interesting as his thoughts about Nina. Merely remembering how incandescent she had looked in the cathedral, her titian-red hair glowing like a candleflame against the velvety blackness of her hat and the high collar of her two-piece mourning costume, gave him a rising in his crotch. Dear God in heaven! She had looked unbelievable—and had behaved unbelievably too, as composed as if the pomp and ceremony of their grandfather's funeral was something she was accustomed to every day of her life.

As his father droned on to William about how pleased he was that William had so easily and quickly established an amicable relationship with Noel, Harry's thoughts turned from the elating prospect of welcoming Nina permanently to Crag-Side, and settled on her appealingly funny-faced sister.

It was only in the cathedral that he had truly noticed her, and then only because of the lovely richness of her singing voice. Once he had noticed her, however, his attention had been held. Not only because her large, honey-brown eyes had reminded him of a lemur he had fallen in love with as a child on his first visit to a zoo, but because it was a face that, once seen, could never be forgotten. And he had most definitely seen it before.

'It was outside Brown & Muff's,' she had said much later when they had returned to Crag-Side with what seemed like an army of mourners, for the traditional cold collation. 'Lottie and I bumped into each other trying to be the first to reach Brown & Muff's revolving doors and Lottie accidentally knocked the new art portfolio I was carrying out of my arms.'

Despite the sombreness of the occasion she had flashed him the widest, most irrepressible smile he had ever seen in his life. 'You bent down and picked it up for me.'

His own grin had nearly split his face. 'And you never did go through the revolving doors!' he had said mock accusingly. 'Where did you go instead?'

With mischief dancing in her eyes she had said, 'Kirkgate Market,' and, a bond of camaraderie effortlessly formed, he had taken her off to show her a portrait of their grandfather and to steer the conversation around to her entrancing, enticing, mesmerizing sister.

'Harry! Are you deaf or are you in a trance?'

Harry blinked, realizing that William was speaking to him and had apparently been doing so for some while.

'For the second time,' William said with exaggerated patience, 'I'm going into

Bradford to meet Noel. He's going to take me in to his art school to show me his work. It must be pretty good because in a couple of months time a London gallery is giving an exhibition of outstanding work from various art schools all over Britain, and some of Noel's paintings are amongst those going to be on show.'

Lottie gaped at him. 'In *London?*' she said incredulously.

William nodded, put his crumpled napkin at the side of his plate and pushed his chair away from the table, rising to his feet.

Lottie blinked. Only days ago she had felt serenely superior to her Sugden cousins. Then she had met them and liked them and had magnanimously been prepared to overlook their social inequality. Now, where talent was concerned, she was beginning to feel positively inferior to them! Rose was studying to be a tapestry designer, Nina designed clothes and had designed and made the amazingly stylish two-piece costume that had turned every head at their grandfather's funeral. And Noel was to have some of his paintings on show in a London gallery—just like a professional artist—just like a *famous* artist!

'I'm coming too,' she said decisively. 'Everyone else is doing interesting things and I'm not going to stay here all day with a stuffy tutor while William and Harry do exciting things with cousin Noel.'

Harry, who had no intention of leaving Crag-Side on the day Nina was to make it her home, said easily, 'I'm not going with William.' He glanced towards his father. 'And I'm not going into the mill today. I'll look through the wool sales figures at home.'

Walter nodded. Every since he had been a small boy Harry had always taken more interest in the family business than William, never missing an opportunity to tag along at his grandfather's side either at the mill, or at Bradford Wool Exchange, or at wool sales. Since the reins of Rimmington's had fallen into his own hands he had had cause to be grateful to Harry's know-how on more than one occasion and was secretly dreading the end of the month when Harry, with William, would be returning to Oxford.

'And so I can go with William, can't I, Papa?' Lottie queried impatiently, breaking in on his thoughts. 'Cousin Noel won't mind and...'

Walter felt a familiar rise of indecisive panic. He wanted his family and Lizzie's family to make up for all the time they had not known each other, to share outings and experiences, to become friends, but what if Noel suggested William and Lottie accompany him back home to Beck-Side Street? It wouldn't matter too much where William was concerned, of course. It would be good for William to see how mill workers, Rimmington's mill workers included, lived. But Lottie...

The thought of his little girl being exposed to the harsh realities and vulgarities of Beck-Side Street made him break out in a cold sweat. Why, why, *why* had Lizzie so stubbornly refused to move her family into Crag-Side? And it was Lizzie who had refused to do so, not Laurence, of that he was sure. He could foresee all sorts of difficulties in the future—difficulties just like the difficulty he was experiencing now.

'I don't think that would be a very good idea...' he began, wishing William or Harry would come to his aid.

William did so, but not in the way he had hoped. 'I think you're mistaken, Father,' he said pleasantly, standing with one hand resting lightly on the back of his dining chair. 'I think it will do Lottie good to see how other people live, and Bradford School of Art isn't exactly disreputable, is it? Next to Manchester School of Art and Glasgow School of Art it's the most prestigious art school outside of London.'

With mixed feelings Walter gave up the battle. Perhaps William was right. Perhaps it would be good for Lottie to see something of Bradford. He, meanwhile, would spend the morning at the mill and then he would drive over to Beck-Side Street where Nina would be packed and waiting for him. He wondered if he would be able to talk Lizzie into accompanying them back to Crag-Side for dinner. Perhaps Laurence would come with her. Despite his many anxieties he felt a shaft of devilish pleasure. Laurence at Crag-Side would have Caleb turning in his grave.

'We're going on a *train?* And a *tram?*' Lottie's eyes danced in delighted anticipation.

'And we'll be walking,' William said warningly, hoping Lottie wasn't going to lose her enthusiasm for the adventure the minute she was faced with one of Bradford's steep cobbled guinnels.

'And might we visit Beck-Side Street?' The long ribbons on Lottie's sailor-hat, black in respect of her grandfather's death, streamed in the breeze as they walked at a brisk pace down Ilkley's main street towards the train station. 'Might we see Rose?'

'I don't know,' William said non-committally, trying to keep the excitement he felt from showing in his voice, 'We'll see.'

As they turned into the station his thoughts were turbulent. Dear Lord, if it once became accepted practice for even Lottie to visit Beck-Side Street, how could his father object to his visiting Sarah's home? And if he couldn't object to his visiting her, how could he object to their relationship? It was, after all, a relationship little different from the one his Aunt had embarked on, so many years ago, with Laurence Sugden. And if his father now found that relationship acceptable...

Oh, Sarah! he thought fervently as he shepherded Lottie aboard the Bradford train. Somehow, some way, we're going to win through! Just have patience, Sarah! Just stay in love with me! *Please* stay in love with me!

With very mixed feelings Rose sat on the end of the bed she and Nina had shared ever since moving into number twenty-six, watching as Nina repacked her large canvas portmanteau for the umpteenth time.

'Winter underwear, hairbrush, hand-mirror...'

'There'll be a dressing-table set on your dressing-table at Crag-Side,' Rose said practically. 'Silver-backed, probably.'

Nina removed the tortoiseshell-backed brush and mirror from the portmanteau and put them back on the bed.

'Art-pads, pastels, crayons...'

'Are you really going to travel between Ilkley and art school every day in a chauffeured motorcar?'

Rose couldn't even begin to imagine what their friends at art school were going to make of Nina's dramatically new, flamboyant lifestyle.

Nina sat back on her heels on the floor, her box of pastels and her crayon case in her lap.

'For as long as I'm still a pupil there, yes.'

Rose's ginger hair looked almost gold as she pushed it away from her face and stared at Nina. 'And just what,' she said at last, 'do you mean by that?'

'I think I may be going to St Martin's College of Art and Design. Uncle Walter has offered to pay my fees and—'

'St Martin's, *London?*'

Nina had the grace to look uncomfortable. Despite their age difference they'd never had secrets from each other and she was very conscious that she hadn't taken Rose into her confidence when coming to the decision as to whether to stay in Beck-Side Street or move to Crag-Side, and she certainly hadn't taken her into her confidence about the conversations she had been having with their uncle.

'It's not an opportunity I can let pass,

Rose,' she said fiercely, the cameo-like perfection of her face taut. 'Just as I can't pass up the opportunity to live at Crag-Side.'

Rose's usually merry face was sombre. She, too, was fascinated by Crag-Side, but not to the extent of leaving home in order to live there. That Nina was going to do so, so unhesitatingly, was something she found very hard to understand. And now Nina was talking of living even further away—of living in London.

'I'll be either in a hostel or staying with friends of Uncle Walter's,' Nina said, reading Rose's thoughts. 'It's what we always planned, Rose. At least, it's what we always planned for me. And now, thanks to Uncle Walter, all those plans are going to come true.'

Rose remained silent. Lots of things they had once only been able to dream of were coming true; they were on friendly, familial terms with their cousins; they were welcome at Crag-Side; there no longer seemed to be a lack of money, though whether that was because their grandfather had left their mother a legacy, or whether it was due to their Uncle Walter's generosity, none of them knew. Why, then, with so many good things happening, did she have such a sense of disquiet? Was it because she knew just how single-minded Nina could be, and because she knew what Nina's ulterior motive was in moving to Crag-Side?

'I don't think cousins are supposed to marry,' Rose said now to her, baldly. 'And if you married William, how could you be a world famous dress designer? Dress designers have to live and work in cities such as London or Paris or Rome or New York. You couldn't be a world-famous dress designer and live at Crag-Side, and as William will one day inherit the mill, and everything that goes with it, how could the two of you ever live anywhere else?'

Nina blushed to the roots of her hair. It had never occurred to her that Rose had read her intentions quite so accurately. 'Cousins often marry in order to secure family dynasties,' she said stiffly. 'Look at the Royal Family—they're always doing it. And besides, I think cousin William and I are *meant* for each other. And that's something you can't know anything about. You're too young.'

Rose wasn't in the habit of keeping her thoughts to herself, but she did so now. To tell Nina that it wasn't William who was interested in her, but Harry, would only complicate matters—and besides, she wasn't so young that she didn't wish *she* was the one Harry was so obviously attracted to.

'If you're going to say goodbye to Jenny's mum, you'd better go round to see her now,' she said, sliding her legs off the bed, knowing she would never be able to compete with Nina in the beauty stakes. 'She won't call in here, not when she knows Uncle Walter is expected any minute.'

'I suppose she's too shy.' Nina closed the portmanteau's lid. 'I wish some of our other neighbours were shy!' She rose to her feet, tucking her butterscotch coloured blouse more neatly into the band of her caramel coloured, ankle-length skirt. 'The last time Uncle Walter visited, Gertie Graham shouted out that he should move in if he liked being in the street so much.' She shuddered expressively. 'Can you imagine the sort of thing she'll call out if William and Harry and Lottie visit?'

Rose could, and didn't think it would matter too much. It was only Gertie's way of being friendly and was something their Rimmington cousins would have to learn to take in their stride.

'Shouldn't you change into black out of respect to grandfather?' she said to Nina as she followed her down the short, curving flight of stairs. 'Noel's wearing a black armband and as you're going to be living at Crag-Side...'

'I don't mind wearing black,' Nina said truthfully, opening the door that blocked the foot of the stairs off from the downstairs room. 'Black suits me. I'll change when I've said goodbye to Jenny's mum.'

'You'd better not be long round there!' Lizzie called out from the scullery where she was washing shirts by hand. 'Your uncle's likely to be here any minute.'

'We'll be five minutes, that's all.' Nina was already at the front door and Lizzie, about to repeat her warning about there being very little time left before Walter arrived, saved her breath. Nina wouldn't be long and if she was to say goodbye to Polly there really wasn't any alternative, for Polly certainly couldn't come round to number twenty-six—not with Walter due at any minute!

'So you're going to be living the life of a rich mill owner's favourite niece, are you?' Polly said teasingly, springy dark curls framing a face of still elfin-like prettiness as she kneaded pastry on the large wooden table that dominated her little living-room.

A smile of sheer delight curved Nina's mouth. 'Yes,' she said, revelling in the knowledge, truthfulness obliging her to add, though I don't think I'm the *favourite* niece. Uncle Walter wanted Rose to live at Crag-Side as well.' She looked across to where Rose was perched on the arm of

Polly's shabby horsehair sofa, as mystified as ever by her younger sister's adamant refusal to do any such thing. 'And Uncle Walter seems to like the fact that Rose, unlike the rest of us, apart from Father, speaks with a Bradford accent,' she said, more mystified than ever. 'He calls her his little Yorkshire Rose.'

Polly picked up her rolling pin and began to roll the pastry out thinly. There had been a time, long ago, when Walter Rimmington had called her his Yorkshire Queen.

The rolling pin ceased moving. She stared sightlessly down at her pastry. Did he, perhaps, sometimes still think of her? Had Rose, with her Yorkshire vowels and bubbly liveliness, reminded him of her?

'I may not be at Crag-Side for very long,' Nina was saying, toying with the enamel mug Polly used as a tart-cutter. 'I may be going to London to study fashion design at St Martin's College of Art and Design.'

Polly scarcely heard her. She knew now, of course, that Caleb Rimmington had been right in giving Walter the ultimatum to either give her up or to give up all hope of inheriting Crag-Side and Rimmington's. What kind of father would he have been if he hadn't done so? He was, after all, a self-made man; a man who had pulled himself up by his own boot straps to be one of the wealthiest and, where textiles were concerned, one of the most influential, in the county. It was only natural that such a man would want his son to marry well.

And Walter, not man enough to defy his father, *had* married well. His bride had been a Harland, and the Harlands of Sutton Place, North Yorkshire, were one of the county's oldest and most prestigious families.

'Noel may move to London, too,' Nina continued, handing Polly the enamel mug, assuming that Polly was satisfied with the thinness of her pastry and was waiting for it. 'Some of his paintings are to be shown in a London exhibition.'

Polly forced her thoughts back to the present. 'So your mother has been telling me,' she said, pressing the rim of the upturned mug onto the pastry and skewering it lightly. 'She's very proud of him. But then,' she added, lifting the mug in order to skewer a second pastry ring, 'she's very proud of all of you, and so she should be.'

Nina had long ago ceased to think of the Wilkinsons as being common, or to fear that contact with them would give her nits. 'I wanted to say goodbye to Jenny as well,' she said now, knowing with rising excitement that it was time to return to number twenty-six; that her uncle might already be there, waiting for her, 'but as she isn't here, will you say goodbye to her for me?'

'Of course I will love, and you just...'

Heavy male footsteps rang out in the echoing passageway.

Polly had been about to tell Nina to take care and to look after herself, especially if she went to London, but the words died on her lips.

She knew those footsteps. They were footsteps she had thought never to hear again. Footsteps that had once been the dearest to her in all the world.

'The door!' she said in panic-stricken urgency to Rose, who was the nearest to it. 'Shut it, Rose! Shut it *now!*'

Startled, Rose rose to her feet. That Polly wanted the door closing before the approaching visitor should emerge from the passageway to find it open, was obvious, but why? Except in the depths of winter, doors were always left open or ajar in Beck-Side Street and unwelcome callers, apart from tallymen, were unknown.

Convinced that the approaching footsteps were those of someone coming in order to try and collect rent money, or for clothes bought on credit, Rose sprang to do Polly's bidding.

She was seconds too late.

As her fingers closed around the door knob the approaching visitor rounded the end of the passageway, standing full square in the open doorway in front of her, a genial smile on his face.

The tension fled from Rose's body. 'Uncle Walter!' Her husky voice was thick with giggles of relief. 'We thought you were a tallyman!'

Walter was vastly amused. He was beginning to enjoy his visits to Beck-Side Street and his forays into a lifestyle so very different to his own. A tallyman indeed! Next thing he knew he'd be taken for a bailiff!

'Your mother said Nina was saying goodbye to your friend's mother,' he said with jovial *bonhomie*, 'she didn't want me to come round, but I thought it only...'

The words died away. As other footsteps, Lizzie's footsteps, came running after him through the passageway, he stared beyond Rose to the slender, petite figure standing at the table in the centre of the little room, a cheap enamel mug clutched in her hands, a dusting of flour on one cheek.

'Polly?' the incredulous whisper was barely audible.

Rose's eyes shot wide. Uncertainly, not sure if she had heard right, she stepped to one side so that Polly was more clearly in her uncle's view.

'Polly?' he said again, his smile gone, not a trace of *bonhomie* remaining. 'Is it really you? Why didn't Lizzie say...why didn't...?'

He swayed slightly, putting one hand on the cold stone of the house wall to steady himself.

Rose's Pekingese eyes widened still further. Nina stared from her uncle to her mother's friend, her jaw hanging open. How could her uncle possibly know Polly Wilkinson? Polly was a *weaver*. Her social world consisted of Beck-Side Street, the mill, an occasional tram ride into the centre of Bradford to shop at Kirkgate Market, and an even more occasional day out on Shipley Glen or Ilkley Moor. How, in the name of all that was wonderful, could her uncle possibly be on first name terms with her?

All the rosy colour had drained from Polly's cheeks. Unsteadily she set the mug down on the table and as she did so Lizzie rounded the end of the covered passage, coming to a breathless halt beside Walter, saying with fraught anxiety, 'I'm sorry, Polly. I tried to stop him, but he wouldn't listen...'

Polly wasn't listening to her either.

As Rose and Nina watched goggle-eyed she stepped from behind her kitchen table and walked towards their poleaxed uncle, her arms welcomingly outstretched, her voice unsteady with emotion as she said, 'Hello, Walter love. It's been a long time, hasn't it? Would you like to come in for a cup of tea? Would you like to make yourself at home?'

## Chapter Eight

'And he *has* made himself at home there,' Harry said wryly, 'because Mrs Wilkinson refuses absolutely to even visit Crag-Side.'

It was May of the following year. Nina and Noel were both back in Yorkshire for a few days, Nina on end of term holiday from St Martin's and Noel because some of his paintings were on show in a Leeds exhibition and he wanted to enjoy in person the acclaim they were receiving.

'Thank goodness,' Lottie said fervently. 'Can you imagine the embarrassment if she were to visit here?'

She had just finished playing a game of mixed doubles with Noel, Nina and Harry, and was now lying exhaustedly flat on her back on the smooth grass beside the tennis-court.

'That should be the least of your worries,' Harry said teasingly, sitting Indian-fashion, his white-trousered legs crossed at the ankle. 'It's what would happen if Father were to marry her that should really be concerning you.'

Lottie gave a cry of horror and sat up abruptly. Rose, her arms hugging her knees, a wide-brimmed cream straw sunhat shielding her freckle-prone skin from the sun, said crossly, 'What would it matter? Why can't you be *pleased* for them? Your father is happy. It should be patently obvious to everyone by now that Polly isn't a gold-digger. If they want to marry, why shouldn't they?'

'Oh Lord, not this old subject *again,*' Nina said wearily, pushing herself up one elbow and reaching for a nearby jug of iced lemon squash. 'If it isn't obvious to you now, Rose, that Polly Wilkinson as mistress of Crag-Side would be a social disaster of the highest order, for *all* of us, then I despair, I really do.'

From under the thick sweep of her lashes she looked across at William. He was being as silent and unforthcoming as ever, but he surely couldn't be *indifferent* to the prospect of his father marrying Polly? Or could he? She suppressed a sigh of intense irritation. All in all, William was proving to be a great disappointment. Despite all her efforts to engage his interest he stubbornly refused to show her anything but cousinly affection. Harry, on the other hand, was wild about her and always had been. But Harry was not heir to Crag-Side and to the mill, and it was Crag-side she ached and yearned for.

'Lottie and Harry and William would

be better off with Polly as a stepmother than with anyone else Uncle Walter might marry,' Rose said stubbornly, hating the affected way of speaking Nina had adopted since becoming a student at St Martin's. 'She's happy-natured and kind and—'

'And she's a *mill worker,'* Lottie said with what she felt was saintly patience. 'I appreciate that she's your friend's mother, and a neighbour, and that you're fond of her, Rose, but Papa would be a laughing-stock if he were to marry her. And so would we.'

William poured himself a glass of squash from the jug and said with an odd edge to his voice, 'What are you most worried about, Lottie? That Mrs Wilkinson will insist on wearing clogs and a shawl at Crag-Side, or that she'll speak to the servants in a broad Yorkshire accent?'

Rose, aware that his sarcasm was a way of showing solidarity with her, flashed him a look of gratitude.

Harry tensed, hoping to God William wasn't about to reveal to the Sugdens that he, too, was in love with a mill worker.

Nina's stomach muscles tightened. She had been right to suspect that William was indifferent to the prospect of his father's marrying Polly. Why he should take such an attitude was, however, a complete mystery to her—as were a lot of other things about him. This time she didn't even attempt to suppress her sigh of irritation. In the six months she had been attending St Martin's she had acquired a gloss of worldly sophistication which had altered her attitude to a lot of things.

Rose, for instance. She no longer felt as close and mentally in tune with Rose. How could she, when Rose insisted not only on remaining with their parents in Beck-Side Street, but on counting Jenny Wilkinson and Micky Porritt her closest friends? As for William... She had had such hopes where William was concerned, but they were hopes that were fast fading.

As Rose began to tediously point out to Lottie that Polly Wilkinson's accent was little broader than the way she, Rose, talked, Nina sipped at the glass of lemon squash she had poured herself and eyed her eldest cousin covertly. He was pleasant looking, but not excessively so. He didn't have the blatant masculinity of some of the young men she had met whilst in London. Young men like Rupert Winterton. Young men with London panache and style. Harry did, though. Harry had enough self-confidence and what her Bohemian college friends called 'chutzpah', to set the Thames alight.

'And *I* live in Beck-Side Street and fit in at Crag-Side,' Rose was saying, refusing to let the subject drop.

Nina raised her eyes to heaven and looked across to see what Noel was making of Rose's idiocy. He was asleep, his hands behind his head, his spiky red hair as untidy as a child's.

'Yes, but you haven't *always* lived in Beck-Side Street,' Lottie was pointing out, trying to be as fair as possible to her best-loved cousin, 'and Mrs Wilkinson has.'

Without turning her head away from Noel, Nina was aware that Harry was looking towards her. She felt an odd sensation in the pit of her stomach. Harry was even more blatantly handsome than Rupert Winterton, but if she were to encourage Harry, even the hope of one day engaging William's interest would be lost to her for ever.

Languidly, as if he were the furthest thing from her mind, she set her glass back down on the grass and turned her head slightly to meet his gaze.

His eyes burned hers, sending shooting stabs of excitement into parts of her body she barely knew existed.

'...at least Polly wouldn't try and impose her will on you all,' Rose was saying with dogged persistence.

Affecting the same indifference with which she had looked towards him, Nina outwardly transferred her attention back to the conversation taking place between Rose and Lottie, a flush of heat staining her cheeks, her pulses racing. Even though she had allowed Rupert Winterton to kiss her, the effect had been nothing like the mere effect of Harry's eyes. As for William...she looked towards his tall, rather angular figure, and knew that even if he was head over heels in love with her, he would never in a million years be able to arouse such a response in her.

'We're never going to see eye to eye on this Rose, so let's talk about something we *can* agree on,' Lottie said practically, her waist-length, near-blonde hair shining like spun silk in the hot sunlight. 'And that is where the best point is going to be for viewing the Coronation. Papa says outside Westminster Abbey, but Noel says there is to be a procession down The Strand and that we stand a much better chance of having a good view of King George and Queen Mary from there.'

Nina rose to her feet, the swirl of her narrowly pleated ankle-length tennis skirt emphasizing her natural grace. 'It's a pity the London house is on the wrong side of the river. It won't be on the route of any procession and we'd have had a super view from the third-floor windows.'

Noel flicked one eye open. 'The third floor is my studio,' he said dryly, still laying with his hands behind his head, 'and even if it overlooked the Abbey itself I'd rather a herd of stampeding elephants invaded it than you and your friends.'

Beneath the casual way they spoke of the house their uncle had rented for their convenience in London, their joy over it was hard to hide. Overlooking Battersea Park, its top floor had been converted into a studio and a motherly resident housekeeper kept an eagle eye on them. Or at least their uncle assumed she did. Nina thought again of Rupert Winterton's kiss and was aware she was being allowed an unconscionable amount of freedom for a girl still a month away from being eighteen; a girl who, only six months ago, had travelled little further than the outskirts of Bradford and had been living in a back-to-back in Beck-Side Street.

Noel was feigning sleep again and she said to everyone, carefully avoiding Harry's eyes, 'The sun's too hot. I'm going to go inside for a while.'

William made a non-committal noise, deep in thoughts of Sarah.

Lottie said, 'I'm not coming in till I've played a game with Rose. She hasn't a clue about the rules and yet she always seems to win.'

Rose, the slights that had been made about Polly still rankling, said tartly, 'I don't know the rules because until you put the nets up last month, I'd never played. We don't have tennis-courts in Beck-Side Street.'

Harry, knowing that neither Lottie or Rose would give up their verbal battle until each believed they were the winner, grinned. Ever since the day of their grandfather's funeral Lottie and Rose had been as thick as thieves, Lottie's only constant complaint being that Rose stubbornly refused to make Crag-Side her home.

He turned slightly, looking over his shoulder, watching Nina as she walked towards the house, her skirt fluttering beguilingly around her legs, the sailor collar of her hip length white tennis shirt giving her a nautical air. His grin deepened. He wondered if she had ever been sailing. He wondered what would happen if the two of them were to find themselves aboard a small boat together, with no one else within hailing distance and land a long way away.

'We play rounders in Beck-Side Street,' Rose said, rising to her feet and picking up Nina's discarded racket. 'Perhaps we could mark out a rounders pitch on the terrace. It's big enough.'

Harry, his eyes still on Nina as she began to climb the terrace steps, stood up, picking up his racket as he did so. 'I think Nina's right about the sun,' he said in the dark, rich voice that so added to his attractiveness, 'I'm going in as well, and if I were you Rose, I'd keep your sun hat on while you're playing. You don't want a touch of sunstroke.'

Rose shot him a swift, happy smile. Though Harry hadn't voiced his opinion when she had been arguing with Lottie over Polly, she knew that if Polly and his father were to marry, he would make no objection.

In the days immediately after their grandfather's funeral all the Rimmingtons had, at one time or another, visited Beck-Side Street. Lottie had regarded her visit as an adventure, but not an adventure she had wanted to repeat. William had been surprisingly keen to visit often, going out of his way to establish friendly relations with her father and to exchange politely awkward pleasantries with the likes of Gertie Graham and Albert Porritt. It had been Harry, though, who had effortlessly fitted in amongst her Beck-Side Street neighbours.

He had shown a genuine interest in Albert's much loved horse. He had rough-housed with a deliriously responsive Bonzo. He had responded to Gertie in her own coin and Gertie's bellying laughter had been heard nearly as far away as Bull Royd. He had met Polly, sensitively making no reference to the fact that he knew of her relationship with his father, knowing that it would deeply embarrass her if he did so. Jenny had been shy of him, but had liked him. Only Micky had persisted in being annoyingly hostile towards him.

'Come on,' Lottie said impatiently, breaking in on her reverie, 'as I've already played a game of doubles and you haven't, I suppose you'll beat me again, but it isn't fair. I've had tennis *tuition*, for goodness sake. What my coach would say if he knew you were beating me every time we played, heaven only knows!'

As the sound of Rose's first serve sounded distantly behind him, Harry took the terrace steps two at a time in swift, easy strides. Nina was no longer in sight but he was fairly sure where he would find her. Even before she had left Crag-Side for London her favourite retreat had always been the winter garden and even now, despite the heat, it was still the pleasantest corner of Crag-Side, for its main decorative feature was a coolly splashing fountain.

Minutes later he entered the winter garden's glaucously green, lily-scented interior and came to an abrupt halt, sucking his breath in sharply.

She was seated on the fountain's bronze rim and as her eyes met his he knew that he had not taken her by surprise but that she had excused herself from the others knowing full well that he would follow her; that she had wanted him to follow her. His throat tightened, the blood surging through his body in a hot tide. During their absence from each other he had had plenty of time to consider the wisdom of embarking on a passionate relationship with her. She was, after all, family. If the relationship should come to an end he couldn't simply walk away from her, never seeing her again. There would be all sorts of difficulties and embarrassments. And he didn't care about them. He didn't care about them because he didn't believe they would ever arise. It wasn't a passing crush he felt for Nina. It was an infatuation deep enough to last a lifetime.

Slowly he propped his tennis racket against the open door and began to walk towards her. Her eyes holding his, she rose to her feet, knowing he was going to kiss her; knowing that she wanted him to kiss her; knowing that she had wanted him to kiss her ever since she had first set eyes on him as he had hunkered down outside Brown Muff's, helping Rose to retrieve her portfolio case.

He came to a halt in front of her, so

near that the back of her legs were pressing against cold, hard bronze.

'There'll be no going back, you know that, don't you?' His eyes burned hers, the tension between them so taut it seemed to crackle like electricity.

She nodded, too confounded by desire to speak, and as he reached out for her she went willingly into his arms, her hands sliding up into the springy coarseness of his hair, her lips parting as his mouth came down on hers, hard and hot and insistent.

Rose came to such an abrupt halt that she nearly fell. In her first serve to Lottie she had broken the strings of her racket and had run after Harry in order to ask if she could borrow his. Now she stood wide-eyed at the entrance to the winter garden, transfixed by the sight of Harry and Nina's passionate embrace.

They were kissing in a way she had never seen people kiss before, not even her parents. With one hand Harry was holding Nina indecently close and with the other he was caressing one of her breasts, his sun-tanned hand dark against the pristine snowiness of her tennis shirt.

They were utterly unaware of her presence; unaware of anything and everything but each other.

As shock froze Rose into immobility she heard Harry groan; heard Nina make a whimpering noise, as if she were in pain. Only she wasn't in pain. She was experiencing an emotion and a sensation way beyond Rose's fifteen-year-old understanding, and Rose knew it.

Clumsily, half-falling, she turned on her heel, not wanting them to know that she had seen them; not knowing which of her violent, conflicting, disturbing reactions was uppermost.

Harry was *her* friend. He had been her friend right from the very beginning of their family reconciliation. There had always been understanding between them—an understanding so complete words were often unnecessary. He knew, for instance, and totally empathized with, her reasons for remaining with her parents in Beck-Side Street instead of moving into Crag-Side. He understood her loyalty to Jenny and Micky. When Lottie was being particularly bossy, or when Nina was being irritatingly pretentious, his eyes would meet hers in shared, exasperated, amusement.

And now Harry was *kissing* Nina! And Nina, who had never made any secret of her hopes where William was concerned, was allowing him to kiss her—and allowing him other, even more shocking liberties as well!

Tears she didn't understand scalded her cheeks as she ran, not knowing where she was running to, only knowing that she wanted to put as much distance between herself and the winter garden as possible.

The ornate iron gates at the end of Crag-Side's lavish driveway opened onto a road that climbed steeply up to Ilkley Moor. Rose, unable to run to her much-loved Beck for comfort, headed like an arrow from a bow for the moor's soothing, cleansing, vastness.

By the time she reached its bracken covered fringe she was panting and exhausted. More confused and unhappy than she could ever remember feeling she threw herself down on springy turf and, staring down towards the distant rooftops of Ilkley, tried to reason out why the sight of Nina, in Harry's arms, had so distressed her.

Was it simply because it was so unexpected? Nina had, after all, never expressed the slightest romantic interest in Harry. It had been William she had so hopefully been setting her cap at. Or was it the sheer passion of their embrace which was so disturbing her?

She circled her knees with her arms. There was no real reason why she should feel so disturbed. Even though she was only fifteen, life in Beck-Side Street had ensured she wasn't a complete innocent. She, too, had been kissed, though not in the way Harry had been kissing Nina. And whereas Nina had obviously been enjoying the experience, she hadn't liked it at all and had told Micky so in no uncertain terms.

She rested her chin on her knees. It was an incident that had nearly brought her friendship with him to an end, only his brusque, not very gracious apology, preserving it.

Her interlinked fingers tightened on each other. She still didn't understand why he should have acted so extraordinarily, nor why Jenny had been so odd with her when she had told her of it. And she certainly didn't understand why Harry, who so often exchanged amused glances with her whenever Nina began talking grandly about St Martin's and London, should now be in love with her. And he quite obviously *was* in love with her, or he wouldn't have been kissing her in such a passionate way.

A bee had begun to circle uncomfortably close to her head and she unclasped her hands, swatting it away. She didn't want Harry to be in love with Nina because...because...

She tried to bring her thoughts to a

logical conclusion and found she couldn't do so.

The bee alighted on a harebell. Two small birds flew, wrangling, into a nearby gorse bush.

*Why* couldn't she do so? Was it because she didn't *want* to do so? Was it because she was *afraid* of doing so?

The answer came back almost instantly. She *was* afraid. And in a moment of stunning self-knowledge, she knew the reason why.

Time seemed to waver and halt. The bee skimmed away. The birds in the gorse bush fell silent.

Clumsily she stumbled to her feet. How could she not have known before? How could she ever have classed her friendship with Harry as being the same as her friendship with Micky, or her friendship with Jenny or Lottie?.

Dazedly she stared down at Ilkley's distant rooftops, knowing that even if she had been aware of her feelings, it would have made no difference. Young men as heart-stoppingly handsome as Harry didn't fall in love with girls with ginger hair and Pekingese eyes. They fell in love with girls like Nina. Girls who were head-turningly beautiful and graceful.

She tilted her chin, the sun hot on her upturned face, knowing that Nina would never again be able to accuse her of being too young to understand things. She wondered how long it would be before Nina noticed the change that had taken place in her, and, when she did notice, what her reaction would be.

Somewhere, far distant, a church clock struck the hour, though what hour she had no idea. Slowly she began to walk back towards the road. Lottie would still be waiting for her, and she wouldn't be waiting patiently. She would be cross; very cross indeed.

'Of course I'm not cross,' Lottie said to Noel, kneeling on the grass a few feet away from him. William had sloped off on some mysterious errand of his own and she was feeling far too pleased at having Noel all to herself to feel anything like crossness. 'I only said I'd give Rose a game because she missed out when the rest of us played doubles.'

Noel, still lying flat on his back, made a disbelieving sound. Lottie was a lot of things, many of them exceedingly entertaining, but she wasn't known for being generously unselfish. If she wasn't miffed that Rose hadn't returned to play their intended game of tennis, it was because it suited her that Rose hadn't done so. Idly, he wondered why. He wasn't left to wonder long.

'Papa says you've been invited to a reception at Leeds Town Hall tonight,' she said with typical forthrightness. 'I've met the Lord Mayor lots of times when I've been to functions with Papa, and he's a pet. I'm sure he wouldn't mind if you took me with you this evening.'

Noel rolled over on to his side, resting his weight on his arm. 'It's an Art and Artists jamboree,' he said dryly. 'I've been invited because my work is currently on show in Leeds. Why would you be interested in being there?'

Lottie took a heather-blue ribbon out of her tennis shirt pocket and began anchoring back the long, satin-smooth fall of her hair. She wanted to be there because he would be there; because if would be fun basking in his reflected glory. *'An amazing talent'*, the arts editor of the *Yorkshire Observer* had written about him. *'A young man whose work shows exciting expressiveness'*.

'Because I'm more experienced at stuffy public social occasions than you are,' she said starkly. 'Since Mama died I've often accompanied Papa to functions. He says it makes them less boring.'

Noel's grey-green eyes flashed with amusement. Lottie had only been eight when her mother had died. If his Uncle Walter had indeed begun taking her to grand dinners and *soirées* at such a ridiculously early age it was no wonder she was now so bossy and precocious.

'I dare say you did make them less boring,' he said amenably, 'but tonight's function is arts orientated. There'll be art buyers and dealers there and it won't be in the least boring. At least not to me.'

Her eyes held his. They were exceptional eyes: a light, clear grey, the irises lamp-black.

'Then take me because I'm *interested* in art,' she said stubbornly.

He grinned, his amusement deepening. If Lottie *was* interested in art, it was a relatively new interest for what she knew about it could be written on the back of a postage stamp.

'No,' he said, well aware that he was the only person in the family who *did* say no to her. 'If I was going to take anyone, I'd take Nina. Have you looked through her portfolio case recently? All her sketched figures look remarkably like you.'

Lottie blinked, so surprised she temporarily abandoned her efforts to persuade him to take her with him that evening. 'Me? But why would she be doing that?' She frowned, bewildered. She and Nina had never hit if off in the totally committed, whole-hearted way she and Rose had done. She had resented the way that Nina, on her first visit to Crag-Side, had refused to be overawed by it, behaving instead as if she were accustomed to such a house when in reality she was accustomed only to a Bradford mill cottage. And she resented the fact that though Nina was only a little over a year her senior, she was allowed to live virtually unchaperoned in London enjoying freedoms she, still under her father's eagle eye, could only dream about.

Her frown deepened. Was Nina making fun of her in some way? The figures Noel was referring to were sticklike clothes-horses for Nina's dress designs, and though Noel seemed to think otherwise, there was really nothing very flattering about having one's likeness used as a clothes-horse. However, if *Noel* was to try and capture her likeness, that would be a very different matter!

She settled herself into a more comfortable position, sitting back on her heels. 'Papa would like you to paint me,' she said, knowing that though her father had never expressed such a wish, he would do once the idea was put into his head.

Noel fell back onto his back, groaning in mock despair. Lottie, aware that her flash of inspiration was going to put him exactly where she wanted him for weeks, possibly months, surveyed him complacently with a pussy cat smile. He would be able to start the portrait tomorrow and would hopefully work on it every day for the rest of his, and Nina's, stay. Then, when the rest of them visited London for the Coronation, she could ask her father if she, too, could stay in the house in Battersea. Not for good, of course—he would never allow that—but just until the portrait was finished.

A flash of movement caught her eyes as someone turned into the distant entrance of the drive. She squinted her eyes against the sun and saw that it was Rose. Without even pausing to wonder where on earth Rose could have been she sprang to her feet, waving both arms in enthusiastic greeting, calling out sunnily, 'Come on! We've a tennis match to play! We can have it finished before teatime if we make a start now!

# Chapter Nine

Sarah Thorpe free-wheeled her bicycle to a halt at the entrance to one of the narrow paths that led from the Allerton side of Chellow Dene woods through to the top end of Haworth Road. It was her's and William's regular meeting place, for it was the nearest thing to secluded countryside west Bradford possessed. It took her twenty minutes of pleasant cycling to reach it from the mill where she worked and once she and William had walked slowly through the woods and reluctantly said goodbye at the other end of them, her way home, down Haworth Road and into Toller Lane, was all downhill.

A smile curved her lips as she slid from the high bicycle saddle. William had obviously slipped away from a posh tennis party in order to drive to meet her for he was dressed in a sports blazer and white tennis flannels.

'Hello love, have you been waiting long?' she asked fondly as he stepped from the shade of the tree he had been leaning against. 'I got here as soon as I could but I had to go on an errand for Pa first.'

He covered the distance between them swiftly, his arms closing lovingly around her waist. 'I've been waiting ten minutes,' he said, breathing in the faint fragrance of rose water that emanated from her hair, savouring a moment of close physical contact that his respect for her ensured would be all too brief. 'It felt like ten hours.'

She pressed her hands against his chest, pushing herself a little away from him so that she could look up into his face. 'I have to be home by six,' she said gently, knowing how intensely disappointed he would be. 'Pa is preaching at Little Horton tonight and he wants me to go with him.'

William wondered whether to suggest he, too, went to Little Horton to hear her lay-preacher father orate, and then thought better of it. It would cause the kind of gossip they desperately wished to avoid and besides, he could hardly go into a Methodist chapel dressed in a sports blazer and tennis flannels.

Reluctantly he removed his hands from around her waist, knowing that if he held her close a second longer he would kiss her; knowing that if he once began kissing her he would never be able to stop.

'Then it doesn't give us much time to talk, love,' he said, taking one of her hands in his and, as they began walking along the narrow pathway, pushing her bicycle along with the other. 'And there's a lot we have to talk about.'

Sarah's hand tightened in his. Whenever William spoke in the tone of voice he was now using, it meant only one thing. He was again tussling with the problem of how to tell his father that he loved her and intended marrying her. A slight shadow touched her eyes. Every moment they shared together was precious and she hated it when, instead of simply taking pleasure in each other's company, they ended up discussing what his father's reaction to her as a daughter-in-law might, or might not be.

It wasn't as if it was an anxiety she shared. Tranquil and serene by nature and possessing a firm belief in her own self-worth, she regarded any difficulty William's father had about her as being his problem, not hers.

'You said you weren't going to worry about it anymore,' she reminded him patiently. 'You said you were simply going to tell him when you were twenty-one.'

'I'm twenty-one in four weeks time,' he said wryly. 'Which is why we have to talk, Sarah. I want you with me when I break the news. And I want you to meet the rest of my family *before* I break the news.'

She looked across at him, her eyes

widening. 'Your brother and sister? I thought you said your sister would be no help at all—that she'd hate the idea of you marrying a mill girl?'

A slight smile touched his narrow, well-shaped mouth. 'So I did—but that was before our Sugden cousins came into our lives. I told you my aunt and uncle live in a street quite near to your own street, didn't I? My father said Rose, my youngest cousin, was more than welcome to come and live at Crag-Side but she turned the offer down. Much as she loves Crag-Side, and I sometimes thinks she loves it more than any of us, she also values her Beck-Side Street friends and is in no hurry to leave them.'

'And?' Sarah prompted, liking the sound of Rose Sugden.

'And Lottie regards Rose more as a sister than a cousin. And as Rose lives in a mill cottage, she's had to revise her snobbish way of thinking quite a lot.'

Sarah remained tactfully silent. She knew that however much Lottie Rimmington's attitudes had changed, they hadn't changed sufficiently enough for her to be happy about her father's romantic friendship with one of the Sugden's neighbours.

The bicycle wheels scrunched over a scattering of loose pebbles. A squirrel, disturbed by the noise, scampered for cover up a nearby tree.

They continued walking, hands tightly clasped, neither of them speaking. William was deep in thought as to how best to introduce Sarah to Harry and Lottie and Rose. Should he do so before Noel and Nina arrived at Crag-Side for his twenty-first birthday party? Or should he wait until he could introduce her to everyone at once?

Sarah's thoughts were equally confused. Why, when William's father was romantically friendly with a Beck-Side Street widow, should he disapprove of her and William's relationship? Apart from age there was, after all, very little difference between herself and Mrs Wilkinson. They both lived in the same working-class neighbourhood; they both worked in local mills. Surely, under the circumstances, William's father would be understanding when William spoke to him, not disapproving?

'I think a Saturday afternoon picnic on Ilkley Moor would be the best idea,' William said, putting an end to her puzzled train of thought. 'Harry can drive Lottie and Rose up there and I'll come for you in Minerva.'

Minerva was the brand name of the imported motorcar he had bought for himself with money left him by his grandfather. He never referred to it as the Minerva, however, only Minerva, as though the motorcar were a person.

'Can we meet where we met today?' Sarah had surprisingly few qualms about meeting Harry and Lottie and Rose for the first time, but she did have qualms where Minerva was concerned. Until now, on the few occasions when William had visited her home, staying for a family high tea of tripe and onions, or black pudding and peas, he had always bicycled there. In her little cul-de-sac a bicycle, even a strange bicycle, attracted little attention. Minerva attracted attention even in the poshest streets of Ilkley and Harrogate.

He nodded, having too much respect for Sarah's parents to even consider the idea of trundling Minerva over their cobbles.

Mr and Mrs Thorpe knew, of course, who he was—and were unimpressed. 'A good name is rather to be chosen than great riches,' Mr Thorpe had said to him, quoting from Proverbs in the gentle, musing manner that made his lay-preacher delivery so oddly effective and so distinctively different to the hell-fire approach of many of his colleagues. 'And a good name, and good character, is what matters in this house, lad,' he had added with true Bradfordian bluntness. 'If your intentions are as honourable as we understand them to be, then you're as welcome to court Sarah as any other fine upstanding young man would be. If they're not, then no amount of mill-owning brass'll make you welcome. You'd best be gone, and gone sharp.'

William hadn't gone. He'd sat down and had a cup of tea and a slice of Mrs Thorpe's mint and currant pasty and by the time he had said his goodbyes he had been reeling in disbelief at the unexpected breadth of Mr Thorpe's self-education. The journals of Dr Johnson; the writings of Charles Wesley; the poetry of John Milton and George Herbert; the novels of Charles Dickens and George Eliot, all were referred to by him in some way or other, and always knowledgeably.

'Why shouldn't Pa be well read?' Sarah had said reasonably when they were next alone. 'He's a lay-preacher and he knows his Bible inside out.'

'Yes, well, I would have expected that,' William had admitted, still dazed at having had lines from Milton's *Paradise Lost* quoted to him by a weaving overlooker, 'but I hadn't expected him to know Milton inside out, or George Herbert either, come to that!'

He said now, slowing to a halt as the woods began to thin and the stile leading out onto Haworth Road came into view.

'I'll meet you at two o'clock on Saturday, and don't worry about picnic food. I'll see to that.' He came to a halt, not wanting to reach the stile; not wanting to have to say goodbye to her.

She rested her head against his shoulder and he unclasped his hand from hers, sliding it around her waist, pulling her even closer.

'I'm not going to wait until my birthday to speak to my father,' he said, his voice raw with resolution. 'I'm going to do so at dinner on Saturday evening. I want us to be able to announce our engagement on my birthday, Sarah. And I want us to be married by Christmas.'

Her eyes widened, deep blue and black-lashed, and the breath caught in his throat. How had a couple as homely as the Thorpes produced a daughter so lovely? Her abundant hair, caught in a high, loose knot, was so dark an auburn as to be almost black. With her delicately winged eyebrows, gently curving cheek bones and innate serenity, she looked more like a Madonna by Raphael or Perugino than a Yorkshire girl brought up in a strict Methodist household.

'Sarah...' Desire was building up inside him hot and fierce and he was terrified he wasn't going to be able to keep control of it. They had to marry soon! They *had* to!

He couldn't continue reining in his need of her, kissing her always with loving tenderness and never with deep passion.

The pressure of her breast, as she leaned in innocent sensuousness against him, was unbearably arousing and he knew he could not trust himself to kiss her goodbye; that to kiss her goodbye now would be to abandon all restraint.

'Sarah...' he said again hoarsely, 'Sarah I...'

As if reading his thoughts; as if sharing the intensity of his need, she turned more fully against him, her eyes holding his, the love in them absolute.

He sucked in his breath and for one brief moment, as sunlight dappled down on them through the leaves of the trees, time seemed to hang suspended.

'I love you,' he said thickly when at last capable of speech. 'You're my fortress and my peace Sarah, and I'll love you till the day I die.'

Her arms slid up and around his neck. 'I'll love you longer, William. I'll love you for always—throughout all eternity.'

It was too much to be borne. He abandoned his hold of her bicycle—abandoned all restraint. As the bicycle toppled into a mat of lily of the valley, his arms closed round her, pressing her in against him in a way he had previously only dreamed of doing, his body hard and urgent as his mouth closed in passionate longing on hers.

Rose, Jenny and Micky surveyed the world from their usual meeting place on top of the midden the Porritt's shared with three other families.

'Will you really see the King and Queen when you go down to London?' Jenny was saying to Rose in awestruck tones. 'Will you be in Westminster Abbey when the King is crowned?'

' 'Course she won't.' Micky was seventeen now and he often found Jenny's fifteen-year-old naïvety intensely irritating. He plucked a blade of grass from a crack in the midden's roof and stuck it in the corner of his mouth, unhappy with himself, unhappy with the world. 'Only proper nobs have seats in the Abbey,' he continued, looking not at her but at Rose, 'and mill owners aren't proper nobs. They're folks like us who just happen to have brass. And they only have brass because folks like you, Jenny, are daft enough to work for 'em.'

Jenny's arms were hugging her knees and her clasped hands tightened together, the knuckles whitening. She hated it when Micky spoke to her in such a belittling way, and she hated it even more when he looked at Rose with such unhappy intensity. Why did it matter where Rose went with her Rimmington cousins? Why was Micky so *resentful* of them?

'Where else would I work if I didn't work in the mill?' she said defensively, wishing he'd pay her just a fraction of the attention he paid Rose. 'Not everyone can be removal men like you and your dad and besides, I *like* working at Lutterworth's. It may be hard work in the weaving but we have a lot of fun, even if we do have to shout at the top of our voices to make ourselves heard.'

Micky made a disparaging noise and rolled the blade of grass to the other side of his mouth. He'd only been in a weaving shed once, when he and his dad had been picking up some shoddy, and no force on earth would get him to go in one again. He didn't like enclosed spaces. He liked being out in the fresh air with the horse and cart, as far out of Bradford and as near to the moors as possible.

'We *will* see King George and Queen Mary,' Rose said, wondering why it was Micky seemed incapable of being civil anymore; wondering why he had changed so. 'There's to be a giant procession through London and we're going to watch it from The Strand.'

Jenny had no idea where or what The

Strand was, but she knew it must be a wonderful vantage point, otherwise the Rimmingtons wouldn't be going to it. Images of horses with brilliantly coloured plumes dancing on top of their heads, and gold carriages, banners, bunting and flags filled her mind, so wonderful she temporarily forgot how miserable Micky had just made her. There would be soldiers in dress uniform, too, and not just ordinary soldiers, but Horse Guards and Grenadier Guards and Beefeaters and...

'Though we won't be in the Abbey, a friend of Nina's will be,' Rose continued, not bragging but stating a truth she knew Jenny would want to know. 'His name is Rupert Winterton and Nina nearly fell off her chair at breakfast when she read his name in *The Times* wedding guest list. He's the youngest duke in England and there was an article about him as well, and a photograph.'

'So?' Micky said belligerently. 'So what does that make him? It doesn't make him any better than other folk, does it? He's only a duke 'cos his father was a duke. He hasn't *earned* being a duke.'

'I never said he *had* earned being a duke,' Rose said exasperatedly. 'I was simply stating a fact. And he can't be the kind of duke you so object to, Micky, or he wouldn't still be at St Martin's, would he?'

Micky didn't know anything about St Martin's, and didn't want to know. He yanked the blade of grass from his mouth and tossed it over the edge of the midden's roof. Things weren't the same any more between himself and Rose and he resented the fact deeply. It was all the Rimmingtons' fault. Until Walter Rimmington had driven his flash motorcar into Beck-Side Street, he and Rose had not only been the best of mates, they'd been equals. Now they were equals no longer. How could they be, when she spent so much time laiking with folk who had more brass than they knew what to do with?

'There's going to be a bonfire in the street to celebrate the Coronation,' Jenny said, hopeful that a changed topic of conversation would put an end to the bickering. 'It'll be fun having a bonfire in June, won't it? Mam's going to put red, white and blue icing on her fairy cakes and Gertie's going to make a trifle.'

Micky made no response. Rose wouldn't be at Beck-Side Street's bonfire. Rose would be in London with the Rimmingtons.

'I'm off to Thornton tomorrow,' he said, his arms clasped loosely around his knees, his feet crossed at the ankle, the steel heel rims on his clogs glinting in the sun. 'I'm moving a widder-lady into a cottage on the edge of t'moor.' He stared down hard at his feet, a pulse throbbing at the corner of his jawline. 'Do you fancy coming?' he asked, as if it wasn't of much interest to him whether they did or not. 'It'll be a grand day out.'

A day out on the horse and cart always was a grand day out and Jenny's face shone in happy anticipation as she said eagerly, 'We'd love to Micky, wouldn't we, Rose?'

Rose shook her head, genuinely disappointed. 'I can't, Jenny. I've promised to go on a family picnic tomorrow and it's a special picnic, not just an ordinary picnic. There's no way I can not go.'

Jenny's radiance evaporated. If Rose didn't go, she couldn't go. Her ma, who was always so sunnily reasonable, had suddenly become very odd about her going out on the cart with Micky if Albert wasn't with them. A whole day out, and on a Saturday when there were so many household chores for her to do, would be completely out of the question.

'I...I don't think I'll be able to come either, Micky,' she said unwillingly. 'I've just remembered how much work there is to do at home on a Saturday and...'

Her voice trailed away, her misery total. Micky wasn't listening to her. He was on his feet, white lines edging the corners of his mouth, fury, resentment, and a misery more than equal to her own, blazing in his eyes.

'Oh, aye, it'll be special all reet!' he shouted, taking Rose so much by surprise that her jaw dropped open and her eyes flew so wide they seemed to fill her entire face. 'Special, because it's yon Rimmingtons you're going jaunting wi'! Well, Rose Sugden, I'll tell you this for nowt, I wish to God Beck-Side Street had never seen sight nor sound of t'bloody Rimmingtons!'

His hair which, as a boy, had always stood straight up in front in an irrepressible cowlick, now fell over his forehead in a manner even Rose had to admit was decidedly attractive. Always tall and skinny, his shoulders had filled out so that, although he was still slenderly built, there was a whippy look to him that told he would be someone to be reckoned with in a fight—and the unleashed anger now coursing through him was evidence enough that he wouldn't need too much excuse to join in any fight that was going.

'Everything was all reet in t'street afore they came...' he continued, breathing hard, his nostrils thin and pinched, '...mixing wi' folk they've no right mixing wi'! We couldn't just tek into our heads to go visiting them, could we? That'd be very different, wouldn't it? So why do they think they can come down here and it'll be all reet wi' us all?'

'I don't know what you mean—' Rose began, trying to interrupt him, far too bewildered to answer his anger with outraged indignation of her own.

He didn't let her even finish her sentence. 'And it *isn't* all reet!' he continued as if she hadn't even attempted to speak. 'They're them and we're us and them pretending to act as if there's no difference, when there's a world o' bloody difference, only confuses folks. It mek's it so's folks don't know where they are and they don't like it.' He ran a hand through his hair, exasperation adding to his anger. 'The only reason Jenny's ma hasn't been shunned by everyone in t'street for having a gentleman friend like Mr Rimmington is because everyone knows he's also your mam's brother. And if you think *that* isn't confusing to folks your mam dress-meks for, then you can bloomin' well think again!'

Rose scrambled to her feet, appalled by how embarrassed Jenny must be feeling. 'That's a rotten thing to say, Micky Porritt!' she flared, the breeze that freshened the tops of the middens blowing strands of ginger hair across her face. 'Why would people shun Jenny's mum just because she's friends with my uncle! He's as single as she is and—'

'Single don't come into it!' It was all Micky could do to stop himself from seizing her by the shoulders and shaking her till her teeth rattled. 'He's not her *class,* can't you see that? Folks like your Uncle Walter don't mix wi' folks like us! And we don't want 'em to neither! They should keep to their own sort and not come sniffing around where they're not wanted!'

Jenny had begun to cry. Neither Micky nor Rose took any notice.

'That's an ugly, *nasty* thing to say!' White-faced and trembling Rose wondered if Micky knew that her uncle wasn't the only Rimmington to have a mill lass as a sweetheart. If he *did* know about William's relationship with Sarah Thorpe he could at least have told her. *She* hadn't known until William had invited her to Saturday's picnic, informing her when he did so that the girl he intended marrying, a girl who lived only three or four streets away from Beck-Side Street and who worked in the weaving at Lutterworth's, would be attending it also.

'Aye, well, if the cap fits,' Micky said tersely, knowing he had said all he wanted to say and knowing it had been far, far too much.

As Rose sucked in her breath, about to make an indignant rejoinder, he turned on his heel. She knew how he felt now and, if she'd listened to him with half an ear, she also knew how other folk felt—and in his opinion it was about bloody time.

'Micky...'

He strode to the edge of the midden and vaulted down from it, the steel on his clogs flashing sparks as they made contact with the paving flags.

What she did about what he'd told her would be up to her, but he knew what he wanted her to do. He wanted her to turn her back on the Rimmingtons. He wanted her to want to be with *him*. He wanted to tell her all about a book he had been reading; a book a schoolteacher he and his dad had moved from one of the smart terraces the other side of Toller Lane into an even smarter house down by Manningham Park, had given him.

The book was all about New Zealand and there were pictures in it. Pictures of wide open countryside; countryside so beautiful and unspoilt it took the breath away. It said in the book that a man could sheep farm in New Zealand. Though Micky was city born and bred, he was also Yorkshire born and bred, and he knew all about sheep. A job as a hand on a New Zealand sheep farm would suit him fine, but he didn't want to go out there by himself. He wanted Rose to go with him. She was sixteen in a few months time and in Bradford plenty of lasses were married at sixteen.

*'Micky!'*

There was no distress in the voice calling after him; no remorse. Instead she sounded outraged—as if she were going to demand that he make an apology.

Not turning his head he dug his hands deep into the pockets of his shabby trousers and, as he entered the passageway leading through to the street, began to whistle. He wasn't going to apologize for what he'd said. It had been the truth, every word of it, by heck it had!

Rose stamped her foot on the midden roof in angry frustration. If Micky expected her to run after him, then he had another think coming because she *wasn't* going to run after him, not now, not ever!

Jenny's crying was now impossible to ignore and Rose, deeply hurt by Micky's savage outburst and more troubled than she wanted to admit by the prospect of Saturday's picnic, said impatiently, 'Do stop snivelling, Jenny. It was me he was angry at, not you.'

Jenny gasped, shocked at Rose's totally uncharacteristic lack of sympathy.

Rose, still standing and looking out over

a back yard filled with the Porritt's washing, was oblivious. Had there been a shred of truth in Micky's accusations? *Were* her neighbours confused and unhappy by her Rimmington relatives' visits to Beck-Side Street? She thought of the easy way Harry fitted in with everyone and, where he was concerned, couldn't bring herself to believe it. Perhaps, though, where her Uncle Walter was concerned, there was truth in what Micky had said. And William? What would the reaction be in Sarah Thorpe's cul-de-sac when William's identity became public knowledge?

As Jenny wiped her tears away with the hem of her working skirt Rose continued to stare out over the Porritt's bleak backyard, the breeze tugging at her hair as she hugged her arms, deep in unhappy thought.

## Chapter Ten

'Aye, li...ttle love, it is a bi...it of a ru...um do,' Laurence Sugden said with difficulty, thinking privately that it was a great deal more than that; that it was history repeating itself with rare old vengeance.

'I don't think it's something recent,' Rose said, frowning slightly. 'I think he and Sarah Thorpe have been sweethearts for a long time.'

She was sitting on a leather pouffe pulled companiably close to his chair and he reached out a prematurely aged hand, touching the top of her head lovingly.

'You mean e...ven from bef...ore William knew ab...out his his fa...ther's friendship with Polly?' he asked quizzically.

Rose nodded. The nice thing about her father was that he always understood things without her having to laboriously spell them out. 'I can understand William having kept his friendship a secret *before* he knew Polly Wilkinson was his father's lady friend,' she continued, her frown deepening, 'but I don't understand why he's continued *keeping* it a secret. I mean, Uncle Walter can't possibly object to Sarah

Thorpe, can he? At least he can't if Sarah's a nice girl and I can't imagine William wanting to marry anyone who wasn't nice.'

Laurence, who had had plenty of experience of the vagaries of human nature, remained silent. On the face of it, of course, Rose was right. How could Walter Rimmington possibly object to his son wanting to marry a decent working-class young woman when he, too, had wanted to marry such a woman—and according to Lizzie, still did.

'Per...haps William knows a side to his fa...ther we don't,' he said perceptively. 'People don't al...ways be...have reasonably, little love. Some...times even people nearest and dear...est to us, take us by complete sur...prise.'

Rose rested her chin on her hand and stared into the fireplace. Even though it was evening, because the weather had been so gloriously hot there was no fire in the grate, only a decorative paper fan to make it look a little less empty.

She didn't know whether her father was right about William knowing a side to her uncle that the rest of them were unaware of, but he was certainly right in saying that even people near and dear could take you by complete surprise. Harry and Nina had, for instance. And Micky certainly had. Even now, several hours later, she couldn't quite believe the savagery with which he had turned on her.

Outside of her family she only had two close friends, and he was one of them. How was it, then, that she had never previously realized how he felt where Harry and William and her Uncle Walter were concerned? And were there other things she hadn't realized? His kiss, for instance. She had simply thought it a ridiculous aberration, but that was before she had come to a realization of her own feelings where Harry was concerned. For the first time it occurred to her that Micky might feel about her as she felt about Harry. And if he did so, then she must have hurt his feelings unbearably.

She sighed. Growing up was proving to be a very complicated business—far more complicated than she had ever envisaged.

'I thi...nk it's ti...me for two mugs of milky co...coa, little love,' her father said tenderly, aware of her dejection, though not of all its causes. 'Co...coa's the best comforter in the wo...rld when you're feeling a bit low.'

She rose to her feet, smiling down at him. 'With a ginger biscuit to go with it?'

'Aye, li...ittle love,' he said, smiling with stroke-stricken lopsidedness, 'a gi...inger biscuit would go do...own a tre...eat.'

From out of nowhere Rose felt tears spring to her eyes. No matter how confusing the rest of life might prove to be, there was one thing that would always be constant—her father's love for her. That would never change; not in a million years.

'I can't believe we're doing this!' Lottie said crossly as Harry drove the open-topped Renault up the hill towards the moor. 'We can't *really* be driving out into the middle of the moor to meet some mill girl William daren't bring to Crag-Side! Some mill girl he wants to introduce to us as our future sister-in-law!

'And cousin-in-law,' Nina added darkly.

They were squeezed with Rose on the Renault's rear seats, a large picnic hamper on their knees.

Noel, seated in the front passenger seat, grinned. William's announcement to them all, that he had been courting a Bradford mill girl for the past two years and intended becoming engaged to her on the evening of his twenty-first birthday, had amused him vastly. What was it with the Rimmington men? Was it some sort of subconscious desire to retain a foothold in the class old Caleb had dragged them out of? Whatever it was, with Walter again embroiled in the relationship Caleb had once thought he had terminated, and with William well and truly embarked on a copycat relationship, Caleb Rimmington was surely turning in his grave.

He looked wryly across at Harry, aware of how much more satisfactory it would be if Harry, not William, was heir to Crag-Side and the mill. William possessed a socialist fervour that could bring nothing but improvements into the lives of Rimmington's workers, but Harry wasn't without a social conscience and his interest in the day-to-day running of Rimmington's was far greater than William's. And Harry was in love with Nina. If Harry and Nina were to marry, and from the besotted way they kept looking at each other and the way they could hardly keep their hands off each other, it was certainly a possibility, then the day would surely come when a Rimmington with Sugden blood would inherit Crag-Side and the mill.

As the Renault swept onto one of the narrow moorland roads and gorse and heather stretched out on either side of them as far as the eye could see, Noel reflected there would be a certain *rightness* about such an event. Seeing one of her grandchildren inheriting everything she had been disinherited from, would surely give his mother deep happiness. And lording it over everyone as a wealthy mill owner's wife would suit Nina down to the ground.

'It's all Papa's fault!' Lottie fumed, hating the way the others had insisted she at least meet Sarah Thorpe. 'If he hadn't set such a bad example—'

'If Sarah Thorpe's a quarter as nice as Polly, William will be very lucky,' Rose interrupted tartly. 'It's what people *are*, that matters Lottie. Not the way they talk or where they live.'

Nina's beautifully curved mouth was as tight as it was possible for it to be. For the first time ever, she was in complete agreement with every word Lottie uttered. Of *course* what they were doing was utterly ludicrous. Whoever heard of anyone being introduced to a future sister-in-law and cousin-in-law at a moorland picnic? That Noel and Rose had been adamant they fall in with William's plans had made her mad enough to spit.

Worse than her anger, though, was the shock she still felt. She had, after all, had romantic hopes of William herself. And to know that those hopes had come to nothing because he was in love with a mill girl from Lutterworth's, a mill girl who, if he married her, would one day be mistress of Crag-Side, had shocked her to such an extent she had thought she was going to have a heart attack. Even now, days later, she still felt a tightness in her chest and a dizzying sense of utter disbelief.

'They're here before us,' Harry said, trundling the Renault off the high track and bouncing it onto springy turf. 'She doesn't look like a Yorkshire girl, does she? At least not from a distance. She looks almost Italian.'

'Then maybe she's brought some ice-cream with her,' Lottie said caustically and then, as the Renault rocked nearer to where William and Sarah were sitting on a tartan travel rug, Minerva parked in lonely grandeur nearby, she added, 'She isn't wearing a shawl. Too hot I suppose.'

William had already risen to his feet, waving cheerily. Rose saw Sarah rise with easy grace to stand a little to one side, and a little behind him. She didn't look overly nervous, nor did she look brazenly overconfident. She was slenderly built and of average height, with a mass of smoke-dark hair caught up in an elegant, loose knot, and there was an overall look of quiet composure about her that reminded Rose of someone, though who, she couldn't quite think.

Harry knew immediately who it was Sarah Thorpe resembled. As he brought the Renault to a shuddering stop and he saw Sarah more clearly, surprise almost robbed him of breath. She possessed the same easy grace as his Aunt Lizzie. Her hair, too, was like his aunt's. Dark and abundant and upswept in exactly the same uncomplicated, yet elegant manner.

He stepped from the Renault in Noel and Nina and Rose's wake, watching as William introduced Sarah to them, aware that his first impressions of her had not been overly fanciful. The quiet dignity and attractive composure with which she was facing Nina and Lottie's open hostility were an exact carbon copy of his Aunt Lizzie's attractive manner. There was a sweetness in her smile, too, that immediately caught his liking.

He moved forward to shake her hand, aware that though Nina and Lottie might be determined not to like, or approve of her, he already instinctively did so, and was certain Noel did also.

'William told me you were partial to mint and currant pasty,' she said to him in a voice which, though typically Bradfordian and flat-vowelled, was pleasantly pitched, 'and so I've brought one with me that I made specially.'

There was lurking laughter in her eyes, as if she were aware of his thoughts. Answering amusement licked through him. Miss Sarah Thorpe was telling him he needn't worry on her account about Nina and Lottie's hostility; that it was a hostility she had expected and was well able to handle; a hostility she had every hope of eventually overcoming.

'Terrific,' he said, smiling broadly. 'I understand you live only a few streets away from Rose. Do you know each other by sight? Her ginger hair is rather hard to forget once seen, isn't it?'

Sarah, aware from the instant she had shaken Rose's hand and looked into her friendly, amber-brown eyes that there was at least one female member of William's family she could count on as a friend, smiled back. It was an intriguing smile, revealing an inner serenity almost Mona Lisa-like, and the last shreds of Harry's doubt as to the wisdom of William's decision, vanished.

'I didn't know who she was until today, but I have seen Rose before,' she said as Noel and William manhandled the picnic hamper from the Renault's rear seat and across to the travel rug. 'She goes out with the Porritt's on their removal cart sometimes, doesn't she?'

Lottie looked as if she were going to choke. Nina, one hand holding a very broad-brimmed, very expensive, cream straw hat in place, resisted the urge to there and then throttle her sister. It was bad enough that as a child Rose had ridden shotgun with the Porritt's on their rackety horse-drawn cart, but that she was still doing it...

'It's a grand old horse the Porritt's have, isn't it?' Harry was saying companionably, for all the world as if he, too, had enjoyed similar days out. 'And they've a grand little dog as well—a little Staffordshire called Bonzo.'

Lottie marched over to the travel rug and sat down on it next to the hamper. She had taken very great care with her dress, far more than she would have usually done for a family picnic. Her pale mauve voile frock skimmed button-boots of ivory kid and she was wearing a rope of pearls that had once belonged to her mother.

Hoping fiercely that Sarah Thorpe, mill girl, would no longer be under any illusions as to the depth of the social gulf dividing them, she began unpacking the hamper.

'Tablecloth, lunch napkins, cutlery case,' she said in a cut glass accent bereft of even the merest hint of Yorkshire flatness. 'Cucumber sandwiches, egg and cress sandwiches, a game pie, a pork and apple pie, a cheese and onion flan.'

As Nina smoothed out the lace-edged tablecloth for her, she set the dishes William had asked Crag-Side's cook to prepare down upon it, crossly reflecting that Sarah Thorpe wouldn't be labouring under any false illusions at all if it weren't that Rose lived so near to her.

'A sherry trifle, a chocolate cake, a fruit cake,' she continued, wondering how she could best get Sarah to understand that Rose's living in Beck-Side Street was an eccentricity that was none of her business.

She placed a plate of scones next to the fruit cake, following it with a plate of vanilla slices.

Sarah, who was accustomed to egg sandwiches, mint and currant pasty and sarsaparilla when it was a special picnic such as a birthday treat, and paste sandwiches, jam tarts and a flask of tea when it wasn't, remained prudently silent. If Lottie was hoping she would betray naïve awe at the sight of such a splendid spread, then Lottie was going to be disappointed for she wasn't even slightly awed, and she didn't think it at all splendid.

Instead, aware of the hunger in homes where men were out of work, or laid off work because of sickness, she thought the amount of food shockingly excessive. There was enough cramming the tablecloth to feed half a dozen destitute families for a week and she was amazed that the Sugdens, at least, didn't realize it.

'Don't worry about anything going to waste,' Rose said, settling herself companionably next to her. 'Anything left over and not half demolished will be on the tea table at the local children's home within half an hour of it being taken back to Crag-Side.'

'A thermos of hot chocolate, a thermos of coffee, a bottle of lemonade, a bottle of shandy,' Lottie said crossly, heaving the last of the picnic items from the hamper. Why on earth had Rose brought up the subject of the orphanage? Of all the many local charities her father generously supported, the orphanage was her own particular favourite. She enjoyed going round there, holding the small babies and playing with the toddlers, and she didn't want Sarah asking William if she, too, could visit it.

'You've just crushed a clump of harebell with the shandy bottle,' Noel said laconically.

It was unheard of for Lottie's short temper ever to be directed in Noel's direction but she said now with crosspatch sharpness, 'No, I haven't. Harebells don't grow on moorland.'

As Harry began slicing the game pie and Nina began passing around china plates, Noel slapped his forehead in mock despair. 'Poor Emily Brontë,' he groaned theatrically. 'How could she have got it so wrong?'

Lottie flushed. She didn't know what he meant, but she did know he was making fun of her and she didn't like it. 'I don't know what you mean,' she said stiffly, unhappily aware of how closely Sarah and William were sitting together, and the almost *sheening* happiness shimmering between them.

'The last paragraph of *Wuthering Heights*,' Noel said, helping himself to a slice of richly-filled pie, 'when Lockwood comes across Cathy's and Edgar Linton's and Heathcliff's graves in the moorland churchyard. There are harebells growing there. How does it go? "I lingered round them, under that benign sky..." ' He came to a halt, unable to remember just what followed.

' "Watched the moths fluttering among the heath and harebells," ' Sarah continued for him in her attractively gentle voice, ' "listened to the soft wind breathing through the grass; and wondered how any one could ever imagine unquiet slumbers, for the sleepers in that quiet earth." '

It was so unexpected a contribution that no one spoke for a few moments and then Noel said, 'That's it, Sarah. It is a pretty memorable piece of writing, isn't it?' He bit into the pie, saying awkwardly with a full mouth, 'I've never been able to understand why everyone refers to *Wuthering Heights* as a love story. It's so macabre it gives me the shivers.'

Nina could have slapped him for talking with his mouth full. It was a commonness she couldn't imagine Sarah Thorpe committing. A light breeze had blown up and was tugging annoyingly at her hat. She took it off, laying it beside her feet. Sarah Thorpe was not at all as she had assumed she would be. She wasn't intimidated by them, as would have been only too understandable. And she wasn't defiantly brazen, as might also have been expected. Instead she possessed an unnerving sense of quiet self-confidence; was relatively well-spoken; obviously intelligent; and last but by no means least, when her mother, Lizzie, had been Sarah's age, she must have looked disquietingly like her.

Rose still couldn't place who it was Sarah reminded her of, but she did know that she liked her enormously. She was also sure that, given time, Lottie would grow to like her too. Even now, Lottie looked slightly less on her high horse than she had when unpacking the picnic hamper. Was that because she couldn't help but be aware of how deeply in love William and Sarah were? Or was it because she was impressed by the way Sarah had so effortlessly, and without the least degree of showing off, finished Noel's quotation from *Wuthering Heights?*

There was no way of telling and Rose didn't trouble to ponder over it. All that mattered was that dinner at Crag-Side on Saturday was not going to be a disaster—and that as far as the present was concerned, Harry was sitting companionably next to her, his hand occasionally brushing hers as he reached for a sandwich or a piece of pie.

'And how's my little Yorkshire Rose?' Walter Rimmington asked genially, beaming at her down the length of the opulently set, white-naperied table. 'It's grand to have you here on a Saturday evening, I only wish your mother and father were with us as well, but your father's never happy about visiting Crag-Side, is he? I don't understand why, when we now get on together like a house on fire, but I respect his feelings. He's a fine man who has battled disablement with a dignity that's truly heroic.'

Rose was just about to tell her uncle how her father had taken up photography again, doing so, of course, with her help. As she opened her mouth, however, Harry's eyes caught hers warningly. Rose's eyes widened. What on earth was the matter? Had something been said that she'd missed? Seeing her bewilderment, Harry flicked a meaningful look towards William and back again, and her bewilderment died, understanding dawning.

Even though the dessert had been served William was still tensely waiting for the right moment in which to announce his, and Sarah's, intention of marrying and his father, in talking about her own father, had given him exactly the kind of lead-in he had been waiting for.

'Don't you think it's a shame that Grandfather was so implacably bull-headed about Uncle Laurence not being of the right class to marry Aunt Lizzie?' he asked, his glass dish of grape jelly untouched in front of him. 'I mean, if Grandfather had taken the trouble to *meet* Uncle Laurence and to get to know him, he would have quickly understand what a very special person he is, and he would have enjoyed his company.'

Walter never liked talking about his father. It always awakened memories of near-choking intimidation. Even now, when he thought what his father's reaction would have been to his renewed affair with Polly, he felt almost faint. Not that his father's worst fears had come to pass, or ever would come to pass, for Polly was adamant she would never make Crag-Side her home. 'Scarborough,' she had said in her cheery, practical way. 'When you can hand the mill and all the trappings that go with it over to William, I'll marry you and we'll live at the seaside, at Scarborough or Brid.'

Scarborough, he had long ago decided. They would live at Scarborough in a house overlooking the north bay. And as far as he was concerned, the day they did so could'nt come a day too soon.

'Aye,' he said now to William, 'when it was business, I doubt if your grandfather made a single wrong judgement throughout his life, but where your Aunt Lizzie and Uncle Laurence were concerned...' He shook his head regretfully. 'Your grandfather's fixed ideas let him down badly there, I'm afraid.'

'And they let him down badly where you were concerned as well, didn't they? And all for no real reason. I mean, it isn't as if we're landed gentry, is it? Three generations ago we Rimmingtons were no different to the Ramsdens, were we? Or to the Thorpes.'

Walter blinked. What on earth had got into William? The kind of family history he was referring to, while no secret, was also no fit subject for a family dinner table. As for Ramsdens and Thorpes...Ramsden was a direct allusion to Polly, for Ramsden had been her maiden name, but who the

Thorpes were was anybody's guess.

'I don't think this is quite the subject for a family dinner table,' he said, aware that though everyone else had finished their pudding William hadn't touched his and didn't look as if he was going to. 'After all, it's all water under the bridge. What matters isn't past family unhappiness but the present, and as far as the present is concerned—'

'As far as the present is concerned I shall be asking your permission to get engaged in a couple of weeks time, Father.'

Walter had been wondering whether he should ring for the dishes to be cleared and the cheese board set on the table and it took him a moment or two to register what William had just said to him.

'Engaged?' His bewilderment was so total as to be comic. *'Engaged?'* He looked in confusion towards Harry.

If the announcement had come from Harry it would have been understandable. Harry's feelings for Nina were no secret and it had already been agreed between himself, and Lizzie and Laurence, that if an engagement were to result it would have their unconditional blessing. William, however, had never given any indication that there was anyone special in his life. There were doubtless some very suitable and attractive young ladies at the tennis club he spent so much time at when home from Oxford, but none of them had ever visited Crag-Side. As for Oxford itself...

As Harry blandly returned his gaze, making no attempt to come to his aid, Walter's thoughts floundered hopelessly. Any girl that was at Oxford would be bound to be frightfully academic and would unnerve him utterly.

'Engaged to whom?' he said unhappily, returning his attention to William. 'I'm afraid I don't understand, William. Where did you meet this young lady? When? How is it you have never previously mentioned her? Never introduced her to us?'

No one moved. It seemed to Rose, seated opposite William, that no one even breathed.

'I've known her for over two years, Father.' William's hands were clasped in front of him on the table, his eyes holding Walter's with fierce intensity. 'Her name is Sarah Thorpe and she's twenty years old and a weaver at Lutterworth's. Her father is a Methodist lay-preacher and...'

Lottie's jaw was so tightly clenched her teeth hurt. There it was, out in the open, and she knew what would happen now. Her father would leap at the opportunity to react in a completely opposite manner to the way his own father had reacted when, years and years ago, he had confronted him with similar news.

Harry, too, was well aware that his father would be feeling as if history were repeating itself. A smile tugged at the corner of his mouth. There'd certainly be no similar sense of *déjà vu* when he broke the news to him that he and Nina wanted to marry.

Noel waited with interest to see how his uncle would react to the news that he hadn't been the only one doing a spot of courting in the back-to-back streets of Bradford.

Nina thanked her lucky stars that no one, apart from Rose, knew she had once had hopes that William would fall in love with, and want to marry, her. To have been publicly rejected in preference to a mill girl, even if the mill girl could quote Emily Brontë, would have been unbearable.

Rose fizzed with excited anticipation. In another second or so William would no longer be in any doubt that his romance with Sarah was going to end happily, and perhaps it wouldn't be too long before her uncle's romance with Polly ended in wedding bells also.

'A weaver...' For a brief moment Walter thought his leg was being pulled, and then William was saying, 'They're a well-educated family. Sarah will want to be married in her Methodist chapel, of course, not a church, but—'

*'No!'* Feeling as if he was choking Walter blundered to his feet, pushing his chair back so violently it toppled over. *'No!'*

Six stunned faces stared back at him, five of them utterly incredulous. Walter was uncaring. He'd known right from the moment he had begun making plans to hand over the running of the mill to William, that William's youth, in the eyes of the men he would have to do business with, would be seen as a handicap. They would doubt his capacity for mature judgement—and if one of William's first actions on becoming master of Rimmington's was to marry a mill girl, they would do more than doubt his judgement, they would put no faith in it whatsoever!

He sucked in a deep, deep breath, knowing he was on the verge of losing happiness with Polly for a second time. William's judgement *had* to be seen as sound because William *had* to take over the running of the mill. If he didn't do so he, Walter, would not be able to marry Polly and live with her in retired domestic bliss at Scarborough. And that was a sacrifice he wasn't prepared to make. Not for William. Not for anyone. It was impossible. Unthinkable.

'It's impossible for you to marry this girl!' he said, his voice clipped, curt, implacable. 'Unthinkable!'

A rage William had never before experienced roared through his veins. He'd *known* his father was going to react in this way! He'd had a sixth sense about it right from the very beginning!

*'Why?'* he demanded, on his feet, his eyes blazing, his lanky body as taut as a coiled spring as he tried to come to terms with the sheer bloody hypocrisy of it. *'For Christ's sake, Father! Why?'*

'Because...because...' Unable to think of a reason that wouldn't reveal the depth of his selfishness Walter floundered, as he always floundered. Why was he having to endure such a scene? His own father wouldn't have endured it for a single second. Why didn't William accept his word as law, as he had had to accept his father's word as law? Frustration at his own inadequacies fuelled his unreasonableness. 'Because I say so!' he fumed, glaring across the table at his blatantly unintimidated son.

Noel cleared his throat. William had already uttered one blasphemy in Rose and Nina and Lottie's presence and though he was far from being a prude, he didn't particularly want him uttering another.

'I think perhaps I should—' he began,

about to suggest he took the girls into the sitting room for coffee.

*'That isn't good enough!'* William was uncaring of Noel's attempted interruption, uncaring of the fact that the girls were listening to every word in round-eyed stupefaction. 'Sarah's a darling girl! She's intelligent, caring, beautiful. And I'm going to marry her! I'm going to marry her whether you approve of my doing so or not!'

It was too much for Walter. For years he'd been bullied by his father. He wasn't now going to be bullied by his son. *'No, you're not!'* he shouted. *'Not if you ever want to be master of Rimmington's! Either you do as I say or you're out! The mill will go to Harry! And so will Crag-Side! And so will every bloody bit of brass as well!'*

William held his father's eyes for a long, long, pitying moment and then he shrugged, patted Harry in a friendly fashion on his shoulder, and walked with terrifying finality from the room.

Walter gaped after him like a beached fish.

Harry crumpled his napkin onto the table, rose to his feet, said crisply, 'Excuse me, everyone,' and strode from the dining-room in William's wake.

Lottie began to cry.

Noel, seated next to her, put an arm

comfortingly around her shoulders.

Rose was too appalled to cry. How could her Uncle Walter have spoken to William in such a fashion? How *could* he? Didn't he know how very hypocritical he was being? Didn't he know how very *unfair* he was being?

Nina had no such thoughts, she was too busy struggling to look suitably distressed. It wasn't easy, for she didn't feel remotely distressed. At the prospect of Harry inheriting Crag-Side and the mill she felt overwhelmingly, staggeringly, *stunningly* euphoric! She wanted to kick off a shoe and send it spinning sky-high. She wanted to dance around the room. Instead, with superhuman restraint, she said, 'Shall I ring for the cheese, Uncle Walter? Shall I ask to have coffee served at the dining table this evening?'

## Chapter Eleven

Dazedly Walter stretched a hand out, reaching for the nearest solid surface. He made contact with the table, knocked a cream jug over, sent a cheese knife skimming to the floor. What on earth had happened? Fifteen minutes ago he had been the happy patriarch of a united family. He had been about to ask William to stay behind when the others went in to the drawing-room for coffee; he had been going to tell him he was handing the mill over to him lock, stock and barrel.

And now? Using the table for support he backed unsteadily towards his chair. Someone had righted it for him. Noel? Nina? He didn't know. He only knew that William had walked out of the room as if he were never going to enter it again, that Lottie was still crying, and that Rose...his Yorkshire Rose...was looking at him out of eyes so appalled his knees felt as if they were turning to jelly.

He sat down heavily. He could take it all back, of course. He could go after William and tell him he had been talking in rash anger, that he shouldn't have done so and had now reconsidered and would be pleased meet the young woman in question. And then what would happen? William would marry her. He would be unable to hand the mill over to him—at least not with any peace of mind. There would then be no Scarborough for himself and Polly, or not in the near future and he couldn't wait for a distant future. Dear God in heaven, hadn't he already waited far too long? Twenty-five years too long?

'I think you should go after William, Uncle Walter,' Rose said unsteadily, uncaring of the fact that it wasn't her place to tell her uncle what he should, or should not do. 'Otherwise I think William may not come back and—'

Walter made a weary, silencing motion with his hand. He wasn't angry at her impertinence. It hadn't even registered on him. 'No,' he said, thinking of Scarborough, knowing that Harry was more than capable of taking over the mill and was committed to it in a way William never had been. 'No. I'm not going to be browbeaten. I've made my mind up. I'm standing by what I said. Harry can have the mill. And he can have it tomorrow.'

Before anyone could make a response there came the sound of the front door being slammed in someone's wake. Seconds later Harry strode into the room.

A Harry so blazingly angry Rose scarcely recognized him.

'William's gone,' he hurled at his father from the wide-open doorway, his legs apart, his hands on his hips, his eyes so dark with outraged fury they looked to be black. 'And he isn't coming back! As for the house and the mill! If you think for one minute I'd take what is rightfully William's you must be stark, staring senseless! I won't accept a single brick or a penny-piece that should be his! Not now! Not ever!'

Nina made an agonized, strangling sound. Harry was oblivious. He'd known for years that his father was weak-willed and that, like most weak-willed characters, he could also be irrationally stubborn, but his stubbornness had never before been cruel or pointless. This time it had been both. This time it had resulted in William leaving Crag-Side, probably for ever, just as their Aunt Lizzie had once done.

'You know what you've done, Father, don't you?' His voice was as cutting as a whip. 'You've split the family, just as Grandfather once split it. William will marry Sarah but he won't bring her here. And he won't bring their children here. You'll grow old not knowing them, just as your father grew old not knowing Noel and Nina and Rose,' and unable to bear the pain and fury and utter frustration he felt for a moment longer, he spun violently on his heel, striding away through the adjoining drawing-room as if he, too, were never going to return.

It took Rose all her will-power not to run after him. She wanted to comfort him; to assure him that nothing would be quite as bad as he thought it would be for the simple reason that neither William nor his father were men of unbending pride. Caleb might have been capable of carrying grudges with him to the grave but neither William nor her uncle were remotely capable of doing so. Only the knowledge that it was Nina's comfort Harry would want, not hers, kept her seated at the table.

Lottie was the first person to move. Very stiffly, keeping tightly hold of Noel's hand, she rose to her feet. Looking across at her father she said in a cracked, strained voice, 'If William doesn't come back I shall never forgive you, Papa.'

Walter didn't answer her. He couldn't. He was way beyond speech. What had happened? How had everything gone so wrong? He'd been firm, for once. Decisive. And still he'd been undermined as he was *always* undermined! If Harry refused to take over the mill... He groaned and lowered his head into his hands. If Harry refused to take over the mill then an early, happy retirement in Scarborough with Polly would remain nothing more than a shimmering mirage.

'He only wanted to do what you once wanted to do,' Lottie continued, her voice so brittle it was a miracle to Rose it didn't break completely. 'And I've met Sarah. We've all met Sarah. She's a grand girl. She wouldn't shame William or show him up. She'd be sensible about the difference in their backgrounds. Even if you're not a quarter as knowledgeable about English literature as she is, she wouldn't have made you feel uncomfortable about it.'

Rose felt as if she were at the Mad Hatter's tea party. First her uncle had behaved in a way she would never have thought him capable of. Then William had reacted with a passion so totally out of character it had stunned everyone present. And now Lottie—Lottie who had been so adamantly hostile towards Sarah—Lottie was championing her!

As Lottie walked from the room, her hand still in Noel's, Rose knew by the set of Noel's shoulders that Lottie had at last achieved what she had long ached to achieve. She had gained his admiration.

'I think...if you'll excuse me, Uncle

Walter...' Nina rose to her feet, her face taut with distress.

Rose felt a rush of warmth towards her. It was unlike Nina to care very greatly about anyone's problems but her own and that she was so distressed now, by William's quarrel with their uncle, just went to show what a very united family they had become.

Walter groaned, his head still in his hands. Rose sighed. She didn't feel in the least like comforting him. He'd brought all his troubles on himself and her sympathies lay entirely with William. He did look abject, though, his shoulders slumped like those of a man of sixty or seventy. With another sigh she moved her chair closer to his. Someone had to make him see how wrong he had been, speaking to William as he had. Someone had to make him see that he had to put things right—and that he had to do so with all possible speed.

'You have to put things right with your father,' Nina said urgently to Harry.

It was the next day. William hadn't returned to the house. Noel had gone to Leeds, taking Lottie with him. Rose was intent on returning to Bradford and Beck-Side Street and Harry, certain he would find William at the Thorpes, had said that he would drive her there.

The family's motorcars were all garaged in what had once been stables and a horsey aroma that reminded Nina of the Porritt's carthorse and Beck-Side Street still hung over the cobbles and empty stalls.

'You have to make sure he knows you didn't really mean it when you said you would never accept Crag-Side or the mill,' she continued, seizing the first moment of privacy that they'd had and hoping Rose wouldn't put in an appearance for several more minutes. 'You have to let him know you were speaking in anger; that you were distressed by his falling out with William and...'

They had reached the Renault by now, she on the passenger side, Harry on the driving side. He stared at her across its open-topped width. Her upswept, deeply waving titian hair was burnished almost gold by the mid-morning sun. Her ivory silk blouse was high at the throat, the sleeves tight at the wrist and fastened by buttons of mother-of-pearl. Her skirt was the colour of rich caramel and from beneath its hem peeped shoes as pale as buttermilk. With the halo-like effect of her hair she looked ethereally lovely; as lovely as an angel in a Pre-Raphaelite painting. But what she was saying wasn't lovely. What she was saying was scarcely believable.

'Of course I meant what I said.' He had been about to open the car door but now he stood, not moving, his eyes holding hers. 'William is the eldest,' he continued, hoping to God he had simply misunderstood her and speaking slowly and carefully so that she shouldn't misunderstand him. 'Crag-Side and the mill go to him. Only if William dies will I inherit them.'

Panic began bubbling deep in the pit of Nina's stomach. All through a wakeful, restless night she had tried to convince herself that Harry hadn't meant what he had said to his father; that out of a sense of fairness he had merely been trying to frighten his father into reconsidering what would, after all, be a very far-reaching decision. And all along, knowing how reckless and, in his own way, how high-principled he was, she had had doubts.

Now, facing him in the bright light of day, her doubts were certainties. Unless she persuaded him otherwise he was going to turn his back on all his father was offering him—and he was going to do so out of a loyalty to William that was entirely unnecessary.

Taking a deep steadying breath, knowing how very, very important it was that he should see things as she saw them, she said in what she hoped was a voice of sweet reason, 'William doesn't *want* your loyalty, Harry. Not where Crag-Side and the mill are concerned. Sarah would hate to be a mill owner's wife. Her mill working friends would have nothing further to do with her and what other friend would she have? William's tennis club friends wouldn't want to know her and William's mill owning acquaintances and their wives certainly wouldn't befriend her. She would be completely isolated...'

'She would have her family.' He was standing with one foot resting on the Renault's broad running board, his hands deep in his trouser pockets, his hair tumbling low over his brow. 'She would have you, me, Rose, Noel, Lottie. Your mother and father. Her own mother and father. That would count for something, surely?'

There was an odd note in his voice; a note she had never heard before; a note that sent fresh waves of panic beating up into her throat. She wasn't convincing him. He wasn't changing his mind. And she knew now that he *had* to change his mind; that if he didn't do so she would never marry him; that his turning his back on Crag-Side and the mill would be an action she would never be able to forgive.

Trying to keep her panic from showing in her voice, she said with passionate intensity, 'Please listen to me, Harry! Even with all our support Sarah wouldn't be happy living at Crag-Side. Forcing her to make such a social leap would be a cruelty to her, not a kindness. And William isn't interested in the mill as you are. You're the one who, whenever the opportunity arises, goes to the London wool sales. You're the one your father talks business with and seeks advice from. You know yourself you're far more cut out to be master of Rimmington's than William is—'

'That's not the point!' He ran a hand through his hair, hardly able to believe they were having such a conversation. How could she think, even for a minute, that he would stand by and watch his father disinherit William? Didn't she understand anything about him? And why were they standing on either side of the Renault like two strangers? What was happening to them for God's sake?

'It's William's *right* to inherit Crag-Side and the mill,' he said, wondering if, because her own parents had nothing to bequeath, she didn't quite understand how inheritance worked.

He began to walk around the Renault towards her, intending to put an end to the nonsense by taking her in his arms.

As he did so two things happened simultaneously. Rose entered the stable yard, hurrying because she knew he had been waiting for her for at least ten minutes, and Nina's tightly-reined self-control slipped at last.

'You're *wrong!*' she flared, her cat-green eyes flashing such sparks he stopped dead in his tracks. 'It isn't his right to inherit it now! Not when your father doesn't want him to inherit it! Not when he's going to marry Sarah Thorpe!'

'What on earth...?' Rose came to a faltering stop.

'*We* should have Crag-Side!' Nina was oblivious of Rose's presence. She couldn't believe Harry could be so stupidly obstinate. If he'd ever lived in a back-to-back in Beck-Side Street he wouldn't be so obstinate! Where did he think they were going to live when they were married? What did he think they were going to live on?

'That's a terrible thing to say!' Rose stared at her, hardly able to believe her ears. 'Last night, at dinner, you were as upset as the rest of us when Uncle Walter said he was going to disinherit William...'

Her words tailed away, sickening understanding dawning. It hadn't been the quarrel between William and his father which had so distressed Nina; it had been the prospect of having Crag-Side so suddenly and tantalizingly placed within her reach only, in the same few moments, to have it snatched away again.

Nina was uncaring of Rose's opinion. All that mattered to her was that Harry should agree with her that Crag-Side should be theirs.

'Crag-Side's never going to be ours,' he said, wishing to God he'd realized earlier the effect his father's words had had on her. At least then he would have been prepared for the present ghastly scene. He would have been able to explain to her with a little more care; to have let her down with a little more gentleness. He ran his hand through his hair yet again, desperately wanting her to understand how impossible her demands were.

'Leastways, it's not going to be ours in the way you want it to be ours,' he added with a conciliating smile. 'We shall be able to live there, of course...'

'Live there?' Nina's eyes blazed like emeralds. 'How can we live there if William and Sarah are living there? If Crag-Side is *theirs?* And what about the mill? Are you going to oversee the running of it for William as if you're one of his employees? As if you're a... a...*skivvy?*'

Rose gasped.

The blood fled from Harry's face. Until now he had assumed that, because of a basic misunderstanding, he and Nina were enduring a nasty scene that would soon be over and would have no far-reaching consequences. Now he knew differently.

Closing the distance between them in one stride he seized hold of her shoulders so hard she cried out in pain. *'Christ Almighty!'* he shouted, not knowing which emotion was uppermost, rage or bewilderment. *'What the devil's got into you, Nina? Yes, if William wants me to, I'll run the mill for him! I'll run it because I want to run it! Because like my grandfather I'm a wool-man to my fingertips!'*

*'But I don't want to be married to a wool-man!'* There was hysteria in her voice now, the word 'wool-man' meaning no more to her than the word 'warehouse-man'. *'I want to be married to a man of consequence!'* and with tears streaming down her face she twisted violently away from him, running out of the stable yard and towards the house as if all the hounds of hell were at her heels.

For a long moment neither Harry nor Rose moved and then, sucking in his breath, his jaw and neck muscles bunched into ugly knots, he wheeled round towards her. 'Get in the car,' he ordered harshly. 'I'm taking you to Bradford.'

'It doesn't matter...' Still hardly able to believe what had just taken place, Rose's voice was little more than a croak. 'You don't have to—'

'Get in!'

He had already seized hold of the Renault's cranking-handle and, not knowing what else to do, she did as she was told.

It was a hideous journey. Harry didn't speak and drove as if he were intent on inadvertently killing them both. When they finally reached Beck-Side Street he didn't vault over the Renault's driver's door and walk her into the house to have a word with her parents, as he usually did. Instead, a pulse throbbing at the corner of his clenched jaw, he roared away over the cobbles intent on tracking down William.

Rose made her way dazedly into the house. How could Nina have behaved so appallingly? She had said terrible things to Harry. Things so terrible she didn't even know how Nina could have thought them.

'Is tha...at you, li...ttle love?' her father called out from the cellar-head where, with difficulty, he was putting the lid back on the biscuit jar. 'Your Mo...ther's over at Ge...rtie's. Did you ha...ave at nice time at Cra...ag-Side? Is everyone ke...eping well?'

'Yes, Pa,' she lied, glad he couldn't see her face; glad her mother was out of the house. 'I've got a bit of a headache, though. I'm going to lay down for a little while.'

Quickly, before he emerged from the cellar-head, she ran up the short, curving flight of stone steps that led to the two bedrooms. She wouldn't say anything to her mother and father about the scene that had taken place at Crag-Side the previous evening. If her Uncle wanted her parents to know about it, then he would tell them about it himself. And she *certainly* wouldn't tell them about the scene that had taken place between Nina and Harry. How could she? How could she possibly find the words?

She sat on the edge of her brass-headed bed, her hands clasped tightly in her lap. What would happen now? Would Nina and Harry's love affair continue? And if it didn't continue, would they still be friends?

Her hands tightened, the knuckles showing white. Unless Nina and Harry were friends, family get-togethers, such as the forthcoming trip to London for the Coronation, would be strained, miserable occasions.

Suddenly, very much, she wanted to be with Micky. Micky was moody at times, but he wasn't likely to suddenly have a tempestuous row with anyone.

She sprang to her feet, clattering down

the stairs, shouting out as she did so, 'My headache's gone now, Pa! I'm just going to Micky's! I won't be long!'

When she returned home three hours later it was to find Noel at home.

'Nina's gone back to London,' he said bluntly, standing on the immaculately white-stoned front doorstep and giving her all the news even before she stepped inside the house. 'William was round a little earlier. He wanted Ma and Pa to know about Sarah, and about the fall-out with his father. He and Sarah are getting married in three weeks time and he'd like us all to be there.'

'And Harry?' Her heart was beating fast and light as she wondered if Harry had been with William; if he was perhaps in the house now, talking to her father. 'Was Harry with William? Is he here now?'

Noel shook his head. 'No. William came by himself.' He gave a wry grin. 'You'll never guess what our surprising cousin is thinking of doing now.'

Still standing on the pavement, well aware that half a dozen neighbours were peering nosily at them from behind crocheted half-curtains, Rose couldn't even begin to guess.

'No,' she said, knowing that if William was marrying Sarah in three weeks time, he certainly wasn't contemplating an early return to Crag-Side, 'I can't.'

'He's hoping to stand as the local Labour candidate in the next election.'

Rose's eyes widened to the size of saucers. 'But that...that would be *wonderful!*'

'A Rimmington as a Bradford Labour candidate?' Noel chuckled, tickled pink by the idea. 'It'd be more than wonderful. It'd be down right amazing. Can you imagine what our grandfather would have said if he'd still been alive? He'd have had a blue fit.'

She stepped up onto the step beside him. 'Do Ma and Pa know?'

'Oh aye.' Noel lapsed into a Bradford accent almost as broad as Micky's. 'Pa's so taken wi' idea he's all set to go out canvassing for him, speech impediment or no speech impediment!'

Three weeks later, when William married Sarah in Bull Royd Methodist Chapel, the only members of the family not present were Walter and Nina. Nina had, however, sent a pretty lace-edged tray cloth to the happy couple as a wedding present and a note, apologizing for her absence and wishing them well.

Noel, who had been back in London for two weeks out of the intervening three, had travelled back to Bradford the previous day. Without telling anyone she was going to do so, Lottie had gone to Bradford's Exchange Railway Station to meet him, running down the platform as he stepped off the train, throwing herself into his arms as if he were a hero returning from the wars.

When the wedding ceremony was over and Thorpes, Sugdens and Rimmingtons had filed out into the June sunshine in William and Sarah's wake, Lizzie had tightened her hold on Laurence's arm.

'Do you see what I see?' she had whispered to him in fierce hope as, in front of them, Noel and Lottie walked out of the church hand in hand. 'Do you think perhaps...?'

He had patted her hand gently. 'Do...on't let's leap to con...clusions, dear hea...rt,' he had said gently, knowing how savagely disappointed she was that Harry and Nina's romance appeared to be over. 'Lo...ttie's little older tha...an Rose, and we wouldn't be ima...gining our Rose in lo...ve with anyone, would we? She's still li...ttle more than a bairn.'

The bairn in question, well aware that now she was sixteen she, too, could have been standing at the altar in bridal white if only the young man she loved, loved her, was smiling brightly, hiding her inner misery as she always hid it. Harry and Nina's love affair might have come to a catastrophic finish, but Harry still loved Nina. She knew that, because he had told her so.

'And I think it'll be all right eventually,' he had said to her, smiling lopsidedly down at her in a way that always made her tummy do somersaults. 'She just doesn't understand the principles governing the inheritance of family property, that's all.'

'That isn't all,' Rose had said bullishly, hating the fact that even after all the terrible things Nina had said to him, he was still trying to find an excuse for her behaviour. 'When Nina wants something for herself she simply doesn't think about other people. She certainly wasn't thinking about William, was she? And why would she want Crag-Side? It isn't as if she'll ever want to live in it—or at least not permanently.'

'What on earth do you mean?'

They had been walking towards the tennis-court, about to have a game, and he stopped, his racket resting against his shoulder as he looked down at her with a perplexed frown.

Rose had given an exasperated shrug. 'London and Paris and Rome,' she had said, wondering how he could possibly have forgotten. 'Nina wants to be an internationally famous dress designer and that's where internationally famous dress designers live. They don't live in Yorkshire, at the edge of the moors.'

An absolutely unreadable expression had crossed his strong-boned face. It was almost as if such a thought had never before occurred to him. Rose had dismissed the notion as ridiculous. Everyone knew that Nina wanted to be an internationally famous dress designer. It was why she was in London, studying at St Martin's.

She was so deep in unhappy thought that for once her sunny smile was absent. Seeing her sunk in deep gloom while everyone around her was boisterously congratulating the bride and groom, Harry walked towards her.

'What's the matter, Funny-Face?' he asked affectionately. 'You look as if you're at a funeral, not a wedding.'

He often called her Funny-Face and until now she had never taken umbrage. Her face *was* a little odd but, as her father had once pointed out to her when, as a child, she had tearfully complained about its oddness, it was *nicely* odd.

'Nothing,' she said stiffly, wishing he would call her Yorkshire Rose, as his father did. 'I was just thinking, that's all.'

'Well, if it makes you look so unhappy, don't.' He stood companionably beside her. He had been William's best man and he looked wonderful, a white bud rose in his lapel buttonhole, his starched linen shirt collar fashionably high, his dark hair curling over it in a way that was positively gypsyish. 'You still haven't been round the mill, have you?' he said suddenly. 'Would you like me to show you round it one day next week?'

All her unhappy thoughts immediately vanished. To go round Rimmington's! And to do so as a member of the family!

'Oh, yes Harry!' she said fiercely. 'Oh, I should like to do that more than anything else in the whole, wide world!'

'We'll start off in the wool-sorting,' he said four days later as they strolled across the cobbled mill yard. 'I've always thought it's what I'd choose to do myself if I was an ordinary mill worker.'

'I've been inside Lutterworth's,' she said, having to walk very quickly to keep pace with him. 'But only the design office and the weaving sheds.'

'And you didn't mind the noise?' He shot her his down-slanting smile and she flushed rosily, happy to be on her own with him; happy to be inside the mill that had dominated her thoughts for so many years.

'No. Just as you think you could enjoy

being a wool-sorter, I think I could enjoy being a weaver, or at least I could if I was allowed to make up my own designs.'

He laughed, amused at the thought of the mayhem that would ensue if his father's weavers were allowed their heads where designs were concerned.

'Have you always been so passionately interested in textile design?' he asked as they left the wool-sorting and made their way towards the scouring.

'Always.' Her eyes shone, testifying to the truth of her response. 'My father used to take me with him to Lutterworth's when he was Head Tapestry Designer there and I was a little girl. I thought it was wonderful. All the different pieces of cloth and the different textures and the colours and patterns. And I'm doing really well in design at school; it won't be long now till I'm finished there. Then when I do, I want to be a Head Tapestry Designer, just like my father.'

They were outside the scouring shed, but the strong stench wasn't bothering her. Not as it would have bothered William, who avoided the scouring sheds like the plague. He tried to imagine Nina in the wool-sorting and the scouring and failed utterly. Nina might want to be a mill owner's wife but she certainly wouldn't want to be familiar with the mill itself.

Just as, in many ways, William didn't.

'This isn't the pleasantest part of the mill,' he said, leading the way into it, realizing for the first time just why it was the two of them had always enjoyed such a sense of compatibility and rapport. It was because they, unlike William and Lottie and Noel and Nina, had inherited their grandfather's passion for a piece of good cloth.

With increasing enjoyment he took her round the wool-combing and the spinning and the twisting. She was far more knowledgeable about everything than he had remotely imagined she would be. With happy enthusiasm he began telling her of just what he hoped to achieve over the next few years.

'And Uncle Walter won't mind you making such radical changes?' she queried, having to raise her voice to a shout as they stepped into the roaring clatter of the weaving shed.

'Pa's always been happy for someone else to do all the hack work for him,' Harry shouted back to her wryly. 'And he doesn't have a passion for the mill in the way I do. He never comes down here unless he really has to, and you can't run a mill like that. The hands don't like it. They'll accept me as his stand-in, though. I spent every free hour of every school holiday I ever had, trotting around the place in Grandfather's wake. He took me to my first wool sale when I was seven and when I was ten I was going with him to Bradford Wool Exchange!'

They lingered for quite a time in the weaving. Rose wanted to see the designs being woven and as the women stood at their looms, shuttles flying, she stopped to shout a friendly few words to one after another of them.

By the time they began making their way back to the offices her legs ached and her voice was hoarse.

'You were quite a hit,' Harry said, pushing open the door of a vast boardroom. In every part of the mill he had introduced her to every overlooker as his cousin. They had all known his grandfather had also been her grandfather. In many respects it had been almost a royal tour, and his only regret was that it was a tour their grandfather hadn't taken with her. 'Do you want to have lunch here, or do you want to go into Bradford to lunch?'

'If we have lunch here can we go to the design offices afterwards? Can I ask your Head Designer why he does so many check and herringbone designs and so few heather mixtures?'

Harry had rolled his eyes to heaven in pretended long-suffering patience, said yes of course they could eat in the boardroom, and wondered why on earth he hadn't spent such a day months and months ago.

Later, as she sat beside him in the Renault and he took a long, scenic route back to Crag-Side over Baildon Moor, he felt buoyantly optimistic for the first time since Nina had rushed off back to London. It was the Coronation in a few days time. With the exception of William, they would all be together again as a family.

He increased speed and Rose gave a cry of delight as the wind tugged even more violently at her hair. He grinned, enjoying her enjoyment, suddenly certain that Nina would be looking forward to the family reunion as fiercely as he was looking forward to it. She would say she was sorry for her hysterical outburst; that she hadn't meant the ugly things she had said; that she loved him as madly as he loved her.

He felt a rising in his crotch just imagining their reconciliation. As William had married so precipitately there was no reason why he and Nina shouldn't marry precipitately also. It was June now. If they became engaged on Coronation Day they could be married by Christmas.

He began to whistle as the Renault plunged down towards Ilkley. By the time he and Nina married his father would, hopefully, have come to his senses over his disapproval of William and Sarah's wedding. They would be able to have a grand wedding reception at Crag-Side, perhaps turn the winter garden into a ballroom...

Rose broke abruptly into his thoughts. 'What on earth is Lottie doing waiting by the gates. Is she waiting for us, do you think? And if so, what on earth for?'

Harry slowed down, shouting out as he did so, 'What the devil are you doing, Sis? Waiting for the postman?'

'No.' As the Renault came to a halt Lottie walked across to them, saying with typical bluntness, 'There's been a telegram from London. Nina is engaged to Rupert Winterton.'

## Chapter Twelve

From that moment on everyone, not only Rose, was aware of a change in Harry. His careless, swashbuckling good humour became a thing of the past. There was a tautness about him, and a tension, that was almost palpable. He didn't go to London with them for the Coronation celebrations, and he didn't return to Oxford at the end of the summer holidays. Instead, still refusing to allow his father to make Rimmington's over to him lock, stock and barrel, he took over its general running, driving to Bradford in the Renault early every morning and not returning until late at night.

In October, after only a few short months of flaunting a diamond that to Rose looked to be as big as the Koh-i-noor, Nina married Rupert Winterton, Duke of Strachan, in a lavish ceremony at St Margaret's, Westminster.

Everyone attended the wedding, even William and Sarah. 'Nina is family,' William had said to Noel when Noel had expressed surprise that he was taking time off from campaigning for a seat in

Bradford's forthcoming by-election, to take Sarah to such a high-society event, 'And so of course I'm going to her wedding, and Sarah will be able to cope. As for Strachan—he's going to have to get used to the fact that he's marrying into a very socially diverse family, and the sooner he does so, the better.'

Two of Rupert's sisters, and Rose and Lottie, were bridesmaids. Rose hated every minute of the experience. She felt hideously disloyal to Harry and the blossom-strewn dress, with its rosy wreath and veil, made her feel like one of the Floras in Botticelli's *The Birth of Spring*.

Her mother, of course, had looked wonderful. Her deep mauve costume, its skirt swirling about her still trim ankles, had been designed by Nina and with it she wore a yard-wide hat in a paler shade of mauve, its brim dripping with hothouse white roses. That she had left for the wedding from a back-street house in Bradford was unbelievable even to Rose. She looked far more elegant than the Dowager Duchess of Strachan who, as unconventional as her son, was draped in purple and red like a Roman Catholic ecclesiastical dignitary.

The reception was held in the groom's town house, just off Park Lane. Sarah, dressed in a simply cut, love-in-the-mist blue suit, looked more bemused than overawed as she politely declined a glass of pink champagne, asking for a glass of lemonade instead.

Neither Rose nor Lottie had any intention of being so northern. 'It's called *oeil-de-perdrix,*' Lottie said knowledgeably as she lifted a glass from a silver tray. 'Harry used to have it served at Crag-Side when his Oxford friends came to stay. First sherry, then *oeil-de-perdrix,* then port and then brandy.' She giggled as the bubbles tickled her nose. 'They used to get awfully squiffy.'

Rose looked across the chandelier-hung room to where Harry was standing, watching tight-lipped and glittering-eyed as Nina and her new husband greeted their still arriving guests.

'He shouldn't have come,' she said to Lottie, her heart hurting. 'He's torturing himself and Nina doesn't care. All she cares about is being the youngest duchess in *Debrett.*'

'He couldn't very well *not* come,' Lottie said, ever practical. She took another sip of champagne and hiccupped. 'Compared to the hordes from Rupert's side of the family, we're putting up a very poor showing numerically. Besides, he knew William was coming and that he was bringing Sarah with him and I think he wanted to give the two of them all the support he could. It's the first time Papa and Sarah have been at the same family event together. I don't think he realized who she was at first, do you? His face was quite comic when the penny finally dropped.'

At Christmas, Walter overcame his pride sufficiently enough to invite Sarah and William to spend Christmas at Crag-Side. He was thanked for his invitation but told they would be going to chapel on Christmas morning and then spending the rest of the day with Sarah's parents. He was, they said, welcome to join them if he so wished.

Walter hadn't so wished. If he was going to spend Christmas in a back-to-back cottage without the convenience of an indoor lavatory, then he'd spend it in Beck-Side Street with his sister and her family, not with William's chapel-going in-laws.

'I think that would be a super idea, Papa,' Lottie said to his vast surprise when he nervously put the idea to her. 'I'm sure Noel would like to spend Christmas in his family home instead of coming here, and as Harry won't care *where* he spends Christmas, let's all crowd into Aunt Lizzie's back-to-back. It'll be fun.'

'And Polly?' Walter asked hopefully, sliding a finger around the inside of a shirt collar that had suddenly become uncomfortably tight. 'She and Jenny will only be next door and...'

Lottie hesitated. A lot of water had run under the bridge since the days when she had so fiercely disapproved of her father's relationship with Polly Wilkinson. She was in love with Noel now, and Noel had no time for snobbishness or class pretentiousness.

'If it would make you happy, Papa,' she said magnanimously, standing up on tiptoe to kiss him on the cheek. 'And only because I know you're trying to make things right again between yourself and William.'

Nina didn't spend Christmas in Bradford. She spent it in Morocco with Rupert.

'Rupert says the light is incredible in Tangiers,' Noel said enviously to his father as they sat around a roaring fire, roasting chestnuts. 'He says he's never painted so well in his life as he is doing at the moment.'

'Tha...t's good.' Laurence liked the fact that Nina had married a young man of serious artistic ability. 'Wh...at did you thi...ink of the Sickert exhibition?' he queried as Rose came and sat on the arm of his chair, sliding an arm around his neck. 'I imagine it wa...as a li...ittle different to the Ger...man Expressionists you so admire.'

Six months later, on Rose's seventeenth birthday, Sarah gave birth to a daughter.

'Her name is Emma Rose,' Sarah said, propped up by a mound of snowy-white pillows as she received her first visitors. 'Isn't she wonderful, Aunt Lizzie? She's got Thorpe eyes and a Rimmington mouth and she has the prettiest smile imaginable.'

'She's a *beauty,'* Lizzie said, picking Emma Rose up tenderly from a crib that had been made out of a spare drawer, and cradling her lovingly.

The house Emma Rose had been born in was William and Sarah's own. A solid family terrace house, similar to the house the Sugden's had lived in, in Jesmond Avenue; it was a fine family home for such a young couple—a home worthy of an ambitious young man who, at twenty-one, was an elected Labour Member of Parliament.

'Nina says she and Rupert will be coming to the christening,' Sarah said, speaking to Rose now as Lizzie's attention was being given fully to Emma Rose. 'She's sent me a christening shawl that must have cost a year's wages. It's far more suitable for

Westminster Abbey than for Bull Royd Methodists!'

Despite not being Methodists, Harry stood as Emma Rose's godfather and Lottie, to her very great surprise, found herself standing as one of Emma Rose's two godmothers.

'This doesn't mean I'm a Methodist now, does it?' she asked Rose anxiously, her hair, now she was eighteen, swept up into a loose, elegant knot.

'No,' Rose said, entertained as always by Lottie's odd mixture of naïvety and sophistication, 'but it does mean you have to take a very personal interest in Emma Rose's welfare and I'm not sure turning up at a Methodist chapel with your hair lightened by peroxide is a good way to start.'

'Lord! It's not so obvious, is it?' Panic-stricken Lottie darted across to the nearest mirror. 'I only rinsed a very small amount of it through my hair, just to brighten it a little.'

'Well, you certainly succeeded. It's just a shame it isn't the same brightness all over. In a strong light you look a little like an albino zebra.'

Apart from the sight of Lottie looking demurely proper as she stood at the front of the chapel, her hair scooped out of sight beneath a dippingly-wide, marguerite-decorated cream straw hat, there were other surprises at the christening. Not only were Thorpes, Sugdens and Rimmingtons in attendance, Polly and Jenny were there too, and Micky Porritt.

At first Rose scarcely recognized him. His unruly hair was brushed so flat to his head, and to such a high gloss, that he looked a complete stranger. Even more perplexing, though, was the fact that he quite obviously wasn't there merely because Jenny was there.

'Mi...icky and Wi...illiam are good pals,' her father whispered to her, seeing her puzzlement. 'Mi...icky canvassed for him du...ring the election.'

'Do you think Micky will ask Jenny to marry him?' Lizzie whispered musingly under cover of the opening bars of 'All Things Bright and Beautiful'.

Rose had been so startled she had dropped her hymn book. Micky marry Jenny? What on earth was her mother talking about? 'Micky and Jenny are good friends,' she whispered back, 'they're not sweethearts.'

Lizzie, singing 'All things wise and wonderful,' in a rich contralto, was unconvinced. It wasn't possible to say what Micky's feelings for Jenny were, but

Jenny's feelings for Micky were written all over her bonny face whenever she looked towards him.

Unknown to Lizzie, when Micky made his proposal of marriage, he did so to Rose, not Jenny. It was September. Rose had left art school and was employed at Rimmington's as a junior textile designer.

'It isn't nepotism,' Harry had said to her when he had offered her the position. 'Your portfolio would get you a job as a junior designer at Salt's, or Lister's, or Lutterworth's, or any other mill in Bradford, but it would be crazy your working for the opposition, wouldn't it?'

Her father, well aware that Harry's remarks about Rose's talent were the literal truth, was so proud he had had tears in his eyes. 'Rimmington's,' he had said expressively, remembering how very much he had once wanted to be a designer at Rimmington's and of how Caleb Rimmington had sworn he would never so much as set foot in Rimmington's mill yard. 'Well, little love, you're certainly on your way to fulfilling all your dreams.'

Micky often met her from work, though out of respect for her position at the mill, never on the cart.

'How about going into t'Park for a walk

round t'lake?' he asked laconically, as he heaved himself away from the wall he had been leaning against whilst waiting for her. 'It's a grand evening. We could mebbe take a boat out.'

Rose hesitated for a second, aware that her Mother would have her tea ready and waiting and that her father would be looking forward to hearing all the details of her day, but Micky was right—it was a lovely evening. The sun was still warm, the bright blue of the sky only slightly tinged with the apricot of approaching dusk.

'Have we to wait for Jenny?' she asked. White-collar workers knocked off a full half-hour before the mill hooter signalled the end of the working day for the rest of the mill workers.

Micky shook his head. 'No sense. T'sun'll be losing its warmth by then and it won't be as nice out on t'lake.'

Aware that there was some truth in his words and aware also that Jenny might not be able to go with them anyway, Rose fell into easy step beside him. She liked Lister Park, or Manningham Park as it was sometimes known. It was only a stone's throw from Lister's Mill and long ago it had been the home of the Lister family. In 1870 Samuel Lister had offered his family home and estate to Bradford Corporation at what was seen as a bargain price of £40,000. A memorial hall, used as a museum and art gallery had been built in its centre and named Cartwright Memorial Hall after Edmund Cartwright, the country parson who had invented the first powered weaving loom.

With wry amusement she wondered what would have happened to Crag-Side if, like the Lister home, it had been built adjacent to the family mill. Once narrow streets of back-to-back cottages had encroached on its grounds it would have been speedily got rid off, just as the Lister estate had been got rid off.

'What are you smiling at?' Micky asked, as they turned in at the park gates. 'You'll be talking to yourself next and you know what'll happen then, you'll be taken away.'

Her smile widened. She never minded Micky's dry banter. Even when the joke was against herself, he always made her giggle. 'I was just wondering what sort of memorial hall my grandfather would have wanted erected at Crag-Side, if Crag-Side had been sold off to the local Corporation.'

Micky made an inarticulate noise that sounded distinctly rude. He didn't like it when she spoke of Crag-Side or brought up the subject of her swank Rimmington cousins. William was different, of course. During the time William had been living with the Thorpes, he'd got to know William well. He had time and admiration for him. William had principles that he'd stood by, even though the financial cost of doing so had been high. William was all right—but he couldn't stand Rose's other two cousins, Lottie and Harry.

Even merely thinking about them made him scowl. Lottie was fast. With her unnaturally gold hair and overly red lips it was a conclusion a blind man could have come to, though Rose appeared to be oblivious of it. As for Harry Rimmington...Micky's fists clenched. Harry bloody Rimmington had it all. A posh family home in Ilkley; a mill he was virtually master of; looks that had girls swooning in droves; and a motorcar with a bonnet as long as an Atlantic liner and a horn as loud as the last trump.

'And what are you looking so fierce about?' Rose asked sunnily as they made their way straight to the lake and the boat-house. 'You look as if you want to punch someone! '

'Aye,' he gave a wry grin, unclenching a fist and jingling the coins he had put in his trouser pocket for the boat ride, 'mebbe I do.'

'You've only got 'alf an 'our,' the boatman said as he held a rowing boat steady for them to step into, 'Then I'm calling all t'boats in, understand?'

Micky didn't bother answering. As far as he was concerned he'd paid his tanner and if he wanted to stay out on the lake till the moon came up, he'd jolly well do so.

Once Rose had safely seated herself, he slung his jacket down beside him and, sitting facing her, took hold of the oars.

'There's summat I want to say to you,' he said as he pulled strongly away towards the nearest of the lake's two duck-infested islands. 'Summat a bit special.'

Rose regarded him warily. Micky was a young man of notoriously few words and if he had something special to say, then it would be just that. It wouldn't be gossip or idle speculation.

'Yes?' she said, aware that the sunlight on the water was creating deep dark jewelled colours of serpentine and jade. If she could re-create the effect in one of her designs...

'I'm thinking of going off to New Zealand,' Micky said, his strong arm muscles rippling beneath the rolled-up sleeves of his shirt as he rounded the first island and headed in the direction of the lonelier, less boat-visited, second island.

'New Zealand?' Rose stared at him in incredulity. '*New Zealand?* Do you know how far away New Zealand is, Micky? It's even further away than Australia! What about your Dad? What about...'

'I'll be taking me Dad wi' me.' They were now at the far end of the lake, where few boats ventured. Satisfied that they were now enjoying as much privacy as could reasonably be found in Bradford on a work-day teatime, he rested on the oars, letting the boat drift towards an overhang of willow.

'I'm going to sheep farm,' he said, his eyes holding hers with fierce intensity. 'I won't have my own sheep farm at first, o' course. But I will eventually.'

Rose believed him. When it came to determination and grit Micky was way ahead of anyone else she knew. Except William and Harry, of course.

'But...it's so far!' She tried to imagine Beck-Side Street without Micky, and without Albert and his horse and cart, and couldn't. 'I'll miss you,' she said inadequately, her voice wobbly, fighting back a sudden onrush of tears.

He leaned towards her, sending the boat rocking wildly, taking her hands in his, holding them so tightly her skin dimpled white beneath the imprint of his thumbs.

'There's no need for you to miss me.' His eyes burned hers. 'I'm a Yorkshireman, Rose. I can't talk fancy...'

Suddenly, with appalled premonition,

Rose knew what it was he was about to say.

She tried to free her hands from his but he wouldn't release them. In the depths of his eyes she could see gold flecks. She wondered why she'd never noticed them before. She wondered why she was suddenly feeling so giddy.

'Micky, please...we haven't time for a serious conversation. Didn't the boatman say we could only be out for half an hour? By the time you row the boat back to the boating shed our time will be up and—'

'I love you, Rose.' There was no sweet tenderness in his voice only blunt, almost savage, forthrightness. 'I've allus loved you, reet from t'start. You're different to other lasses. You look different and you act different.' He leaned even further towards her, her hands clasped in his. 'We could mek a fine life for ourselves in New Zealand. There's mountains and rivers, and there's becks just like t'Bradford Beck, but far bonnier.' There was fierce eagerness in his voice. 'I've got photographs I could show you...'

As a proposal of marriage it wasn't a very romantic one, but Rose knew it had come from the depths of his heart and she felt sick with distress at the thought of how much she was about to hurt him.

'Micky, I can't...' she began, and got no further.

'Don't tell me you can't marry me and come wi' me because of Harry Rimmington or t'mill!' White lines edged his mouth and his skin was taut across his cheekbones. 'Ever since your sister ditched him Harry Rimmington's been sowing wild oats from here to Land's End, and well you know it! As for t'mill...'

He couldn't go on. There was no point. Her little monkey face was as stricken as if he'd just told her of the death of a close relative. His chest felt so tight he thought it was going to explode. He'd thought she would at least have known of Harry Rimmington's indiscriminate womanizing, but her reaction was enough to tell him that she hadn't and that his proposing to her was a complete waste of time. Rose wasn't going to marry him, or anyone else, not while she was still carrying such a torch for Harry.

'You're daft!' he exploded, letting go of her hands so suddenly the boat began rocking like a bottle top again. 'Harry bloody Rimmington is in love with your sister, not you!' He seized hold of the oars, pulling not for the opposite end of the lake and the boat-house, but for the stretch of tree-shaded bank nearest to them. 'You'll be a spinster for t'rest of your life if you wait for him to marry you!—a spinster never going any farther than Scarborough or Brid and never seeing any more of life than t'four walls of Rimmington's bloody design office!'

The rowing boat banged perilously into the bank and Micky shipped oars.

'And instead of that, we could be married!' He sprang to his feet, sending the boat rocking more violently than ever. 'We could have bairns and be living in the most beautiful country in the whole wide world! And if that isn't being daft, Rose Sugden, I don't know what the heck is!' And as she grabbed for the oars in order to steady the boat, he made a leap for the bank, striding off through the thick belt of trees without a backward glance.

For a brief, rash second Rose was tempted to follow him. If she did, though, what could she possibly say to him? She couldn't tell him she had changed her mind and that she did want to marry him and that if he wanted her to go to the ends of the earth with him, then of course she would do so. She loved him dearly, but she wasn't *in* love with him. She was in love with Harry.

Tears burned the backs of her eyes. Was it true what Micky had said about Harry? Certainly Micky wouldn't have said such a thing if he hadn't believed it to be true.

With her heart hurting she dipped the oars cumbersomely into the water. She knew there were evenings when Harry drove away from Rimmington's heading not towards Ilkley, and home, but eastwards towards Leeds, or sometimes even south-west, towards Manchester. Was he conducting love affairs there? In the not too distant future would he turn up at Crag-Side with a strange young woman on his arm and would he expect her, Rose, to be happy for him?

The sky was now a deep, warm apricot, but she was oblivious of its loveliness. In so many ways, as cousins and as friends, she and Harry were as close as two people could possible be. Yet just as she wasn't in love with Micky, so Harry wasn't in love with her. And there was nothing she could do about it. Nothing at all. In bleak misery she continued to pull inexpertly on the oars, weaving an erratic course back to the waiting boatman.

Christmas 1912 was spent at Crag-Side. Polly resolutely refused to join them there for it and so, for the second year, did William and Sarah. As Nina had declared as early as December the first that nothing in the world would prevent her and Rupert from being at Crag-Side for Christmas, Harry had announced he would be spending the festive season in Scotland, with friends.

'I like the fact that Harry is keeping up with the friends he made whilst at Oxford, but I wish he hadn't chosen to do so at Christmas-time,' Walter grumbled, unhappy that Polly wouldn't be more accommodating, unhappy that he still hadn't succeeded in bringing about a proper reconciliation between himself and William.

'You can't expect Harry to want to spend Christmas with Nina and Rupert,' Lottie said practically. 'I just hope to goodness Rupert proves to be jolly company and doesn't huddle in a corner with Noel, talking art all the time.'

Rupert certainly spent a lot of time talking art with Noel, but not to the extent that he was a bore. As Lottie said after their first hectic family evening together, when Rupert had organized the noisiest, most boisterous Christmas party games they'd ever played and had kept them convulsed in laughter the entire evening, 'Life couldn't possibly be boring with Rupert, could it? No wonder Neen fell in love with him!'

In spring, Noel had his first exhibition at a major gallery. His radical combination of subject matter and style, northern industrial landscapes painted with freely applied brushwork and in vibrant, often non-natural colour, attracted instant attention. The Cork Street dealer exhibiting his works had been one who had been supportive of him since his Bradford School of Art days, and the prices he demanded—and got—for the new work, made Noel's head reel.

Lottie was delirious with pride. Wanting to be with Noel as much as possible, and unable for reasons of propriety to stay with him in the house her father was still renting for him in Battersea, she stayed with Nina and Rupert in their elegant town house for week after successive week.

'I don't like it,' Walter said with crotchety bad temper to anyone who would listen. 'Crag-Side is becoming like a morgue with only Harry and me rattling around in it. Rose won't come and live here. Polly won't come and live here. William and Sarah visit, but they won't come and live here either. It's a ridiculous state of affairs, especially so as I no longer want to live here either. Scarborough, that's where I want to be. I want to be at Scarborough with Polly.'

By May he had had enough. Though William was still refusing to be reinstated as his heir and Harry was still pig-headedly refusing to be heir in William's stead, the mill was being run by Harry with absolutely no help nor hindrance from himself. And as that was the case, Walter could see no reason whatsoever for not behaving as if the mill *was* Harry's total responsibility. He would leave Crag-Side by the end of the month and set up home with Polly in Scarborough. They'd have to be married first, of course, but that was no problem. No one would make any objections to that now, not even Lottie.

Euphoric that at last he could see the future clearly, Walter waited for an evening when Rose was at Crag-Side with them, to appraise Harry of his decision.

'There'll be no real difference to anything,' he said, wondering why the devil it had taken him so long to realize it, 'the only real difference will be that I'll be living at Scarborough, not Crag-Side.'

He waited happily for Harry to agree with him. Instead, there was a long, long silence. At last Harry crumpled his napkin, laying it on the table beside his plate, saying reluctantly, 'I'm sorry, Pa. I'm really and truly very sorry, but I'm afraid things aren't so simple.'

Walter blinked. How could things not be so simple? He wasn't asking Harry to compromise his principles, was he? He wasn't asking for *anything*.

'How? Why?' he demanded, wondering

why the devil it was nothing he ever planned or anticipated ever went smoothly.

For a terrible moment Rose thought Harry was going to announce he was leaving Crag-Side and the mill to marry a girl from Leeds or Manchester. Instead he said, 'The news has been so bad for so long where Britain's relations with Germany are concerned that when I heard the latest, that Germany is boosting its peacetime army by a third, I decided it was time to do the obvious.'

'The obvious?' Walter stared at him as if he was talking Chinese. 'The obvious? What in tarnation's name is the obvious?'

'I've enlisted. Sorry Pa, but there it is. In four weeks time the mill will be all yours again and I'll be bashing it out at an officer cadet training camp.'

## Chapter Thirteen

Not for the first time Rose felt as if events were moving far too fast for her to be able to keep up with them.

'War? But there isn't going to be a war!' She looked from Harry to her Uncle, seized by sudden doubt. 'There isn't, is there, Uncle Walter?'

Walter didn't answer her. He was slumped in his carver dining chair, a defeated man. With a mill to run and no son to run it for him, his dreams of Scarborough were as far from being realized as ever. He wondered gloomily if he should abandon them altogether. Perhaps he should just sell up and give the proceeds to charity and move in with Polly in Beck-Side Street.

'I'm afraid it looks very much as if there *is* going to be a war with Germany,' Harry said sombrely, unaware of the bizarre direction his father's thoughts were taking. 'And if there is, Rose, I want to be in a decent regiment, not conscripted at the last moment in to some ragtag and bobtail outfit.'

Cold ice was trickling down Rose's

spine. War. And Harry in the thick of it. It didn't bear thinking about. What if he were injured? Dear God in heaven—what if he were *killed?* And even if God were very, very good and there was no war, if Harry were a regular soldier she would hardly ever see him. Their wonderful working camaraderie at the mill would be at an end. He would only be home on leave and how often would that be? She didn't know the first thing about the Army, but she was certain such leaves would be both short and infrequent.

Suddenly aware of how much his talk of impending war had shocked, and perhaps even frightened her, he flashed her a down-slanting smile, saying flippantly, 'Won't you love me when I'm in uniform, Funny-Face?'

'Not if you get killed in it,' she said, forcing herself to answer him just as teasingly, wishing with all her heart she could have said instead, 'Of course I'll still love you. I'll always love you. I wouldn't know how to begin to stop loving you.'

'Uncle Walter is awfully lonely at Crag-Side now Harry is at officer training,' Rose said six weeks later to her mother. 'I know I've always said that I wouldn't live at Crag-Side, but I think now perhaps it's time I did live there. At least for a little while...'

'So do I,' Lizzie said, smiling with love at her tender-hearted daughter. 'Walter couldn't possibly be lonely if you were living with him and he certainly needs someone to cheer him up. Polly says he's as miserable as a wet weekend these days.'

'He wouldn't be if she'd marry him.'

'And live at Crag-Side?' Lizzie asked with a raised eyebrow. 'No, Rose. Polly's got more sense than that. She knows what's right for her and Walter, and when Harry realizes there isn't going to be a war and returns to Civvy Street and the mill, then she and Walter will marry and live quietly at Scarborough.'

'And I think Ha...arry *has* over-re...acted,' her father said to her that evening as he read his evening paper. 'There may be war ag...ain in the Ba...lkans, but Sir Edward Grey will keep Britain uninvo...lved.'

'But what if there comes a time when we *shouldn't* be uninvolved?' Rose asked doubtfully, sitting on the pouffe near his feet, a sketch-book on her knee, a box of pastels by her side. 'This isn't the first war there's been in the Balkans, is it? And every time trouble flares up there the shock waves ripple out a little wider and a little wider.'

Laurence lowered his newspaper and surveyed her over the top of it. Ever since Harry had enlisted, Rose had been following the chaotic political situation in eastern Europe with keen interest.

'Well, it's true Aus...tria has a ve...sted interest in the squ...abbling now going on, esp...ecially where Russia's inter...est in it is con...cerned, but Grey's line is that we should stay ne...utral and, as I trust our Fo...reign Secretary's judgement, I'm in agr...eement with him.'

'I'm not,' Micky said flatly, carrying a nosebag of feed out to his horse as it stood patiently in the street between the shafts of the removal cart. 'Not when Kaiser Bill's hand in glove wi' t'Austrians and allus strutting abaht in military uniform.'

'Is that why you've not...not...' Rose didn't finish her sentence. She had been going to say, 'not gone to New Zealand,' but realized that she couldn't. New Zealand, and his proposal to her, was absolutely never mentioned between them.

'Aye,' he said, snapping the nosebag into place, knowing very well what it was she had been going to say, 'When war comes and I'm away fighting, Dad'll be better off on his own in Beck-Side Street than he would be on his todd at t'other side of t'world.'

'Mr Churchill thinks there's going to be a war,' Jenny said as she and Rose met after work for a friendly walk around the Park lake.

'Uncle Walter thinks Churchill's an irresponsible warmonger.'

Jenny chewed the corner of her lip. By the tone of her voice, Rose obviously disagreed with her uncle's opinion. She, too, fond as she had become of her mother's unlikely gentleman friend, thought that Mr Churchill's views were perhaps better informed.

'If there is a war, Micky will join up the day it's declared,' she said bleakly, 'and so will Charlie Thorpe.'

'Charlie Thorpe?' Rose spied an empty park seat and, not wanting to walk to the far end of the lake where she would be reminded of Micky's proposal to her, began steering Jenny towards it. 'Who's Charlie Thorpe? Is he related to Sarah?'

Jenny nodded, a faint wash of colour heightening her cheeks. 'He's her cousin. He isn't a mill worker. He's a motorbus driver.'

For a moment Rose looked at her, frankly disbelieving, and then, as Jenny refused to meet her eyes, she exclaimed in high delight, 'And you fancy him, Jenny Wilkinson! You do! I can tell!'

Now that she was no longer living in Beck-Side Street she missed out on lots of local gossip and she hadn't had a glimmer of a suspicion that there was now a young man in Jenny's life.

'What is he like?' she asked curiously as they seated themselves on a park seat which gave both a wonderful view of the lake and, through the trees ringing it, a glimpse of Cartwright Hall as well. 'Is there an understanding between you? Does Sarah know of it? Why on earth haven't you told me before?'

Jenny still avoided her eyes, looking intently instead at a bevy of ducks skimming gracefully across the burnished shield of the water.

'I was hoping you, or Micky, would tell me what's happened between the two of you before I did so,' she said, taking Rose by complete surprise. 'I know that something *has* happened between the two of you because you're so different with each other. You're...strained somehow.'

Rose frowned. She hadn't told Jenny about Micky's proposal of marriage because somehow it hadn't seemed right to do so. Apart from the fact that she was sure Micky wouldn't want anyone to know of it, she hadn't forgotten Jenny's reaction when, a long time ago, she had told her of how Micky had once kissed her; nor of her mother's assumption, at Emma Rose's christening, that Micky and Jenny were sweethearts.

Intuitively realizing that the truth might be very important, she said reluctantly, 'A few months ago Micky asked me to marry him.'

'And to go to New Zealand with him?' Jenny still wasn't looking at her, but though Rose couldn't see her eyes, there was no mistaking the hurt in her voice.

Appalled, she realized how very, very blind she'd been, and that she had probably been so for a long, long time.

'Yes,' she said at last, with even more reluctance. 'Yes, he did ask me to go to New Zealand with him.'

Even though Jenny's face was still averted in profile from hers, Rose could see tears glinting on her eyelashes.

'He's asked me if I'm interested in going to New Zealand as well,' she said bleakly. 'He hasn't asked me to marry him...not yet. And now I know that he asked you first, I'm not going to give him the opportunity to.'

'But...but if you're in love with him...' Rose began awkwardly, floundering for words in a way that would have done credit to her uncle.

'Oh aye, I love him.' Jenny turned her head at last, her eyes meeting Rose's. 'I love him far too much to ever be happy wi' him knowing that he'd much rather be married to you. Knowing it's you he really loves, and that I'm just second-best.' There was passionate bitterness in her voice now, a bitterness Rose hadn't thought Jenny capable of. 'And I don't want to be second-best! I want to be first! And wi' Charlie I *am* first!'

As the summer progressed even Walter and Polly's relationship underwent a kind of metamorphosis.

'I don't see why I shouldn't just *visit* Crag-Side,' Polly said to Lizzie as they pegged their week's laundry on a clothes-line that stretched from one side of Beck-Side to the other. 'I mean, it isn't as if Walter is a public figure in the way his father was, is it? He wants Harry to take that aspect of being the owner of Rimmington's over from him. And I do have connections to Crag-Side, don't I? You and me are friends and you were born there, and Rose lives there, and I don't suppose anyone who'd be nasty about it, will know about it, will they?'

Walter drove her to Crag-Side on a gloriously hot August day. The sky was a brassy blue bowl, the air milk-warm, the heather-covered moorland a purple-rich feast of colour.

'I could get used to this, Walter love,' she said, seated beside him in the Renault in her Sunday best. 'I've been over the top of the moors before, but it was a heck of a hike! Doing it like this could easily make me forget what my legs are for!'

When they turned in between Crag-Side's high, wrought iron gates, and she got her first sight of the house, she sucked in her breath, letting it out slowly on a long sigh of wonderment.

Walter didn't blame her. Standing four-square, massive and magnificent, Crag-Side was looking its best.

Her speechless wonderment didn't last long. 'Blooming heck, love,' she said with a little choke of laughter as the Renault came to a halt before the wide and shallow stone steps leading up to the main entrance, 'Your father certainly did himself proud when he built this little lot, didn't he? You could fit Cartwright Hall into it four times over!'

Later, as he showed off Crag-Side's splendidly vast interior, she hugged his arm, saying with a throaty chuckle in her voice, 'Now I know why you want to marry me, love. You just want me to do the perishing cleaning!'

Polly wasn't the only one beginning to enjoy a heady life-style. In London, Lottie was having a whale of a time. Despite their Bohemianism, Nina and Rupert moved in very exalted circles and Lottie happily scampered in their wake.

The young and glamorous Duke and Duchess of Strachan, and the Duchess of Strachan's even younger, sizzlingly extrovert cousin, attended summer balls in a string of grand London houses: Derby, Lansdowne, Bridgewater, Londonderry. There were parties in tented marquees in great gardens, and parties on luxurious private launches on the Thames. There were evenings of riotous party games and guessing games and charades and, as autumn approached, much concert and opera and ballet-going.

Rupert was a young man who could keep even the staidest table in a constant roar and though Noel's creative juices were in full flow and he was working harder than he'd ever worked before in his life, he often accompanied them, sitting with his arm around Lottie's shoulders, laughing until his sides ached at Rupert's magical combination of wit and inspired lunacy.

Some early mornings before going home the three of them would swim at the exclusive Bath Club in Berkeley Street,

Nina and Lottie vying with each other as to who could execute the most perfect swallow-dive or swim the farthest underwater. Later they would disappear for a restorative half hour in the Turkish 'hot' room, gossiping and giggling and enjoying ice-creams that Rupert had had sent in to them from nearby Gunter's.

Nina's talent as a designer of lush and exotic day and evening gowns became the talk of what was fast becoming known as the Strachan 'set' and everyone who was anyone wanted to wear a gown designed by the sparklingly effervescent, luminously beautiful, young Duchess. Lottie, who had once taken umbrage at Nina using her likeness in her fashion drawings, now happily acted as a live clothes-horse for her, wearing wildly imaginative gowns inspired by the visiting Imperial Russian Ballet, or the latest Art Nouveau exhibition at the Royal Academy.

As the easy intimacy between herself and Nina increased, Lottie even found herself wondering if it were Nina now, and not Rose, who was her 'best' friend. She certainly found herself feeling far more at home in London than she did in Yorkshire. Noel, too, despite the flat northern vowels he refused on principle to eradicate from his speech, was firmly entrenched in Nina and Rupert's glitzy, influential, unconventional, 'fast' circle of friends.

Lottie, believing wholeheartedly in his talent, was fiercely ambitious for him.

'I suggested to the Russian Ambassador that you paint a mural for his Embassy,' she said to him blithely after the Ambassador, Count Benckendorff, had waltzed her nearly off her feet at a ball at Landsdowne House. On another occasion, when Count Benckendorff had introduced her at an Embassy function to his fellow countryman, the great Chaliapin, she had said later to Noel equally blithely, 'I told Chaliapin you would be able to do the most wonderful portrait of him. Just think of it, darling! All of London would know about it and you would be *inundated* with commissions!'

In vain Noel tried to make her understand that he wasn't a mural painter, nor a portrait artist. He might as well have been speaking to thin air. Lottie continued her self-appointed task of being a one-woman Noel Sugden publicity band, determined that his name should be on the lips of everyone who was anyone of consequence.

She was also determined to be worthy of him. In an effort to make up for an education that had consisted entirely of being tutored at home, and that she now knew to have been pitifully inadequate and shamefully skimpy, she set about educating herself. She attended lectures at all the leading art galleries and museums, went to concerts, learned reams of poetry and chunks of Shakespeare off by heart and, to Noel's vast amusement, even attended drawing classes at the Slade.

They were lovers now. In the sophisticated, unshockable circle in which they moved, no eyebrows were raised. Unknown to Walter, and with Nina's connivance, the live-in housekeeper at the Battersea house was dismissed and Lottie spent more and more time there with Noel, only gathering up her belongings and bolting back to Nina and Rupert's town house when Walter made a fleeting parental visit.

By the end of the year, as William and Sarah moved into a small flat conveniently adjacent to the Houses of Parliament and Harry received his officer's stripes and Rose increasingly became Walter's right-hand where the running of Rimmington's was concerned, Lottie was knee-deep in highly eligible prospective suitors.

Idolizing only Noel, she rejected them all, but was vastly pleased by their attentions.

'Count Benckendorff says my hair is like spun gold,' she said, her legs curled beneath her as, from the comfort of a battered *chaise-longue,* she watched him work on a large canvas.

Any hope she had had of trying to arouse his jealousy died an instant death.

'Benckendorff would think differently if he knew the gold came from a bottle,' he said with a chuckle, not taking his eyes from his work. 'Can you get me some more turpentine, love? I've run right out.'

'Just because we've got through the year without war being declared doesn't mean to say there isn't still going to be a war,' Harry said to Rose as he drove her back to Crag-Side after a visit to Beck-Side Street.

It was the New Year and he was home on leave. They had just spent a very jolly evening with her parents and with William and Sarah and little Emma Rose, and Rose was splendidly wrapped up against the cold, a cossack-style hat crammed low over her ears, her gloved hands buried deep in the silk-lined warmth of a fur muff.

'But what if there isn't a war this year either?' she asked, hoping passionately that there wouldn't be. 'Will you still stay in the Army? Your Father is hopeless at running the mill,' she added as they sped out of Bradford on the Ilkley road. 'He just has no *enthusiasm* for it.'

Harry grimaced. 'I can't just bob out

of the Army at a moment's notice, Funny-Face,' he said, well aware that his Father wasn't doing an ace job where Rimmington's was concerned. 'And even if I could, now isn't the time for me to be doing so. There's still trouble in the Balkans...'

'But no one's taking it seriously, are they?' Beneath the stylishly elegant hat, a hat which had been his Christmas present to her, her gamine-like face was all eyes and mouth. 'The diplomats have had the situation under control for so long, they're not likely to let it get out of control now, are they?'

It was a brilliantly clear night. In the velvet-dark sky the stars looked bright enough, and near enough, to touch. Rose burrowed her hands deeper into her muff. She didn't want to waste part of their precious time together, talking about the likelihood, or non-likelihood, of war. Ever since he had arrived home on leave her heart had been singing with happiness. He hadn't visited Leeds or Manchester. He'd spent all his time with her at Crag-Side, Beck-Side Street, or the mill.

Although it had been wonderful having a family get-together at Crag-Side, spending the evenings in the Chinese drawing-room in front of a roaring coal fire and playing word games and guessing games and charades, their visit together to the mill, when he had asked *her* to take *him* around it, had been an experience so special she knew she would never forget it.

'Getting the dyers to dye the tops in that dazzling shade of midnight blue and emerald green was a masterstroke, Rose,' he had said admiringly. 'Did you have to stand over them to get such unusual shades?'

'I told them I wanted the tops to look like Lister Park lake under a hot summer sun,' she had said, delighted he was so pleased with the colour mix in the finished, woven cloth.

Now he said in answer to her last question, 'I think diplomatic neutrality may have gone as far as it can, Rose.' The hard, exciting line of his mouth was sombre. 'When people flout all the principles of civilized behaviour so openly, there comes a time when it's impossible to stand back, hands in pockets. When it comes to right and wrong, what do you do? You have to be on the side of right, don't you? There's no other option.'

They had driven the rest of the way to Crag-Side in unhappy, contemplative silence, she knowing that of course under those circumstances there would be no option for him, and that there would be none for William or Noel, either; he more certain than ever that within the year he would be in full battle rig, fighting the Germans and their allies.

The next day, despite the harsh cold, they went for a walk on the moor.

'I think I love the moor even better in winter than I do in summer,' she had said, striding out beside him over the rough, hard-frosted ground, 'There's an extra grandeur about it in winter, isn't there?' She was buried deep in a heavy tweed coat, swathed in woollen scarves, cossack-hatted and muffed. 'It's so...lonely. It seems to roll on endlessly.'

'Even to the crack of doom?' he had asked, laughing down at her.

She was holding his arm so as not to twist an ankle on the frozen, hummocky ground and she hugged it tighter, laughing back at him, her eyes sparkling with happiness, her cheeks rosy with cold.

He halted, as if a thought had suddenly robbed him of breath, staring down at her with a dazed expression in his eyes.

Her laughter died an instant death. 'What is it?' she asked anxiously, hoping he wasn't going to start talking about a possible war again; hoping he wasn't suddenly feeling ill.

His mouth tugged into a smile. 'Nothing, Funny-Face,' he said reassuringly, patting her gloved hand. 'Shall we try and walk as far as the cairn? Have you enough breath for it?'

She nodded, her breath smoking in the freezing air, wishing with all her heart that his pet name for her were 'sweetheart', or 'dear love', or 'darling.'

There had been a moment, when he had given her the fox fur hat and matching muff, when she had almost been able to pretend that she *was* his dear love. They had been the kind of presents she could imagine him giving Nina. They had made her feel wonderfully feminine and wearing them, feeling as if she had stepped from the pages of a Russian novel, she had been able, for the first time in her life, to believe herself beautiful.

When he returned to camp she had felt utterly bereft. The weather hadn't helped. Snow had fallen heavily, making the roads between Ilkley and Bradford impassable. When it had first been forecast, she had returned to Beck-Side Street with enough clothes to see her through a few short weeks. Together with Jenny she tramped every morning through knee-deep drifts as far as Toller Lane where they would say goodbye, Jenny then ploughing on towards Lutterworth's while she struggled in the direction of Rimmington's.

The misery of the weather wasn't helped

by the fact that her father wasn't very well, and hadn't been ever since Christmas.

'I'm ju...st tired, li...ttle love,' he would say to her whenever she expressed concern. 'Dr Todd says I'll be fi...ine and dandy by the spri...ing.'

He wasn't. He was worse. In April, when international as well as home news reached a new all-time low, Albania threatening war on Greece, Russia announcing it was quadrupling its army, Germany announcing it was launching fourteen new warships, suffragettes setting London buildings on fire and civil war breaking out in Ireland, Dr Todd announced that the infection Laurence had been unable to shake off was, in fact, tubercular.

*'What does that mean?'* Nina had wired frantically from Paris where she and Rupert were staying at the George V.

*'How ill is Dad?'* Noel had wired from London. *'Should I come home?'*

*'Keep me in touch with what's happening,'* Harry had wired from deepest Surrey. *'I'll be with you within a few hours if you need me.'*

On the first of May, as Beck-Side Street children and their schoolteachers partied in a field adjoining the Beck, taking it in turns to dance around a gaily decorated maypole, the long colourful ribbons they held weaving exotic patterns as they did so, Laurence smiled up at Lizzie in whose arms he was lying, patted her hand lovingly and, as peacefully as he had lived, died.

Rose couldn't believe it. It was as if the world had ended. She was so shocked she couldn't cry; so shocked that even when Harry arrived, hard on the heels of Noel and Lottie and William and Sarah, she barely noticed his presence. Like a mantra, the words, 'My father's dead. I'm never going to see him again. Not ever!' beat round and round in her brain as ceaselessly as waves pounding a beach.

She remembered how, when she had been a very small girl, he had taught her to see the beauty in simple, everyday objects; how he had taught her that even mill chimneys could be beautiful. She remembered their photography expeditions together; the way he had so gallantly come to terms with his cruel disablement; the way he had never once raised his voice, much less his hand, to her.

The whole of Beck-Side Street turned out for the funeral. 'He was a gent,' Gertie said, weeping into a ragged piece of white cloth that, saved from an end-piece at the mill, served her as a handkerchief.

'Your Pa was a real trouper,' Albert said, his eyes overly bright, the same battered trilby he had worn the day he had moved them into the street, crammed on to the back of his head. 'In his own quiet way he was a hero, a real hero.'

Nina and Rupert arrived, Nina so distraught as to be on the point of collapse.

Walter helped Noel and William and Harry to carry the coffin. A sheaf of white, hot-house roses lay on top of it.

'Rosa alba,' Harry had said thickly, his arm around Rose's shoulder's. 'The White Rose of York. Yorkshire flowers for a true Yorkshireman.'

The mourners following the horse-drawn hearse to the church were the most motley collection Beck-Side Street had ever seen, or was ever likely to see. A widow who enjoyed the reputation of being the neatest dressmaker in west Bradford and who looked, and carried herself, like a dowager duchess. A pukka young duke and duchess. A red-haired young man who, even dressed in mourning, carried the stamp of 'artist' all over him. An ex-weaver from Rimmington's, so vast in bulk she resembled a moving mountain. The wealthy owner of Rimmington's, astrakhan-coated and black top-hatted. An elderly removal man cum rag-and-bone man, black ribbon tied around one arm of his shabby coat and around the crown of his even shabbier hat. A young lady whose mourning clothes shrieked out that they had cost more than the average working man earned in a year, her hair, beneath her black veiled hat, the improbable colour of sun-ripened barley. A young weaver from Lutterworth's and her middle-aged, still pretty, mother. A young army officer wearing the distinctive uniform of an élite regiment. A Labour Member of Parliament and his wife. A locally well-renowned and respected Methodist lay-preacher. A young man with a pugnacious set to his lean shoulders and a faint, lingering smell of horse about him. An array of mill-working neighbours, some wearing clogs because they possessed no other footwear.

United in a sense of loss they followed the coffin and, afterwards, all crammed into the Sugden's back-to-back for a traditional funeral repast of ham salad and cups of scalding hot tea.

'What will Mother do now?' Nina asked Rose, her skin still as flawless as finest porcelain despite the river of tears she had shed.

Rose, aware that her own grief had physically done her no favours whatsoever, and uncaring, said bleakly, 'I don't know. I suppose she'll stay here. I'll come back and live with her, so that she won't be on her own and—'

'There's no need.' The speaker was William. 'Mother wants to move in with us. It's a good idea, if you think about it. Sarah's often without adult company when the House is sitting and I'm in London, so Mother will be company for her. And Mother adores Emma Rose and will be kept busy, helping to look after her.'

It was a good idea, but it did absolutely nothing to ease the heavy burden of Rose's grief. It meant there would no longer be a home for her in Beck-Side Street. Never again would she live in back-to-back cosiness with Polly and Jenny, nor in a house where Albert and Gertie called in unexpectedly at any times of the day, for a cheery word. From now on, her home would be at Crag-Side. And when her Uncle finally married Polly and moved to Scarborough? She closed the thought from her mind. It was enough, at the moment, that she had lost her dearly loved father. Compared to that loss, everything else was trivial.

## Chapter Fourteen

For the next few weeks, with Harry back at camp, William irregularly commuting between London and Bradford, Noel, Nina and Lottie in London and her mother living with Sarah, work was Rose's salvation.

She was far more than a junior textile designer now. In all but name she ran the Department and, in many ways, was on the brink of running the entire mill.

'What do you think of this, Rose?' Walter would ask as they ate dinner together at Crag-Side in lonely grandeur. 'Should I do this? What do you think of our taking on this government contract? What do you think Harry would do? What do you think Harry would think?'

His questions and prevarications were endless and all Rose could do in advising him was to learn everything she could about the running of Rimmington's, use her common sense and, above all, keep her fingers firmly crossed.

In June she was deeply shocked by the assassination in Sarajevo of Archduke Franz Ferdinand, heir to the Habsburg throne, but it still didn't occur to her that Harry's predictions of a war between Great Britain and Germany were on the brink of being fulfilled.

'Grey's neutralist policy will keep us out of trouble,' Walter said to her reassuringly. 'This new trouble in the Balkans will blow over just like all the other spots of trouble there have blown over.'

In this, as in so many other things, Walter was wrong. Ultimatums were issued. Armies were mobilized. The Kaiser declared war on his cousin, the Czar, and then on France. Great Britain told Germany it was standing by the Treaty of London which guaranteed Belgian neutrality and that it would protect the French coastline. Germany ignored the warning and, on the 4th of August, a British Bank Holiday, German armies invaded Belgium. By midnight of the same day, Britain and Germany were at war.

'Thank God!' Lottie said fervently. 'No more shilly-shallying! No more spineless neutrality! Bullies shouldn't be endured and now that nasty old bully, the Kaiser, will get what he deserves! A bloody nose!'

She and Noel had been spending the holiday weekend at Crag-Side and were sitting with Rose, William and Sarah, by the edge of the tennis-court.

'And what about all the thousands who'll be conscripted into his army and who don't deserve a bloody nose and will simply die obeying orders?' Noel said so caustically that Lottie's carefully pencilled eyebrows flew nearly into her hair.

Emma Rose had been happily picking daisies and was now beginning to eat them. Sarah scooped her up in her arms and, as she removed the daisies from Emma Rose's chubby fist, said, 'But when there's open conflict between good and evil, when one's very principles are at stake, surely wars have to be fought then, Noel?'

Noel rose to his feet and looked around at them all, the sun glinting like fire on his mahogany-red hair. 'Not by me, they don't,' he said starkly. 'Not when to do so would be to flout *my* principles. I've given this a lot of thought over the last few months and the conclusion I've come to, is that I don't intend either enlisting or being conscripted.'

'I'm sorry?' William wondered if he'd missed something Noel had been saying. He certainly wasn't making sense. As a healthy twenty-two-year-old not in a reserved occupation, Noel wasn't going to have any alternative but to enlist or wait for his conscription papers.

Noel didn't look at him. He looked at Lottie. 'I'm not going to fight,' he said bluntly. 'I'm a creative artist, not a legalized murderer. I'm going to stand by my principles and declare myself a conscientious objector.'

For a moment no one spoke or moved. Rose was dizzyingly trying to come to terms with just what being a conscientious objector was going to entail for Noel. Sarah, despite her belief that there *were* such things as righteous wars, and that the present war, as far as Great Britain and her Allies were concerned, certainly fell into such a category, was quietly admiring. After all, it was no use having principles and beliefs if, when the crunch came, you didn't stand up for them, no matter how unpopular standing up for them might be.

It was William who put his reaction into words first. 'Become a conscientious objector? A *conchie?*' He rose to his feet, running a hand through his hair. 'You can't be serious, Noel! How can you stay home *painting* when other chaps will be fighting for *your* king, *your* country, *your* freedoms?'

'I doubt if I'll be doing much painting,' Noel said dryly. 'I rather suspect I'll be down a coalmine somewhere, or in a steelworks, or—'

'I don't believe you.' It was Lottie. Ashen-faced, she sprang to her feet, facing him. 'Tell me this is a sick joke, Noel. Tell me you don't mean it. *Please, please tell me you don't mean it!*'

He gazed at her in helpless despair. He had hoped she would react differently. He had hoped that, as always previously, she would be his fiercest, staunchest ally. And he knew now he'd been hoping in vain. Lottie, with her direct, no-nonsense, confrontational approach to life, was mentally incapable of understanding the stance he was taking.

'I'm sorry, love,' he said, knowing how fiercely she wanted him to be the hero above all other heroes; the knight on a white charger who would cover himself with glory on the battlefield. 'I should have told you how I felt sooner...'

'Oh God!' Tears were pouring down her face. 'Oh Christ!' Shaking violently, uncaring of how she was shocking Sarah with her blasphemies, she began struggling with the ring that had unofficially graced the fourth finger of her left hand all during the summer. 'I can't believe this!' She was hyperventilating, her breath ragged. 'I can't live with this! I can't endure the pain of it! The man I wanted to marry, a coward! My *cousin,* a coward!' She wrenched the ring from her finger, flinging it down in front of him on the daisy-starred grass. 'I want to die with the shame of it. I wish I *was* dead! I wish *both* of us were dead!'

She fell down on to her knees, covering

her face with her hands, sobbing as if she would never stop.

Noel made no move towards her. His face contorted with pain, he turned on his heel, striding away from them as if he were striding out of their lives for ever.

Rose ran after him, but couldn't keep up with him. Without returning to the house for his weekend bag he headed straight down into Ilkley, making for the railway station. He knew that Rose would do her damnedest to understand, and that, God willing, Harry would understand, but that no one else would.

Grimly he swung himself aboard a London-bound train. From now on, until the war in whichever way, ended, he was going to be on his own with only white feathers for company. He wondered if Lottie would send him one. He wondered if human hearts could break, and if his were doing so.

William, hoping to God that news of Noel's decision wouldn't reach the ears of his electorate, joined the London Volunteer Defence Force.

Rupert joined an élite regiment.

In Bradford, the number of volunteers was such that the town formed its own battalion, the 1st Bradford Pals Battalion. Micky was one of the first young men through the recruiting office doors. Hard on his heels was Charlie Thorpe.

Lottie, on hearing that Nina's friend, the Duchess of Sutherland, was taking a Red Cross Hospital to France and that she was taking her daughters and her daughters' friends with her as nursing staff, immediately wrote to her, asking if she could accompany their party as a volunteer nurse.

Nina offered her services to Guy's Hospital, putting her patriotism to the test by wearing a monstrous uniform.

*'The dress is made out of purple and white striped material that wouldn't disgrace a tent,'* she wrote to Rose. *'It fits like a tent, too. I swear Gertie Graham could wear it and have room to spare. I bunch the whole hideous thing together with a belt and then, for the crowning touch, don black wool stockings and flat black shoes! If Rupert could see me he would have ten fits!'*

For the early months of the war, during the period when everyone was confidently predicting it 'would be over by Christmas,' and that 'we'll soon roll 'em up', Rose worked long fourteen-hour days at the mill. There was no designing new patterns now. Only the overseeing of the fulfilling of a huge government contract for khaki, khaki, and yet more khaki and, constantly, the long, agonizing wait for letters from Harry.

As a regular serving officer he had been despatched to the front almost immediately. In August he was in the thick of the bloodbath that was Mons. In September he was part of the Allied armies' retreat from the Marne. In October he was one of the countless many fighting back towards the Marne, recovering ground once lost and enabling British and Allied newspapers to print banner headlines declaring: 'PARIS SAVED: GERMANS IN RETREAT!'

*'One thing is for certain,'* he wrote to her grimly in November, *'and that is that the war isn't going to be over by Christmas. There are times when I doubt it will even be over by next Christmas.'*

In the New Year it looked as if Harry's predictions were, once again, going to be proved correct. The German retreat was limited. Both sides resorted to constructing defence-works and a line of trenches extended from Nieuport on the Belgian coast, all the way through Ypres, Arras, Soissons and Rheims, to Verdun. Neither side advanced, or retreated, more than a few miserable miles.

*'It's deadlock,'* Harry wrote to her in

February, *'and it's being suffered under conditions beyond description. I don't want to write of it, Funny-Face. I can't write of it. I just want to think of Crag-Side, and the mill, and wonderful, wonderful, heather-covered Ilkley Moor.'*

On the Eastern Front, in April, the Allies despatched troops to Gallipoli in order to try and seize the forts guarding the approach to Constantinople, thereby opening up a route to assist the beleaguered Russians. Rupert sailed with them.

The Commander-in-charge of the operation, knowing the Turks would be manning the heights in massive numbers above the narrow beach on which his men were to land, devised an approach reminiscent of that once used by the Ancient Greeks at nearby Troy. Instead of an apparently innocent wooden horse, however, he used an apparently innocent sea-horse, a collier, the *River Clyde.*

Huge openings were cut in the *River Clyde's* sides in order that, as soon as it was run aground, the troops could pour from it.

When they did so, they did not succeed in taking the Turks by surprise. Instead, they ran headlong into hell. Beating a way ashore under the murderous onslaught of the Turkish guns, the sea stained red with the blood of the dying and dead, Rupert was one of the few who gained the beach. Amid the mayhem and carnage he found there, he rallied the remnants of his battalion and, achieving the impossible, captured the Turkish-defended heights. There, engaged like a gladiator in brutal hand-to-hand fighting, fearless and courageous and twenty-five years old, he died a hero's death.

On hearing the news, Rose left immediately for London. Nina was beyond comfort; beyond any kind of rational behaviour. For once in her life, Rose was out of her depth.

*'I think Neen's losing her reason,'* she wrote to William. *'She doesn't even seem to be aware of my presence. Ma might be able to get some response from her, but no matter how hard I try, I can't.'*

Lizzie, still in mourning for Laurence, travelled down to London and installed herself in the Strachan town house. Rose returned to Crag-Side.

Rimmington's was now in production virtually around the clock and it was she, not Walter, who dealt with suppliers and customers. With Belgian and French textile mills occupied by the Germans, and Russian and Polish mills devastated, Rimmington's was receiving orders not only from France, but from Serbia and Russia as well.

*'Keep up the good work, Funny-Face,'* Harry had written from the front. *'Grandfather would be proud of you!'*

In June the Thorpe family received news that Charlie had been seriously wounded and moved to a field hospital at Boulogne.

*'As soon as he opened his mouth I knew he was from Bradford,'* Lottie wrote to Rose. *'And then he said he'd like to show me a photograph of his sweetheart and he asked me to open his wallet for him and what do I see? I see my father's lady friend's daughter smiling sunnily up at me! If Papa marries Mrs Wilkinson and Charlie Thorpe marries Jenny, does that mean I'll be related to Charlie? It would make the head of a banshee whirl! The next bit isn't nice, but has to be told. Charlie Thorpe's left leg was amputated the evening he was brought in here. Break the news to Jenny gently. At least Charlie's now out of the war and will soon be on his way home to her.'*

At the end of June, Rose fell ill with a particularly vicious form of influenza. At the beginning of July Harry came home on leave. There was no possibility of any trips out together, either to the mill or to the moors. All she could do was lie back against her pillows, her temperature, according to Walter, 'soaring off the thermometer', and rejoice in the fact that, after nearly a year at the front, she could feast her eyes on him, reassuring herself that he, at least, was still blessedly all in one piece.

'Charlie Thorpe's home,' she said to him as he sat by her bed, holding her hand for all the world as if she were his sweetheart and not his 'funny-faced' cousin. 'It's terrible to see him limping down Beck-Side Street with a crutch, one empty trouser leg pinned up out of the way. Jenny is being very brave and very practical about it. She says she'd rather have him home and alive with only one leg, than two-legged and dead in Flanders.'

It was while Harry was home that the news came that Rupert was be awarded a posthumous Victoria Cross.

'I wrote a sympathy letter to Nina immediately I knew of Rupert's death,' Harry said, not making eye contact with her but staring intently at a bowl of marigolds on her bedside table. 'She knows I'm home and she's invited me to spend my last couple of days leave in London. Your mother's kept me in touch with what's been happening down there. It seems Neen's taken Rupert's death very hard.'

'Yes.' There was such a lump in her throat she could hardly force the word out. She knew what would happen when Harry saw Nina again. Nina would turn to him for comfort and Harry, loving her as he had always loved her, would give that comfort. And then? After Nina had grieved for Rupert, would she and Harry marry? It would be what Harry would want. It was what Harry had always wanted.

Within days of Harry's returning to Flanders, via a brief stay with Lizzie and Nina in London, Jenny and Charlie were married in Bull Royd Methodist Church.

Not having a father, Jenny had asked Walter if he would give her away. 'I'd be proud to, my dear,' he had said, deeply touched, knowing how it would set tongues talking and not caring.

Sitting at the front of the church with her mother and William and Sarah, Rose had had to blink hard to keep tears away as she watched Jenny walk down the short aisle.

Her wedding-dress was of misty lavender-blue silk. She had made it herself, cleverly cutting the long sweeping skirt on the bias so that it swirled around her ankles. With her hair prettily decorated by crimson roses, a posy of them in her hands, she walked, radiant with happiness, to stand at Charlie's side.

There was a card, wishing her and Charlie well, from Noel. Although there was, as yet, only talk of conscription, he had informed the authorities that if and when it came he would be burning his conscription papers and, as that was to be the case, that he would appreciate being delegated without further delay to non-combative war work. No one in the family knew what kind of response he had received to his demand, but the wedding card had been posted from Wales. Micky, too, contacted Jenny on her wedding day. *'Have a smashing day, stop,'* his censored-marked telegram read. *'You're marrying a grand bloke, stop. All best wishes, stop. Micky.'*

'Where the devil is young Micky?' Gertie Graham asked Rose at the wedding reception in the church hall. 'Albert says he gets a postcard now and then with bugger all but censor marks on it. If we and the Frenchies get together for a big autumn push as folks are saying we're going to do, will he be in t'thick of that, do you think? He always did like to be in t'thick of things, didn't he?'

In September, taking part in the great autumn offensive on the Western front, Micky was certainly in the thick of things.

' "Where's tha' bin?" is the first question I shall blooming well ask him, first time he comes home,' Albert grumbled to Lizzie as they studied the latest news reports from the front in the *Bradford Daily Argus*. 'What the heck's the use of letting the boys write home, if they can't say nowt about where they are or what the heck they're doing?'

'If he's taking part in the autumn offensive with the British 1 Corps, he must be in the fighting around Loos,' Lizzie said, spreading out a map of France and Belgium on Sarah's kitchen table. When they could both see it clearly she returned her attention to the newspaper. 'Marshall Joffre is quoted here as saying, "After a new and very violent bombardment our infantry rushed forward to assault German lines. The enemy has suffered very considerable losses from our fire and in the hand-to-hand fighting." '

'I don't like t'sound of that,' Albert had said baldly. 'Trench fighting's bad enough, but 'and-to-'and is worse. Still, if anyone'll get the Germans running for 'ome, it's our Micky. 'E 'as a devil of a temper when 'e's roused!'

The offensive failed. No ground worth mentioning was taken—and that which was taken was subsequently lost. British casualties amounted to over 60,000, but Micky Porritt was not among them. To the vast relief of his family and friends Micky Porritt, cursing like a trooper and clinging to the dream of a sheep-farm half a world away, lived to fight another day. And another. And another.

'Harry was right, wasn't he, when he said it wouldn't even be over by this Christmas?' Rose said to Walter as he drove her home from the mill in the Renault. 'And not only is it not going to be over by this Christmas, there doesn't look much chance of it being over by *next* Christmas. Not unless this terrible stalemate is broken.'

The weather was so cold she was wearing her cossack-style hat and matching muff.

'It has to be broken,' Walter said grimly, aware that luck couldn't continue to favour Harry indefinitely. 'The new Ministry of Munitions might be the trick. Now its formed, the army in France should have all the supplies they need.'

'To do what with?' Rose asked exasperatedly. 'To make offensives from trenches over barbed-wired ground, in order to gain or retake a few hundred yards of waist-deep mud and to be mown down in their hundreds, in their *thousands,* as they make the attempt?'

He didn't answer her, because he didn't know what to say. Instead he put his foot down harder than ever on the Renault's accelerator pedal. The latest published casualty figures had been monstrous. They'd been so enormous they had been past all belief. An entire generation was being mown down. And to what purpose, dear Christ? he asked silently as the gas-lights of Ilkley came in to view. To what *purpose?*

The Western front, running from Ostend across Flanders and then assuming a deep salient above Paris before swinging East to Verdun, had scarcely changed over the last twelve months. No ground was being won. No opposing army was being thrashed into retreat. An enemy surrender was as remote a prospect now as it had ever been. And every day that passed made Harry's continuing survival a little less likely. Or did so unless he were injured and sent back behind the lines. Or unless he lost a limb, as poor bloody Charlie Thorpe had lost a limb.

He made a despairing, inarticulate sound in his throat and Rose said tentatively, 'I have an idea I'd like to put to you, Uncle Walter. It's about Crag-Side, not the mill.'

In the winter darkness the car began the climb up out of the centre of Ilkley.

Walter changed gear. He didn't like driving, but he had no option now. Every able-bodied man in the country had volunteered for one of the Services. Or nearly every man. Noel hadn't and Walter couldn't quite make out how he felt about that. It wasn't general knowledge at the mill, thank goodness. With so many of his former employees now fighting in Flanders or Palestine or Egypt or God-only-knew where else, it would have been a humiliation impossible to survive if it were known his nephew was a conscientious objector.

'He's still contributing to the war effort,' Lizzie had said to him fiercely, explaining how Noel had abandoned his painting and gone to work in a Welsh mine. 'He hates and loathes it underground, but it's his way of helping to fight the war.'

The fact that Rose was speaking to him impinged at last on his consciousness.

'And Crag-Side is certainly big enough,' she was saying eagerly. 'It will make a *wonderful* convalescent home for wounded servicemen. I've done some measuring up and I think we could make a ward for at least ten patients in the Chinese drawing-room and if we empty the winter garden of plants it would hold another twelve.

The walls will need hanging with glazed linen—or at least that's what Lottie advised when I wrote to her with the idea...'

'Lottie?' Walter braked the Renault to a halt outside Crag-Side's vast gates. 'You've written to Lottie about converting Crag-Side into a convalescent home?'

Rose nodded, or nodded as much as she was able to from under the sumptuous weight of her fur hat.

'She thinks it's a wonderful idea and can't understand why we never thought of it before. She said the best room to turn into an operating theatre would be the bedroom that used to be William's as it has a centre skylight as well as huge windows. She also thinks we should be able to manage quite well with a nursing sister, two trained nurses and a healthy number of VAD's to assist.'

Walter groaned. If Rose had involved Lottie in her plans then there was no help for it, Crag-Side was as good as a convalescent home already.

He struggled out of the car in order to open the gates. No longer with the Duchess of Sutherland's hospital at Boulogne, Lottie's bossy efficiency was now being giving full rein in a field hospital far closer to the front. A friend of William's, a young second lieutenant, had been hospitalized there and had written to

William, *'Your sister wears a big organdie Red Cross headpiece which doesn't quite disguise her golden hair. She looks like a veritable angel from heaven and where the wounded are concerned she is an angel. She's also, when it comes to any attempted interference by military old busy-bodies, as tough as old boots! If she says a man isn't fit to return to the front, not even General Haigh himself would succeed in countermanding her!'*

He pulled open the heavy gates. There was more than a dash of his father in Lottie—and in his little Yorkshire Rose. He shook his head bemusedly. They were grand girls—girls to be proud of—and if they had decided that Crag-Side was to be a convalescent home, then who was he to argue with them?

In Wales—without art, without Lottie, without the rest of his family, Noel was surviving as best he could. He hated the work. He had chosen it, knowing he would hate it, seeing it as a penance for his not suffering the hell of the trenches. He hated the claustrophobia; the dark; the coal dust that seeped into his every pore; the callouses that deformed his hands. Above all, he hated the social isolation. There was no one he could talk art with. No one he could remotely count as being a friend. Unskilled, he could only do the most menial of jobs and his fellows down the pit, Welshmen to a man, regarded him with undisguised suspicion. With his tall, lean build, he was as physically ill-equipped to be a miner as he was mentally ill-equipped to be one. But day after day he stuck it out. And day after day he thought of Lottie.

He knew now that he had never valued her enough; that he had always taken her adoration totally for granted; that he had passively, and with mild amusement, *allowed* himself to be loved by her. Now, too late, he knew he had never troubled to truly love her back. And now, too late, he knew how deeply he needed her; how deeply, in his own self-centred way, he loved her.

In January, conscription, which he had always known was only a matter of time, came into effect.

*'The House voted overwhelmingly tonight in favour of the Conscription Bill,'* William wrote to him from London. *'You may like to know that I, like the majority of Labour MP's, voted against it. The Home Secretary feels so strongly he has resigned over the issue. I imagine life is going to be extremely tough now for single young men who feel as you do. You'll be called before a military tribunal and*

*what will happen to you then, the Lord alone knows.'*

What happened, was that to his great surprise and to everyone else's intense relief, he was classified as being employed on essential war work.

*'At least we're spared the ignominy of Noel being publicly labelled a conchie,'* Nina wrote to Lottie from London. *'As for me—I don't care about anything anymore. What is there to care about? I've decided that instead of pining myself to death, I may as well party myself to death. Rupert would understand. Mother won't.'*

Lizzie didn't. 'She's behaving outrageously,' she said wearily to Sarah on her return to Bradford. 'I simply couldn't stay and stand by, watching her destroy her reputation and her health—and I couldn't have done anything *but* stand by as she won't listen to a word I, or anyone else, says.'

'I thought she might have continued with her nursing,' Sarah said, lifting a wriggling and soapily wet Emma Rose from a small tin bath in front of the sitting-room fire.

Lizzie handed her a warmed towel. 'She hasn't been back to Guy's since she received the news of Rupert's death. None of her high-society friends seem to think her behaviour outrageous. Their code seems to be to dance and drink and to behave as if there's going to be no tomorrow.'

'For many of them, there won't be.'

A spasm crossed Lizzie's face. Sarah was right. Perhaps even Nina and her friends were right. 'Dear God,' she said devoutly, turning her wedding ring round and round on her finger, 'how much longer is it going to go on for, Sarah? When is it going to end?'

## Chapter Fifteen

By the beginning of the summer, under Rose's energetic supervision, Crag-Side was transformed into a convalescence home. Most of the patients were officers. Nearly all of them were under the age of thirty. Nearly all had lost a limb. Many had lost two. Many had been blinded during the gas attacks at Ypres and Loos.

'By the time the war is over I doubt if there'll be an able-bodied man left,' Josie Warrender, one of the VADs, said wryly to Rose as they stowed freshly laundered bed-sheets into a high linen cupboard. 'My mother always said I was leaving finding a husband a little late. I'm beginning to think she may have been right!'

Rose stood on tiptoe in order to slide a pile of pillowcases away. She liked Josie. Tall and statuesque, with a square-jawed face and a mass of dark hair, she was a New Zealander and she possessed a direct, effervescent quality that reminded Rose of Lottie.

'If you do grow into an old maid, you'll have plenty of company,' she said to her cheerily, popping a bag of dried lavender on top of the pillowcases. 'Me for one.'

'It's to be the biggest offensive ever,' Jenny said when Rose visited her later that day. 'They're calling it the Somme Campaign and the West Yorkshire Regiment is taking part. Two of its battalions are made up entirely of Bradford Pals, which means nearly everyone we know who is in uniform will be in it. I went to church to pray yesterday. I just can't bear the thought of more of Charlie's friends dying or being maimed.'

Neither could Rose. Particularly she couldn't bear the thought of Micky being killed or maimed.

*'It's the boredom that's the worst,'* he had lied on the last postcard she had received from him. *'I have a hammock of sorts and I lie in it and try to shut the never-ending noise out of my head and think instead of the moors, and the horse and cart, and the pictures in my book of New Zealand.'*

Within days The *Bradford Daily Telegraph* was leaving Bradfordians in no doubt as to the calamitous way the campaign had opened.

*'At 7.30am, on the morning of July 3rd, the artillery barrage was lifted and the British, three battalions of the West Yorkshire*

*Regiment prominent among them, went over the top in waves, each man carrying 70 pounds of equipment. The objective was to seize some 4,000 yards of enemy territory in the first day. It was an objective that was not attained. In the first five minutes of the battle thousands were cut down by relentless enemy fire. By nightfall many battalions numbered barely a hundred men...'*

Rose had been unable to read on.

'The casualty figures!' her mother had said when the first list had been published, tears streaming down her face. 'Have you seen the latest casualty figures, Rose? The Bradford Pals have been nearly wiped out. Already the list of those killed is over a thousand names long, and names are still coming in! Gertie Graham's nephew has been killed. Albert's sister's boy has been killed. Dr Todd's son has been killed. Do you remember Mr Jabez who delivered our coal when we lived in Jesmond Avenue? He's lost all three of his boys. There's scarcely a street or a cul-de-sc in the city that hasn't suffered a loss.'

In sick dread Rose had forced herself to read each new casualty list as it was published. Harry's name didn't appear, nor did Micky's. And Noel, at least, was safe. Working deep underground in his Welsh pit, Noel would survive the war.

It was a straw to cling to; the only certain thing in a world which had spiralled into unimaginable hell.

'There's been a major pit disaster,' William said to her, telephoning from London, his voice made indistinct by static. 'News has just come in of it. More than 400 men are trapped by fire underground...'

'Which pit?' Her voice cut across his, choked with fear. He wouldn't be telephoning her if it weren't Noel's pit. Noel, who she had thought safe. Noel, who was going to survive the war no matter who else died. *'Which pit?'*

Walter drove her and her mother through the night to South Wales. Dawn was breaking as the Renault climbed the steeply climbing cobbled streets of the Welsh village that had been Noel's home for nearly two years. None of them had visited him here, for he hadn't wanted them to visit him. None of them had seen him since he had left Crag-Side so abruptly, leaving his weekend travelling bag behind him in his room. To all intents and purposes it had been exactly as if he, like Harry and Micky, had left two summers ago for Flanders.

The doors of the pit cottages all opened directly onto the street, as did the doors in Beck-Side Street. Had Noel managed to feel at home here? In which pit cottage had he lived? Were any of the hundreds of women standing silently around the pit-head, his landlady? Question after question whirled in Rose's brain as she fought to contain the fear consuming her. *Was Noel amongst those trapped underground by fire? Was Noel dead?*

Despite the ostentation of the Renault they received no preferential treatment when they reached the pit-head. They were just three more relatives, waiting desperately in the pale light of early morning for news.

'It was an explosion,' one woman, a shawl pulled close around her head and shoulders, said to Lizzie. 'They must have been able to hear it in Swansea. It ripped through the pit just after the night shift went down. My man's a day man, thank God, but my nephew's still missing. There's been no one brought out alive since midnight.'

'They got close on 300 out immediately after the explosion,' Walter said when he came back to them after speaking to pit officials. 'Noel's name isn't amongst them. That doesn't mean, of course, that he isn't safe. Lists can't be accurate under these conditions—'

'If he was safe he would be here,' Lizzie

said starkly, holding on to Rose's arm. 'He would have seen the car, sought us out—'

'Your boy may be helping with the rescue attempt,' another voice, a male voice, said quietly from behind them, and then someone else said, their voice raw with hope, 'The cage is coming up again. There may be some more survivors!'

There were, but Noel wasn't among them. William arrived. In his capacity as an MP he talked to the men in charge of the rescue attempt and was able to relay back up-to-date, reliable information to those waiting outside the Pit gates.

'There's a section of the mine they think the fire hasn't broken through to. The question is, how long can any men trapped there survive? A rescue party is trying to reach them via a disused mine entrance on the other side of the hill.'

'They'll never make it,' the quiet male voice said again with dreadful certainty. 'I know this mine. I've worked it all my life. If there's fire down there, there'll be methane too. Methane gas is deadly. Whoever is going down now isn't going to come out alive.'

There was more restless movement amongst the crowd. A stoutly-built woman walked out of the pit yard saying to those who clustered around her, desperate for news, 'The Jenkinson boys have gone down, and Tom Burton and Evan Evans, and the English boy...'

'English? Did you say English?' Rose left her mother's side and pushed her way through to the front of those massing round the latest news-bearer.

'Aye, *cariad,*' the woman said gently, noting the colour of her hair. 'He'll be your brother, will he? He's been working with the main rescue party these six hours past and now he's gone down again, though I doubt he'll have any success.'

Relief roared through Rose so intense she swayed on her feet. Until a little while ago Noel had still been alive! And if this next rescue attempt failed? If he were trapped underground? If he were to be overcome by methane gas? With fresh fear flooding through her she began pushing her way back to her mother and William. A young woman in the crowd began saying the Lord's Prayer. Others joined in.

At eight o' clock chipped enamel mugs of steaming tea were handed round. At ten o'clock the woman who had broken the news of the latest rescue attempt said to Rose, 'Would your Mammy like some *cawl?* My girl's brought a jug up and there's plenty to spare.'

Not knowing what *cawl* was, but knowing

it would be something sustaining, Rose accepted her offer with gratitude.

'It's soup,' Lizzie said to her, her hands wrapped about the mug that had previously held tea. 'There's bacon in it. What's happening, Rose? Why is there no news? *What's happening?*'

It was midday when the news broke that men were being brought up via the shaft to the old workings. *'They're alive!'* went up the cry. *'Only twenty of them, but they're alive!'*

Some of the men walked out into the blessed light of day. Others, rescuers as well as rescued, were carried out on stretchers. Among them was Noel.

'He's broke his back, *Duw,*' a weary coal and smoke-blackened figure said to her as she rushed up to the stretcher, her mother and Walter and William only feet behind her. 'The timber supports in the old working were so rotten they were giving way all the time we were down there. He shored the exit timber up for as long as he could and then, as we got the last of those trapped out, it gave way. He may be an Englishman, but he's a hero, *Duw.* A real hero.'

*'At present he's in Swansea General Hospital,'* Rose wrote to Lottie from Wales. *'They're*

*not sure yet whether he'll ever walk again. As soon as he's well enough he'll be transferred to Crag-Side to convalesce.'*

*'There's talk of a civilian medal for bravery,'* William wrote to Lottie from Westminster. *'If he hadn't physically shored up the timbers for as long as he did, his companions would never have got the last of the trapped men out. How he did it beats me. He's built like a lath, not a Hercules.'*

*'Thank God he injured his back and not his hands,'* Nina wrote to Lottie from her London town house. *'I know it will be terrible if he can't walk again, but it would be even more terrible if he'd lost his ability to paint.'*

At Christmas, Nina arrived at Crag-Side with a gentleman-friend in tow. He was twenty years her senior, a landed lord and a member of the Government. 'He's exactly what Nina needs,' Lizzie said to the rest of the family in deep relief. 'He'll steady her. He also says that now Lloyd George is Prime Minister we can look forward to a speedy end to the war. Pray God he's right!'

He wasn't. At Easter, when Noel was ferried by ambulance from Swansea to Crag-Side, a fresh offensive was launched by the Allies against the famous Hindenburg Line, opposite Arras. *'Thank God it's a party I haven't been invited to,'* Harry wrote to Rose. *'I'm behind lines at the moment and may be for some time.'*

Rose's initial relief on reading his postcard was followed immediately by fear. Was he behind lines because he was injured? If he was, why was he reluctant to tell her? Had he lost an arm? A leg? Had he written a more informative letter to Nina?

*'Everyone thinks there'll be a difference now the Yanks have finally pitched in,'* Micky wrote to her gloomily from somewhere in Picardy. *'I don't. They're all talk and no blooming action.'*

Neither she, nor anyone else, knew of any other two young men who had survived uninjured at the front for as long as Micky and Harry.

'You'd think, wi' both of them being Yorkshire lads, they'd 'ave fought side by side by now, wouldn't you?' Albert said to Lizzie and Sarah, smoothing Micky's latest pencil-written missive out on his knee so that he could read it aloud to them. 'If they 'ave, Micky's never mentioned it. Not that he mentions a lot.' He peered down at Micky's faintly scrawled message. 'He must 'ave written this against a tent-pole.

A bow-legged spider could 'ave made a better job of it.'

Rose divided her time between helping the nursing staff at Crag-Side and supervising the running of the mill. In many respects the war had simplified things where the mill was concerned. There was no more competitive tendering, instead the Army allocated orders and a newly formed Wool Control Board dictated the amount of wool to be made available for civilian manufacturing purposes.

'And as women are now doing men's work in the mill, we're paying them men's wages,' she said to Noel as he sat on the terrace in a wheelchair, a sketch-book on his lap. 'You'd think all the other mills would be doing the same, but they're not. The General Union of Textile Workers is having a rare old ding-dong with some local mills. Rimmington's, you'll be pleased to know, is a shining light when it comes to conditions and terms of employment.'

He didn't answer her. He wasn't even listening to her. Across the vast sward of sun-kissed lawn, dotted with patients' day-beds and wheelchairs, a slender figure was walking briskly towards the foot of the terrace steps. She had a suitcase in one hand, a summer coat over her arm. Her once waist-length hair had been bobbed and there was elegant self-assurance in every line of her body.

'Lottie,' he said, his sketch-book slithering to the ground as he grasped the arms of his wheelchair so tightly Rose was sure he was going to miraculously rise from it and run. *'Lottie!'*

One look at Lottie's face was enough to tell Rose that her visit was no casual visit; that she wasn't home on leave; that she was home for good. Home, because Noel was home. Home, because she intended nursing him back to health. Home, because she now knew that there was more than one kind of courage and because she would never, as long as she lived, accuse Noel of cowardice again.

'Can you hear the larks?' Harry asked his adjutant. 'You'd think the guns would send them fleeing miles away, wouldn't you? Yet every time there's as much as a ten-minute break in the firing you can hear them singing as if their hearts will burst.'

'They don't sing so chirpy a few miles back, sir,' his adjutant said with a cheeky grin. 'The French farmers shoot 'em for pies. I reckon the little bleeders think they're safe here. Every sod in sight has a rifle but we don't make much of a mark with 'em, do we? The Germans are exactly where they were three bleeding year ago and I doubt a battalion of the West Yorkshire's joining us for our next little scramble is going to make much difference.'

Harry gave a weary grin. He never minded his adjutant speaking to him with familiarity. They'd been through too much together. Insubordination was quite another thing, of course. The French had been plagued by it to such an extent in some cases it had developed into outright mutiny. He slid his gun into his holster. If the new men assigned to him were Bradford Pals there'd be no question of insubordination from any of them. They would be battle-hardened soldiers. They would be the very best soldiers any man could possibly command.

Walking over creaking duckboards, he set off to inspect them. Bradford. It seemed a million miles away. Another world away. He wondered if there were still rowing boats on Lister Park lake. He wondered if Rose still went into the park with Jenny or if, now Jenny was a married woman, they no longer enjoyed such jaunts together.

'It wasn't the girl I saw you with at Brighton,' one of his men was singing, 'So who—who—who's your lady friend?'

He knew who he wanted his lady friend

to be. He'd known for a long time now. The damn thing was, though, he didn't know how to go about telling her. She'd always believed him to be in love with Nina. For far too long, *he'd* always believed himself to be in love with Nina. When the scales had finally fallen from his eyes he'd felt like a man bereaved, certain he would never again feel an emotion so deep.

And then, high up on the moors, he'd looked down into Rose's upturned, sunnily smiling face, and he'd known that everything that had gone before had been nothing but heady, fevered, youthful infatuation. It was Rose that was his real love; his true love. It was his fiercely loyal friend, with her irrepressible sense of fun and sure and certain values, that was his rock and his still centre, his searing flame and his peace.

'Is it true the Big Push is on for tomorrow night, sir?' a 'Mons-man', a gold wound-stripe on his sleeve, asked him.

'I haven't had confirmation yet, Sergeant,' Harry said easily. 'There'll be a briefing the minute I hear.'

He wondered what Rose's reaction would be when he told her he loved her. He wondered if, by some miracle, she would say she could learn to love him. Would they live at Crag-Side together for the rest of their lives? Would they run the mill together? Would they...?

'Sergeant Porritt's platoon is over at number 3 machine-gun post, sir,' his adjutant said, interrupting his thoughts.

'Porritt?' Harry nearly lost his footing on the narrow duckboard. 'Did you say Porritt?'

'I did, sir. He's a bolshie bugger but he's been out here ever since day one and he's won himself so many medals the bits of ribbon would decorate a maypole.'

Despite his weariness Harry chuckled. Sergeant Porritt had to be Micky Porritt. Micky had always been bolshie. Especially with him.

Quickening his pace he strode swiftly past a group of men sorting out a large ammo box and swung himself down into the machine-gun station. The men lounging there, taking what uncomfortable rest they could, sprang hastily to attention.

He looked immediately towards their sergeant, his grin widening. It *was* Micky. There was a hardness and a maturity about him that hadn't been there previously, and he was even broader in the shoulders and more muscular in the arms than when he'd seen him last, but it was Micky all right.

'It's grand to see you, Micky,' he said, meaning every word of it.

'Sir,' Micky saluted.

'Stand easy,' Harry said to Micky's

platoon, saying to Micky, 'I thought we were never going to meet up. You were at Loos, weren't you?'

'Yes, sir.' Micky remained tight-lipped and taciturn. Three bleeding years he'd been in bleeding Flanders and he had to end up taking orders from a Rimmington—and Harry bleeding Rimmington at that!

The edge vanished off Harry's pleasure. There was going to be no friendly reminiscences of Bradford with Micky. Just as, when Micky had been been living in Beck-Side Street he had clearly shown he had no time for 'toffs', so he was showing now that he had no intention of being matey with an officer.

'You know that tomorrow is most likely going to be a Big One, don't you?' Harry said, surprised at how fiercely disappointed he was. He would have liked to have talked about Beck-Side Street, to have exchanged amusing anecdotes about Gertie and Albert, to have asked if Albert's old horse was still alive and if Bonzo was still plaguing the life out of any stranger who might walk down the street.

'Yes, sir.' There was a note of weariness in Micky's voice. Another 'Big One'. Another God Almighty 'Big Push'. Christ, but he'd seen his fair share of them since Mons. And he'd seen his fair share of officers, and those higher in command, leading from the rear. Much as it would have given him great satisfaction to believe Harry bleeding Rimmington fell into such a category, he doubted it. Word was Rimmington was that bloody rarity, an officer who was respected by his men.

' 'E leads from the front,' he'd overheard one of Rimmington's men say to one of his own privates, 'an' when we march, 'e marches with us. 'E don't ride on a bloody horse like some of 'em.'

'I'll be giving a briefing at 1900 hours, Sergeant,' Harry said, knowing that the battle to be friends with Micky was one battle he seemed destined to lose. 'Tell your men to get as much rest as they can. They're very likely going to need it.'

When Harry received his orders for the next day he passed a hand over his eyes. What was the point? What was the bloody point? He'd give the order to go over the top into no man's land and he'd come back, if he came back at all, with only a third, maybe only a quarter, of his men. How many letters to parents and wives had he written over the last three years? *'I am sorry to have to tell you...it will console you to know he was a highly efficient young man, and popular among his comrades...your grief is shared by every man in his battalion...'*

And in forty-eight hours he would, if he were still alive, be writing more.

'Officially,' he said to the officers grouped around him, 'tomorrow's objective is to straighten out the salient around Ypres and attract the enemy's reserves. Unofficially, it stands every chance of being a massacre. We'll be going in without any element of surprise, thanks to the prolonged preparatory bombardment.' He ran a hand through his thick shock of hair. 'When, in the name of Christ, are the powers-that-be going to realize that preparatory bombardment pounds the ground into a swamp, making it impassable and our task impossible?'

'When hell freezes over, sir,' one of his lieutenants said bitterly.

At the back of the dugout Micky remained silently impressed. There was a frankness in Harry Rimmington's manner with his men that aroused respect. He didn't give them any of the, 'Come on, gallant lads, into battle victorious,' rubbish. He'd be a good man to serve under in a tight spot, and tomorrow was going to be a very tight spot. He thought of his New Zealand book and the photographs of the mountains and the sheep farms and rushing rivers. He wouldn't be cheated out of it by any Hun, by hell he wouldn't! He'd survived so long out of sheer bloody cussedness and he'd survive till the last shout, by hell he would!

At 0500 hours the barrage started up and the German batteries began replying. In a front-line trench with his men, waiting for Rimmington's signal to 'go over', Micky felt his stomach muscles tighten. Low air-bursts were already falling all round them and every now and then a shower of hit sandbags whirled high into the air. But no bodies with them. Not yet.

Micky ran his eyes over his platoon. They were white-faced but resolute. He'd never had to shoot a deserter yet, thank God. At twenty-two he was the eldest. 'Lucky Porritt' they called him, because they knew how long he'd been out there. 'Lucky Porritt's platoon's the platoon to be in,' they said. He knew. He'd heard it over and over again. His hand tightened on the stock of his rifle. Pray God they were proved right today.

At last the order came down the line: *'Fix bayonets!'*

'All right lads,' he said, 'only a few minutes more, so hold steady now!'

They were all Bradford Pals, survivors from the Somme. Eddie Firth came from Eccleshill. Young Barraclough from Wyke. Two more were from the west side of the city. Micky had been a class above them at Whetley Lane Infants.

The guns were lifting. He could see Harry Rimmington looking intently at a pocket watch. He thought briefly of Albert and the horse and Bonzo. And Rose, of course. He always thought of Rose at moments like this. He didn't see Rimmington give the signal, but he heard it.

*'Come on, lads,'* he yelled at the top of his lungs as the whistles blew and machine-guns rattled from the enemy lines. *'Let's be having you!'*

He was the first over the top, dropping down onto muddied ground, one man with his platoon behind him and two hundred others at their heels.

Ahead of him was a sea of poppy-speckled corn. The sound of the guns was deafening, but he was still on his feet, still running, and so were his men.

*'Come on lads!'* he yelled again, the corn flying flat around him as the enemy trenches came into view; as the mouths of the guns came into view. *'Let's show 'em! Let's make Bradford proud of us!'*

Harry was sprinting, breasting the corn. He heard a big one sail over his head, saw the world flash and felt the ground dance. There were screams. Shouts for stretcher bearers. *'Come on men!'* he bellowed. *'Come on!'*

The enemy wire was in sight now. As men all around him fell dying and wounded he saw Micky's platoon reach it.

Enemy machine-gun fire laced into them. He saw khaki-clad figures toppling onto the barbs.

*'Give covering fire!'* he shouted at the top of his lungs and, as a shell barrage from behind them fell short, spinning the bodies on the wire into a spurning bloody fountain of broken limbs. *'Hold off the bombers, for Christ's sake! Hold off!'*

They made the German front trenches. With bayonets bloodied to the hilt they took them. Hours—days—years later it seemed, the world again fell silent. Or nearly silent. From out in no man's land a wounded boy was calling for his mother.

Harry slumped back against a wall of mud. He was bleeding from the chest but he'd packed the wound as best he could. 'How long has that boy been crying for help?' he asked hoarsely, struggling to button his tunic jacket over the bulky improvised dressing.

'Dunno, sir. He'll be quiet soon, sir.'

Harry shook his head, blinking a blood-red mist from his eyes. He had lost over half his men. Micky had survived, though.

Micky would very likely get yet another ribbon for his personal maypole—or would do so if he had any say in the matter. It had been Micky's platoon which had first gained the German front-line trench and had silenced the machine-gun company causing them most losses.

The wounded boy cried out again.

Harry groaned. He couldn't detail anyone to bring the boy in. Now that it was dusk, the least sign of movement would draw the attention of the long-distance gun batteries of both sides, making it a near suicidal mission.

He struggled to his feet. 'Give me covering fire,' he said tersely, knowing that if anyone was going to have to do it, he would have to do it.

'I don't think your idea is a very good one, sir,' his Regimental Sergeant-Major said bluntly. 'You're bleeding, sir...'

Harry knew he was bleeding and now so did everyone else, for the blood had begun to ooze through the thickness of his jacket.

'...and if his Company's stretcher bearers couldn't reach him...'

'I'll cover you.' It was Micky. His face was all sharp angles. Nose. Cheekbones. Jaw. He and his Bradford Pals had knocked an entire machine-gun company out, racing up to it at point-blank range, overcoming it in the bloodiest of hand-to-hand fighting.

'Thank you, Sergeant Porritt,' he said quietly and then turned, hauling himself up and over the lip of the earthwork, weaving and ducking and diving as the long-distance guns opened up as he had known they would open up, holding the blood-sodden rags to his chest as he ran in the direction of the cries: *'Hilf mir, Mutter! Hilf mir, Mutter!'*

From that day on there was no question of Micky treating Harry with disdain. Throughout the remainder of the fighting at Ypres, after Harry had recovered from his wound, they fought side-by-side, or as near to side-by-side as it was possible for them to do. They were together at Passchendaele and they were together when, in the spring of 1918, a flood of German troops inundated forty miles of the British front.

'If this isn't going to be the end of it, I don't know what is,' Micky had said sourly, as Harry handed him a roll-up. 'Don't suppose I'll get to New Zealand then, will I?'

'You'll get to New Zealand,' Harry had said, wondering just when the orders for a massive counter-attack would come. 'Did I tell you William's written to me with the news that Nina's to marry again? He's a lord and he's in the War Cabinet.'

Micky grunted. He'd never had any time for Nina Sugden. She and Rose were as different as chalk and cheese. He remembered that Harry had once been in love with Nina and that, according to Rose, he still was.

'You don't mind?' he asked, blowing a ring of blue smoke into air that was, for once, blessedly free of the smoke of guns.

Harry lifted an eyebrow. It was a question he had never thought to be asked by Micky. 'No,' he said truthfully. 'I still love her as a cousin, but I'm not in love with her and don't think now that I ever was. I was infatuated though. As infatuated as it's possible to be.'

'What happened?' Micky knew, of course, that Nina had very speedily married a duke; a duke who had won a posthumous VC at Gallipoli, but he didn't know what had gone wrong between Harry and Nina before that. Rose had never told him. He didn't think she'd even told Jenny.

Harry was silent for a moment, thinking of the ugly row in the stable yard at Crag-Side. 'We didn't think the same way about things,' he said at last. 'Things that were important to her, weren't important to me, and vice versa.'

It was Micky's turn to be silent. Only

one thing was important to him. New Zealand. He'd be on a boat out there the minute the war was over. He inhaled deeply, regarded the tip of his roll-up with studied interest, and said, 'What will you do when it's over?'

Harry grinned. 'What I'll do when it's over is to ask the girl I *do* love if she'll marry me, and then we'll live happily ever after at Crag-Side, in sight of wonderful, wonderful Ilkley Moor!'

*'That's what he says he's going to do anyway,'* Micky wrote to Jenny. *'Who the girl is, I don't know. The guns started up before I could ask. It's good news about the baby. Maybe this lot will finally be over before it's born. Give my best to Charlie.'*

Jenny pondered long and hard before showing the letter to Rose. She knew that after Nina had been widowed, Rose had believed Nina and Harry would eventually marry. What Rose felt now she knew that that would never happen, Jenny didn't know. She only knew that it wouldn't be right to allow Rose to live in fresh, fierce hope where Harry Rimmington was concerned. Not if all such hope was going to be in vain.

It was June when she finally plucked up the courage to show her Micky's hastily scribbled, pencilled letter. They were seated on their favourite park bench in Lister Park, enjoying a rare afternoon out together. The newspapers had been full of the news that the Germans were gaining ground again, reaching and crossing the River Aisne at several strategic points, but they had had much happier things to talk about. Her coming baby; her mother's move to a modest family villa at Scarborough where Walter soon hoped to join her; Lottie and Noel's forthcoming wedding.

'It's a pity Noel won't be able to walk Lottie down the aisle,' Rose said, throwing some crumbs into the lake for the birds, 'but though he can now walk a few steps, he isn't up to anything more ambitious.'

'Rose, I...' She took the letter out of her maternity smock pocket and laid it on her lap.

'Lottie desperately wants Harry to be home for the wedding, but he says home leave is so out of the question and that she and Noel must just go ahead and—'

'Rose, there's something I have to show you.'

At the tone in Jenny's voice Rose forgot all about the ducks. For the first time she became aware of the letter on Jenny's lap.

'It isn't news of a death,' Jenny said hastily as the blood drained from Rose's face. 'It's from Micky. He's all right, he isn't injured, but...'

Rose picked the letter up. Like all Micky's letters, it was very short.

'I didn't know whether you already knew,' Jenny said awkwardly. 'And if you didn't, I thought perhaps it would be best if you did know and—'

'Yes.' Rose could hardly frame the word. She felt sick and giddy. It was so unexpected. If, before Nina's remarriage, it had been the news that he was to marry Nina, then at least it wouldn't have been a thunderbolt from the blue. As it was...

'Are you all right, Rose?' Jenny was asking anxiously. 'Do you think we should be going home?'

Rose didn't answer her. She couldn't. Home. Home for her was now Crag-Side, and Crag-Side was where Harry would bring his bride. She couldn't live there then. It would be an utter impossibility. It would be beyond all bearing.

'Perhaps if we had a cup of tea in Cartwright Hall café?' Jenny was suggesting, appalled by the pallor of Rose's face, wondering if she had done the right thing in showing her the letter, wondering how on earth Rose was going to get home to Ilkley.

'Yes.' With a supreme effort Rose tried to rally herself. It was no use behaving as if she were in a Greek tragedy. She had always known that though she and Harry would be best friends for as long as they both had breath in their bodies, he was never going to be her lover. She remembered his trips to Leeds and Manchester in the days after Nina had become engaged to Rupert. Was the girl he intended marrying as soon as the war was over, a girl he had met then? There really didn't seem to be any other option—unless she were a French girl—a girl he had met, perhaps, on leave in Paris.

## Chapter Sixteen

During the next few months, as the tide of the war turned and the Allies began to sweep all before them, delivering crushing blows to the Germans all along the front line, Rose pondered her future.

She had known, almost from the very first moment of reading Micky's letter, that she wouldn't stay on at Crag-Side, and in the same instant she had known that she wouldn't ask William and Sarah if she could make her home with them. They already had her mother living with them, and Sarah was now expecting another baby. A spinster cousin taking up lodgings beneath his roof was an inconvenience William could well do without.

Where, then, would she go? What would she do? The minute Harry was home he would take over the running of Rimmington's. Everyone knew now that William, by choice, would never do so and that it was only a matter of time before Harry, knowing the burden he would be lifting from William's shoulders, became not only Rimmington's *de facto* master, but its legal master as well.

She thought about offering her services as a designer to one of the other Bradford mills. Lister's, perhaps. Or Lutterworth's, but she didn't think about it for long. How could she work in another mill, within sight of Rimmington's? How, indeed, could she even remain in Bradford?

It was Josie who inadvertently came up with the answer to her problem.

'Have you heard the latest good news?' she asked her cheerily one morning as, together, they wheeled a patient's bed out into the September warmth of the terrace. 'The Germans are retreating as fast as their legs will carry them. The war really *is* going to be over by Christmas this year, and the minute hostilities are over I'm going to head back home, to New Zealand.'

Rose had stared at her, transfixed. New Zealand was as far away as anyone could possibly get from Bradford. In New Zealand she would never have to suffer the pain of seeing Harry with his new wife. In New Zealand she would have friends, for as well as Josie, Micky would be there.

'Can I come with you?' she asked, her fingers tightening around the iron rail of the bed-head. 'Can I stay with your family for a little while? Until I can get myself a job and a place of my own?'

Josie gurgled with delighted laughter.

'Find a place of your own? My parents have one of the biggest sheep farms in the country! You can move in for good without anyone batting an eyelid!'

Rose had written a letter to Harry, telling him of her plans, but she hadn't posted it. She didn't intend posting it until she was on the point of leaving. Instead she wrote him other letters. She told him that Jenny had given birth to a baby boy; that Noel and Lottie had married and that though Noel hadn't been able to walk his bride down the aisle, he had stood unaided by her side during the service. She told him that his father now spent nearly all his time with Polly in Scarborough and that they were only waiting for his return home in order that they could have a wedding at which all the family would be present. Then, in November, when the Armistice was signed, she posted her letter telling him that she was accompanying Josie Warrender to New Zealand.

*'There isn't really anything to keep me at Crag-Side any longer,'* she had written. *'New Zealand will be a fresh beginning for me. Wish me luck. I wish you all the luck there is in the world.'*

In the silvery pale light of early morning, a light breeze blew across what had once been no man's land. Harry shivered and pulled on gauntletted gloves. The war was over but it would be months before the giant machinery of the war wound down and every man who had served in it, and survived it, was home again. He, however, was lucky. This leave had been in the pipeline for months and it couldn't possibly have come at a better moment. He stamped his booted feet against the cold. This time tomorrow he'd be home. This time tomorrow he would be at Crag-Side with Rose.

*'Post, sir!'* a private shouted, running breathlessly up to him. 'Thought I wasn't going to catch you, Sir! Have a nice leave, Sir! Give my best to dear old Blighty!'

He opened the letter as his adjutant drove him away from camp and towards the railway station. Seconds later he knew that if he hadn't already been on his way home, he would have immediately gone AWOL. New Zealand? *New Zealand?* A fresh beginning! What was she talking about, for Christ's sake! She couldn't make a fresh beginning on her own. They were going to make a fresh beginning together! A panic he had never before experienced, not even on the battlefield, roared through him. Christ Almighty, but he couldn't lose her now! Not before he had at least told her how he felt about her! Not when he might, just might, be able to persuade her to stay—when he might be able to persuade her to begin caring for him a different way—to love him as he loved her.

*'Faster, man!'* he shouted at his adjutant in a way so totally unexpected and out of character that his adjutant nearly drove into a ditch. *'Faster!'*

The train to the port was so interminably slow he thought he was going to have a nervous breakdown. When he reached the port it was chock-a-block with troops and the first boat he could get a passage on was a night-boat.

Time after time he read and reread her letter. She hadn't said *when* she was setting sail, only *'by the time you receive this I will be on my way with Josie to Wellington.'* Would they be leaving from Southampton? Had they got a passage on a troopship? Why had she never given him any indication that she, like Micky, was thinking of emigrating?

*'Dover!'* someone called out. 'I can see 'er through the dawn mist and she don't 'alf look a grand sight!'

He got a seat on a London-bound train, jammed between an American soldier and a woman so fat she was bigger than

Gertie Graham. What would he do if he didn't get home in time and she had already left? He couldn't follow her, or not immediately. He would have to wait for his discharge and that could take weeks, possibly months.

At Charing Cross he battled through the rejoicing crowds to Kings Cross and a train north. Had it been Micky who had put the idea of New Zealand into her head? Even if she wanted to go there, why would she want to leave before he had returned home and she could say a proper goodbye to him? What was going on? Why, why, *why* hadn't he told her months ago, *years* ago, that she was the love of his life and that he'd have no joy, nor peace, without her?

*'Leeds!'* the conductor called out. *'All change for Bradford! Ilkley! York!'*

It was mid-afternoon by the time the taxi deposited him at the foot of the sweeping stone steps leading to Crag-Side's impressive front door. The door was ajar. Two suitcases were propped against it.

He burst into the marble-floored hall, saying to a startled looking girl in nurse's uniform, 'Rose? Is she still here? Are these her bags? *Is she still here?'*

'She's up on the moor,' the girl said, eyeing his broad shoulders and near-black eyes and hair appreciatively. 'She and

Nurse Warrender are leaving in an hour's time for Southampton...'

He turned on his heels, running out through the open door, taking the wide stone steps two at a time, running back down the drive, out of the gates, up the tree-lined road that led to the moor. Running, running, running, his heart pumping as if it were going to burst.

It was very quiet on the moors. In the November mist a few sheep huddled forlornly. With her fur hat low over her ears, and her gloved hands tucked deep into the warmth of her muff, Rose walked over frost-hard ground towards the cairn. She had wanted to look out from it over a vast vista of rolling, heather-covered moorland, just as she had once done with Harry. Then, though, it had been a bright, clear day. Now, in keeping with her mood, the day was bleak, the low-lying clouds dank and oppressive.

She removed a hand from her muff, touching the freezing cold stones of the cairn with a gloved fingertip. Perhaps it was just as well that now the time had come to say goodbye to Yorkshire, Yorkshire was hidden from her. If it hadn't been, if she had been able to look to the north-east and see the moor rolling purple-hazed for mile after mile and then south, to where Crag-Side's decorative chimney pots peeped, barely visible above the tops of its surrounding trees, then her inner resolve might very well have failed her.

She took a small stone she had taken from Crag-Side's rockery out of her coat pocket and placed it on top of the cairn and then, tears stinging her eyes, she turned to leave.

It was then, as she did so, that the clouds suddenly lifted and parted, revealing a hard, bright, azure sky. Distantly she could see the grey rooftops of Ilkley; a little nearer, the chimney pots and treetops of Crag-Side, and nearer still, a running figure. A figure running in her direction. A figure uniformed and toughly built. A figure running with athletic strength and muscular control. A figure she had been determined never to set eyes on again, knowing that if she did so her heart would surely break. A figure she loved with every fibre of her being.

*'Rose!'* he shouted breathlessly as he raced towards her over the frosted heather. *'ROSE!'*

She stood there, rooted to the spot, unable to move. Rose, not Funny-Face. He hardly ever called her Rose. Why was he calling her Rose now? Why was he running towards her with such frantic urgency? What had happened? Was he bringing bad news? Had Micky, in the very last days of the war, been fatally wounded?

As the yards between them closed and she saw the intensity of his expression, the look almost of fear on his face, her own fear escalated so that she could scarcely breathe.

*'What is it?'* she demanded in terror as he caught hold of her, his arms going round her, *'Has someone died? Is it Micky? Is it...?'*

'No one's died.' He was panting harshly, sucking in air in great breathless gasps. 'It's just that...I thought I was going to be too late...' His voice cracked in a way she had never heard it crack before. He was holding her, too, in a way he had never previously held her; holding her as if he would never, ever, let her go. 'Don't leave,' he gasped abruptly, hugging her against him so tightly she thought her bones were going to break. 'Don't leave. Not yet. Not now. Not till I've talked to you. I've got so much to say, Rose. So much to say that I ought to have said long ago.'

His eyes were burning hers. She could feel his heart slamming. She could feel her own self-control beginning to slip. She didn't want this. She didn't want him to tell her about the girl he loved; the girl he was going to marry. She couldn't survive the pain of it.

'I know,' she said stiffly, through lips that felt frozen with far more than cold. 'You're to be married. Micky wrote to Jenny. I thought it would be best...I didn't want to be here when...' She couldn't go on. The tears she had fought against so hard and for so long, were choking her throat. They were also on her eyelashes, blurring her vision so that she could no longer see him clearly; so that he looked to be almost as stunned and incredulous as she had felt when she had first seen him running towards her.

'Is that why you're leaving?' His voice was as stunned as his expression and there was something else in his voice; a change of mood so drastic she felt dizzily disorientated. *'You're leaving because you think I'm going to marry?'*

He sounded euphoric. He sounded as if it was the most wonderful news he had ever heard.

She nodded, knowing her tears were now streaking her cheeks and no longer caring. He knew now how she felt about him, so what point was there in further deception?

'Rose, *Rose.*' He was tilting her face to his, wiping her tears away tenderly with a fingertip, his voice just as tender as his touch; just as caressing. 'I do want to marry, Rose,' he was saying unsteadily, looking down into her saucer-eyed, funny, *beautiful*, face. 'I want to marry *you*. I don't know why I never realized years and years ago that it was you I loved, but I realize it now.'

If his arms hadn't been so securely around her, she would have fallen. Somewhere very near to them a bird had begun to sing. Even though it was November and therefore impossible, Rose was sure it was a lark.

'Can you forgive me being so stupid?' he was asking, his hair tumbling low over his brows just as it had the first time they had met, hunkered down opposite each other on the pavement outside Brown & Muff's. 'Can you learn to love me, as I love you, Rose? As I will always love you?'

Tears continued to roll down her face, but they were tears of joy now, not tears of anguish.

'I don't have to learn.' Her heart was filled with such wild elation she didn't known how she could possibly contain it. 'I love you already. I've loved you for so long, Harry, I can't remember a time when I didn't love you.'

Beneath the fiery fox fur of her hat her toffee-brown eyes were shining, her beguiling little monkey face, radiant.

'And you'll marry me?' His voice was thick with urgency and desire and absolute love. 'You'll marry me just as soon as we can gather everyone together for the biggest family wedding ever?'

She nodded, laughing through her tears, and at long, long last, he lowered his head to hers, covering her mouth with his, his lips hot and sweet and all she had ever dreamed they would be.

Later, much later, as, with their arms around each other's waists, her head resting lovingly on his shoulder, they began to walk back across the moor in the direction of Crag-Side, she said musingly, 'Micky won't be leaving Flanders for New Zealand without coming home first, will he?'

Harry turned his head, flashing her the down-slanting smile that always sent excitement spiralling through her. 'No. He'll have to come back to Blighty to be demobbed. Were you worrying he wouldn't be at our wedding?'

'No.' His army jacket was rough beneath her cheek as she smiled rosily up at him. 'It's just that by the time he's home for our wedding there'll be someone in New Zealand who will be very, very pleased to meet him. I want to give him her address before he sails.'

She thought of Micky's broad, superbly fit physique and her smile deepened. Josie was going to fall in love with Micky at first sight and Micky was going to find himself working on a sheep farm sooner than even he could anticipate.

A sense of deep, all-pervading joy flooded over her. The war was over, the future was golden, and the world was a beautiful place. 'Let's run!' she said impulsively, hugging Harry's arm as Crag-Side came into view. 'Let's run all the way home!'

The publishers hope that this book has given you enjoyable reading. Large Print Books are especially designed to be as easy to see and hold as possible. If you wish a complete list of our books, please ask at your local library or write directly to: Magna Large Print Books, Long Preston, North Yorkshire, BD23 4ND, England.